Final Portrait

Kellie Sisson Snider

Writers Club Press
San Jose · New York · Lincoln · Shanghai

Final Portrait
Copyright © 2000 by Kellie Sisson Snider

ISBN: 0-595-00045-2

Published by Writers Club Press, an imprint of iUniverse.com, Inc.

For information address:
iUniverse.com, Inc.
620 North 48th Street
Suite 201
Lincoln, NE 68504-3467
www.iuniverse.com

URL: http://www.writersclub.com

Contents

To my husband Richard Allen Snider

What a strange thing is memory, and hope; one looks backward, the other forward. The one is of today, the other is the Tomorrow…memory is a painter, it paints pictures of the past and of the day.
  Grandma Moses, *My Life's History*, Aotto Kallir, ed. 1947

Prologue

New Orleans is hot and wet. In order to live there comfortably, one must wear loose cotton shirts and be forgiving of wrinkles and the order-less things humidity does to one's hair. Men wear light sear sucker suits if they must dress for work; Women who are comfortable in their bones slide their bare feet into shoes that are open and close to the ground. This results in a waving gait that urges air to move freely under their skirts.

Being born and raised in New Orleans is to exist in an exotic and independent place that just happens to exist within a governing country that is large and homogenous, and more than a bit condescending to this errant and lazy step child. New Orleans is the home of river boats, jazz, crooked politicians and tall, cold hurricanes in flared glasses. You can get drunk there any time of the day or night- nothing ever closes. Tourists flap down Bourbon Street at all hours, addled by heat and libation, unaware that the lights distort the proffered titillation. The strippers are old and have stretch marks left by illegitimate kids they had when they were far too young. The Dixie Land musicians are sick and tired of it all and are only there just to try to lose themselves one more night. They want to play the horn so deep it hurts, they just wish someone who wasn't drunk on beer slurped from plastic cups or the excitement of being away from home for a week could hear it and would just simply sink inside the story the notes have to tell. All art tells a story, they would say. It ain't just about a song. Its about everything.

New Orleans lays at the open mouth of the Mississippi, but it is not as far as you can go. There are places further south, places so close to the ocean that they sometimes get sucked in. Places called Belle Chasse and Sulphur, Morgan City and Venice. Places that are evacuated every year for hurricanes and rebuilt in bits and pieces from time to time when the storm knocks them down.

The language of that foreign place resembles the one used by the rest of the larger country, but is, in fact, all its own. The Cajun dialect, an amalgam of French and English that has steeped in long isolation in the bayous, is loose and lazy like the hips of pregnant women, ripe with idiom and its own peculiar melody. It is not the rounded drawl of the less far South; In Georgia, for example, one speaks spherical English, round and lazy but with esteemed blood. Cajun talk is not the easy English adaptation of the western places; it does not plod like a horse's walk, it is not nasal so that the lips can stay nearly closed to keep the dry dust out. It is a rich, open and hearty voice that comes from the depths of experience. It is like the soup they call gumbo, spicy and thick, into which anything at all might be put, and probably is. It knows how the Grand Mama's Grand Mere came from the south of France and already knew how to cook with spices to save the food from spoiling in the heat and how the Grand Pere learned to catch 'dem srimps' (the shrimp) and 'de gator' (the alligator). When the Papa wants to let you know he ain't kiddin' or lyin', he calls you Cher. Then you know you got yourself a deal.

The language and the people even have their own surnames that are as popular as Smith or Jones to the rest of the states, but more tied to the bayou and some mysterious place across the sea. Kate Breaux (pronounced Broh') was a native of New Orleans. So was her neighbor, Cassandra Dee Orgeron (Oh'-zher-on). And the boy Cassandra would marry, Danny Boudreaux (Boo-Droh'), and of course his sister, Helen Boudreaux, who grew up on the river with her bare feet in the mud. Their names came over across the sea from France so long ago that no one remembers exactly how. The names are nearly as old as France, too, older than the United States, New Orleans' patronizing benefactor. And they belong to New Orleans now.

Kate Breaux and Cassandra Dee Orgeron were seventeen years old in nineteen seventy two when this story began. Or rather, when the telling commenced. The story started years before that, in two separate secrets, dark and disturbing. Cassandra and Kate lived in New Orleans all their lives, just like their parents had, and their parents' parents and ancestors yet before them.

They lived in houses that had been in New Orleans for more than a hundred years, maybe two hundred. They were in constant need of repair after facing the ravages of so many hot, wet years, stricken by hurricanes, teased by daily afternoon rain. Some of these long narrow houses, lost the fight and were desperate shacks now. Others retained their dignity through the sweat of caring residents. These houses were called Shot Gun Houses because, it was said, if you shot a gun through the front door the bullet would go right through the back. It might be a Daddy, you know, who fired that shot, avenging his yet unmarried, pregnant daughter. Beware the vengeful father. Beware his heartsick child.

On every corner in The French Quarter, or somewhere along each street, you can find original paintings of famous New Orleans land marks to help you remember that you were there, in case you drink too much and forget. In the middle nineteen seventies Kate Breaux spent some time painting paintings you might see in one of those places.

These days you might only see the prints of those originals. The originals would be quite costly today, and increasingly rare.

If you should go New Orleans and want to buy a painting, Kate would tell you to wait until you see a picture that tells you a story. Don't buy paintings simply because they are of the places you visited. Think little of whether the picture is pretty. And by all means skip the one that matches your couch. Look for a story in the painting, one that will know how to tell itself. Don't even buy it if it tells your companion a story, for that is her painting, not yours. And when you have found your story-telling painting, then listen. Very carefully, listen.

Everyone has a different story even when they walk under the same wet sky every day of their lives. Even when the same wickedness approaches them in the same dark mask, no two stories are ever the same. For everyone makes her story her own. Everyone interprets the plot in her own style, and decides whether to give the antagonist her heart or her fist, her peace or her fury. And how she interprets the story has everything to do with how her story will end.

Sometime, if you live all your life at the mouth of the Mississippi, you might chance upon a moment that is so special it bonds you to the place so strongly you know you'll never leave. One night you might walk across Jackson Square after it has rained and all the tourists have run for cover inside restaurants and hotel rooms and before they have ventured outside again. You might see the light of the street lamps glance off the rain darkened sidewalks and brick lined streets. You might smell the scents of all those years of living weighted down around you in the wetness from the sky. And as you listen to your shoes slapping one after the other on that wet pavement, you might hear in the distance a saxophone playing - and once you hear it, you will forget who you are with and what you are doing. You will hear a single thread of melody that tells a story so mournful and deep that it makes your soul weep and you will either want to end it all and die, or you will find the courage to walk purposefully on, watching and learning, to live another story.

One

The Secrets Of
The Faithful

It would have been my nature to tell a story succinctly, in the patterns of light and dark, the play of a color against its compliment on the canvas. To linger on a subject too long meant getting too attached, becoming too vulnerable. It meant eventually being victimized by my own need. If Helen Boudreaux hadn't come to me I would only have illustrated Cassandra's story, absorbing her anguish until I could feel my love expanding like a fetus, gestating it until it spilled out of my brush in a fury. Yet, I would not have seen past the silhouette. No lingering look at what I had borne would precede selling it away, no grieving like a child who's been sexual too soon, who knows she can't be the mother she should be, who knows all too well she has to let go.

This story can't be told on one canvas, no matter how wide, no matter how tightly it is stretched. My young life turned into an unintentional sacrifice while I was waiting to see what was supposed to happen.

My father said that sacrifice was also an investment. I suppose he was right. I have collected dividends.

I coped by asking, "What am I learning?" I decided that when I started getting the same answer over and over again I would be finished with it and move on. But already I'm getting old. I've asked and asked and the answer is still changing.

I know that what they teach you in church isn't any kind of answer. At least not my church, and certainly not Cassandra's. It is particularly untrue when they say that life is supposed to be happy. Happiness is such a small part of it. It's just the reflection.

Cassandra Dee Orgeron was my best friend. She lived two doors down from me on New Orleans' old Jefferson Avenue in a small white house shaded by seven towering cypress trees. She had a white cat that she treated like a baby doll. Her mother was a devout fundamentalist Christian. She took the children to church at least three times a week no matter what. Mr. Orgeron went along on Sundays to keep up appearances, part of being a good businessman, but he grimaced throughout the sermons and his wife prodded his shoulder with her elbow, while displaying nothing but rapt attention on her face.

There was a lot of talk about God and even more about Jesus, and more still about their Reverend Bill Billings. But what seemed the most real was that for them, church was the axis of morality. My family was Catholic, but not pious, yet we, too, assigned all the virtues to Christianity's keeping.

Even as a child I could tell that things in their life were not as they seemed. Now, looking back across all these years it seems that their religion was more of an addiction. Lists of rules about how to live dominated Mrs. Orgeron's life and were pressed upon her family. No one could remember all those rules, much less live up to their demands. What seems apparent to me now is that people weren't what mattered.

At least not if those people were still children. Female children had it worst of all.

Cassandra struggled to be so pious, so devout, so true to what she was taught that you could almost believe it. She read her Bible, she went to church, she prayed with her head bowed before eating lunch in the school cafeteria. She ignored the snickers at her blatant religiousness. But when something God or Mrs. Orgeron wouldn't approve of was going on- when boys were telling dirty jokes or girls were bragging in the rest room about how far they went the night before, Cassandra was always a little too captivated, not with mere curiosity, but with desire. Cassandra would linger on the edges of the group of students who stood smoking near the pampas grass behind the football field, even though they taunted her and tried to scare her away. Cassandra kept her Bible on top of her schoolbooks like a talisman, but her expression betrayed her hunger. Once a sneering boy offered her a cigarette, and she hesitated for almost a second before she ran across the school yard, with the cool kids' laughter causing her cheeks to burn and her eyes to well with tears.

The fear of the Lord was strong, and hovered around Cassandra every waking moment. Mrs. Orgeron often said, "All have sinned and fallen short of the glory of God." She said, "The wages of sin is death."

"If that is true," Cassandra told me much later, "Some pretty uncontrollable things end up as death sentences."

Add to that, "Whatsoever a man thinketh, so is he," and even one's thoughts condemn.

I remember how furious Mrs. Orgeron was the time Cassandra vomited on the floor of her first grade Sunday school class and had to be taken home. I watched from the street as Mrs. Orgeron stomped angrily into the house ahead of Cassie's small trembling self. With the door standing open I could hear her high-heeled Sunday dress shoes hammering the hardwood floor even from my hiding place outside near the hedge. I sneaked up behind the Orgeron's wrought iron railing in the clandestine shade. Cassandra stood on the porch crying in desperate gasps, shaking. She leaned forward holding her soiled Sunday dress away from her tender little legs until Mrs. Orgeron reached out through the door and grabbed her arm, pulling her inside. All I saw was that big arm, and my Cassie was gone.

After a while Mrs. Orgeron left the house without Cassandra. She came back another hour later with Mr. Orgeron who had stayed until the church service ended.

I told my mother about it later that night. I broke the damning sacred oath of childhood: Never tell. I didn't mean to tell but I kept thinking how scared it would make me to be left alone, especially when I was sick. I fretted about it all day, going outside from time to time to peer at Cassandra's window from behind our hedge. Finally I couldn't stand it any longer and I had to tell. Mama breathed deeply and wiped her face with the frayed red checkered dishtowel she had dried the dinner plates with. She said that if she was only alone a few minutes then it wasn't a problem she could do anything about now.

I remember thinking that if I were a grown up I would do something. If I were a mother I'd go over there and go in that house and sit on the edge of Cassie's bed and take her temperature. I'd tell Mrs. Orgeron you can't leave six-year-olds alone for even a minute when they are sick or they'll be scared. What if she had vomited again? Who would help her rinse her mouth? Who would take her a drink of water in bed? Who would touch her forehead with the coolness of her palm and say, "Poor Sweet One, I'm going to help you get better. You rest and I'll be here if you need me"?

Now I am a grown up and I have an idea why some people don't get involved. Getting involved means being blamed for the very wrongs you wanted to correct. Getting involved means standing out in a crowd. Getting involved means giving up everything you thought was your own.

Cassandra was as different from me as was possible. Although we were together we grew up differently. She was terrified of solitude, always wanted people around, talked constantly. I was shy. I didn't like crowds and I didn't like talking out loud much, except when there were only one or two people around that I knew very well. Mostly I kept my thoughts to myself.

Cassandra Dee Orgeron looked petite and fragile, but to me she seemed to be wound up tight like a jack-in-the-box, ready to spring. She dressed in fluffy gingham and long calico dresses we called Maxis. She had a closet full of girlish dresses with lace and sashes and puffy sleeves. But I could see her struggling to contain something fierce within herself.

I wore the teenager's uniform for the nineteen seventies: jeans and tee shirts and sandals imported from Mexico with rubber tires for soles. Cassie's mother said it wasn't proper, the way I dressed. She told Cassandra she didn't understand why my mother would let me dress like a boy. There was something in the Bible about it, Cassie told me. I never told my mother because I was afraid she might ask our priest and maybe he would agree. Mama probably wouldn't go to the priest, but it wasn't worth the risk. As far as I knew, God was God, and the rules must be pretty much the same no matter what church you went to. It just seemed like jeans were a pretty silly thing for God to waste time on.

All her childhood Cassandra dreamed of getting married as soon as she could find a boy who would have her. She probably began dreaming of it as soon as she learned that being married meant leaving. She was a flower girl in a wedding when she was five years old. She looked like a tiny porcelain doll in that little lavender gown. Her mother fretted that she would cry or mess up the ceremony in some other unforgivable way, but she didn't. She lock stepped all the way down the aisle and went to stand next to the groom for an almost imperceptible instant before she moved to her place at the left side. I remember sitting with my mother and thinking how pretty Cassie was, my heart pounding for her. I don't even remember who was being married that day.

I remember that our neighbor, Miss Lizzie, from across the street was there, too. She baby-sat for me sometimes when my parents wanted to go out alone. She was gentle and had deep lines shooting out from her eyes because she smiled a lot. She wore her gray hair in a long braid wrapped around and around her head. She looked over at me and grinned. I blushed. She was sitting with an older girl I didn't know. Mostly I remember Cassandra.

By fifteen Cassandra was afraid she would never meet Mr. Right. By seventeen she was frantic, and by high school graduation she was desperate. I wasn't concerned about boys at all. I sometimes wondered why, but I was most content to sit with Cassandra, or to be alone, painting and watching. I wasn't truly satisfied, but I couldn't interest myself in daydreaming about boys, going to dances, the latest fashions. I was not anxious, but still I waited for some passion to possess me. I hadn't been taught passion. My mother was stoic and reserved, my father passive. So far the closest thing I had to a passion was art, but even that wasn't mere passion. It was existence. I couldn't imagine not painting. I carried a sketch pad the way other girls carried a purse. I made an entry in it each night, as another girl would write, Dear Diary. I thought in pictures rather than words, and still prefer to, even though the world insists that I write and speak. My mother said I was a late bloomer and for some reason that seemed answer enough for my differences. I waited for the passion to be born within me and while I waited, no one else seemed to notice.

My size must have put the boys off. I was never asked for dates. Or maybe there was something more basic about me that didn't attract them. I wasn't sure. I was insecure in their presence. I couldn't giggle about them over lunch. I wondered when I would find them interesting.

I was a full head and shoulders taller than Cassandra. I painted a portrait of the two of us when we were in high school and it looked as if we were of two different breeds. My art teacher said I had gotten my proportions all wrong. But he had never met her. I was big and angular, hands as long as spatulas, points and corners everywhere. Cassandra was petite, just slightly more than frail, gently curving all over. Her hands were barely able to grasp a tea glass. I remember noticing that even during that brief time she was a mother herself she still had to hold her glass with two hands.

I stood in the back of the chorus at school because otherwise no one could see over my head. Boys in our school didn't like big girls, strong girls, unless we could play baseball. I was both big and strong but baseball was beyond my talents and beneath my interest. Cassandra suggested I slouch in order to look smaller, but it was uncomfortable and made me feel silly, so I didn't try to get dates with boys. I felt good in my strength, I was glad I didn't have to ask anyone to help me lift and carry and reach high things. I did it myself. I assumed my time would come- people told me it would. Still I was lonely, wondering what would become of me. What did happen to strong girls who didn't particularly care about boys? I knew that I could do nothing about it but wait for an answer.

Cassandra couldn't afford to wait. Each day she was spouseless was another day in her suffocating house. Her mother's broad bosom was made firm by strict undergarments and her sharp breath pounded as she quoted scripture after scripture for Cassandra to memorize day in and day out. Cassandra needed to find her escape, not only from the home that was a prison, but also from the faith in a damning God that would not listen when she cried at night, that did not see her tremble. She struggled to desire the conformity that kept her there. She felt her rebellion growing and it scared her half to death.

I could see she was filled with richness and wanderlust. I saw it much of the time. She was not suited to the silent life of a submissive minister's wife. That's why I wanted to paint her so often. To show her that she was enough. But also to try to see beneath her false piousness.

I was ordinary and plain. That was the way I liked to be, so that I didn't draw too much attention. I couldn't pay attention to the world if I was being watched. Besides, I didn't understand my place in it and didn't want to take any chances. But Cassandra longed to be special, to be extraordinary. The last thing she wanted to do was fit in. But it was against her religion for women to be brilliant and she was afraid that being extraordinary would damn her. In the end, of course, it did.

Cassandra's father owned an antique store on Magazine Street. It seemed to me that Eugene Orgeron never paid any attention to Cassandra except to criticize her mistakes, to scorn their efforts. She was a girl, a disappointment from birth.

Mr. Orgeron was an alcoholic. Even though my family knew it as well as we knew his family went to church three times a week, we pretended there was nothing wrong except that Cassandra's dad was very strict and that it was no one else's business. We never called him cruel. After all, he was a Father. It was his right to do as he saw fit. With paternity came the assumption of wisdom.

Cassandra's mother was so righteous, so God fearing, that no one dared mention that she was married to a drunk. But she was. In fact, one rarely dared speak to her at all. She was quick with a reprimand and a quoted scripture. No casual conversations took place with Mrs. Orgeron in the grocery check out lane.

In their house I saw a picture of her before her children were born. She was a pretty, strong farm girl. During her marriage she gained weight each year while trying to stabilize her family. Perhaps she realized that fierceness was not enough to subdue her husband. Perhaps she felt that she would be able to weigh him down like a vast stone foundation if she couldn't contain him any other way.

When Cassandra came to my house she nearly drove my parents crazy with her chatter. She called them 'Mom' and 'Dad' and they nodded and smiled at her through clenched teeth. Since she was my friend, they accepted her like they accepted all the guests who entered our house. If you were in our home you were made to feel welcome. But Cassandra crept through her own house silently like a hungry mouse, hiding from something unfathomable that waited for her in dark corners.

Cassandra lapped up the attention she got in my home. She wasn't used to feeling special. Just my mother bringing us glasses of tea or offering her a cookie made her feel like a princess. You could see it in her eyes. They sparkled with delight, and she savored her treats slowly as if they were magic potions of hope.

My parents accepted me and I took it for granted. That's the way parents treated their children, I thought. If anything, my parents were reluctant to interfere in my life at all. They had darkness of their own. But Cassandra was amazed that I would casually share my thoughts and experiences with my parents over dinner. It didn't occur to me not to. My parents were never judgmental. They just listened and loved me. I'm so glad I never had to wonder if they loved me.

My mother had her own cross to bear, even so. I knew from early on that Mama was prone to fits of sadness. Over a period of days she would grow irritable, then quiet, and finally unable to move from the couch or her bed unless some pressing business forced her to. She forgot things and she cried often, but would never say about what. But mostly Mama was capable and intelligent. Mostly Mama was fine.

After we graduated from high school I went on to Delgado junior college. I wanted to do my art so I painted and I studied. I enjoyed riding up St. Charles Avenue on the streetcar, even when I had to carry my portfolio under my arm and bumped against the other passengers. I felt sheltered by the towering cypress trees forming that benevolent canopy over the street. I was caressed by the same wet heat I later found oppressive.

Cassandra dropped out of secretarial school at Delgado after one semester because her mother said she was wasting her time, that the right boy would come along soon. Her father's eyes narrowed and he kept silent. Mrs. Orgeron insisted that Cassandra needed to be spending her time filling her hope chest, dreaming of a white wedding, and studying the Bible so she could be a good wife.

Someone who didn't know Cassandra might have thought she didn't fight it. She struggled to maintain a grip on the pious life she wished she wanted to live, but the dissident in the darkest recesses of her heart tore her fingers back and pressed sharp temptations against her spirit. The only way she could see to get out was to follow the evil she'd been shielded from for so long.

Cassandra knew passages from the Bible better than anyone I have ever known, except, perhaps, for her mother. She could quote a scripture for every occasion, her brown eyes gently closed, her brown bobbed hair dancing from side to side. She would draw on a beatific expression as she chanted, intoxicated by the cadence and the hope. She had read the whole Bible and memorized great long passages by the time she started junior high, and by the end of high school she knew every single word of the four gospels, chapter and verse from Matthew to John. She knew almost all of Acts and Romans, and selections from both letters to the Corinthians. Even though I was a Christian I wouldn't even have known the names of those books had she not been my friend. She worked on learning more passages each evening with her mother treading heavily across the floor behind her chair at the table after dinner. She clicked steadily back and forth in her brown flats, listening, checking, getting Cassandra ready to marry a preacher someday. Cassandra worked herself weary, hoping that being saved would somehow begin to work its magic and stop the longing and the hurt.

During our sophomore year in high school I painted "White on White", a portrait of Cassandra dressed in a white eyelet blouse with a matching skirt, holding the white Bible she had received at her Baptism, sitting in a white wicker chair, surrounded by the chaste white calla lilies in our backyard. I was frustrated because I wasn't able to project the tranquillity I had intended into the scene. I wanted to paint what Cassandra believed about herself. In the painting, Cassandra looked as if she would bolt and run at any moment, like a brown rabbit ready to flee. The piousness of the upward gaze came across as fear on canvas. While I was painting I cursed my lack of skill. After that little piece was completed and hanging in my bedroom I looked at her real face only to see that fear was what was really there.

Cassandra saw the honesty in my paintings long before I did. As time went on, the truth became more evident in each of the canvasses on which I captured her likeness. In time she would loathe those paintings. They said too much and they said it out loud to anyone who would stop for a bare moment and look.

New Orleans was predominantly Catholic in faith. We Catholics let the priest take care of such details as Bible reading for us. At least that's the way it was in my family. My Great- Aunt Ruby had always gone to mass each morning, but she was long dead by the time I reached high school. We rarely ever went to mass except on Easter and for Christmas. I was baptized and confirmed, of course. I studied Catechism in junior high and my confirmation portrait hung in the hall of our house. My parents let me go to church with Cassandra a few times, but they didn't feel very comfortable about it.

Many years later my father told me that he had been concerned that I was going to be converted and that I would start quoting scriptures the way Cassandra did. My mother rarely went to church even on holy days because she said it made her feel too guilty and too sad. But my father would have dealt with it, he said. I had a good mind and could decide for myself, he said.

Cassandra's mother only approved of her when she was studying the Bible or talking about it. Religion was referred to in every conversation, even if they were just talking about which dish washing detergent worked best. The Lord must have blessed the makers of Ivory, because it stood head and shoulders above Lux. Thank God for letting us learn the secret of making fluffy biscuits and crisp fried chicken. Jesus cared so much for Aunt Geraldine that He didn't let her suffer, but let her die peacefully in her sleep in her own home. They never mentioned that Aunt Geraldine was found next to an empty bottle of sleeping pills in a bed full of her own excrement. There are some kinds of pain even Jesus couldn't take away.

Between the pages of the Bible, Cassandra learned that she didn't have the luxury of unconditional love either in her house or in heaven. She knew she had to toe the line or God and her parents would cast her out of their lives. For eighteen years she struggled to find the peace that passes understanding, the hope that she would be on the receiving end of God's grace. She tried to believe that it would be enough if this life offered her nothing and heaven was all there was. But she knew deep in her heart that even if God cared he couldn't do anything for her. She knew the words her church mentors would say to reassure her that God did care. They would say, "God watches over the sparrow, and he'll watch over you," the words of a hymn taken from some place in the Bible. In her heart, where it counted, Cassandra knew it wasn't true. Cassandra knew what her fluffy white cat did to sparrows. The sparrows didn't stand a chance.

If God heard her begging in her prayers that her mother would stop hitting her with the belt before her skin grew welts, He never let on. But she prayed anyway. God never stopped her father from drinking and saying and doing the ripping things he did. God should have gotten involved long before her father did the things that drove Cassandra out, but by the time we crossed the stage at the end of high school it was too late. Things were too far gone already.

When we were juniors in high school I asked her how she stood it. I didn't even know the half of it then. We hardly ever talked about her pain, but this day it was so apparent that after we settled into our seats on the streetcar I just asked. She hadn't done something her mother had expected. I forget what. Memorize a chapter of the Bible, wash the dishes, feed the cat. She was sixteen years old and she couldn't sit flat on her bottom because it was so blistered and sore.

"Why don't you tell someone? Reverend Billings or the school counselor?"

She set her jaw and said to the Louisiana History book she had opened on her lap, "Spare the rod and spoil the child." I must have looked as confounded as I felt because she added, "God does this to make his power manifest in me. My job is to honor my father and mother."

She was the only real friend I had, but I knew then that she couldn't let me be close. She was full of foreboding I couldn't understand. I offered to talk to my parents and help her figure out what to do, but my offer was kept at arm's length by God's will and the words of the scriptures imparted to me through the mouth of Cassandra Dee Orgeron.

Cassandra needed liberation from her demons so badly that by the last day of school she had decided in her secret heart to break her oaths to God and betray her beliefs. It was the day before graduation when she told me what she wanted to do.

"I want to go drinking. Let's go to the Quarter and get drunk."

"Get drunk?" I laughed. "Do you want to invite your mother?"

"Look at me, Kate," she said. We were hustling out the door after our last class, our arms swinging free of our usual load of books. "I am serious. If I regret it I will confess and repent but right now I can't stand this any more. I feel like I've been sleeping with my brain in a girdle all my life, and I can't do it any more."

I shook my head and sarcastically said, "Who are you going with?"

"You!" She pulled at my elbow and I pulled it away.

"Oh, no! Not me! Find someone else!" I sped up and walked ahead of her through the gauntlet of the school corridor, lockers slamming, bodies bumping, tearful good-byes in progress, year books being signed.

"There isn't any one else." Cassandra kept up with me by jogging on tiptoes in her white Mary Janes and knee socks. Her plaintive expression surprised me. "I already asked Susan Brinsky and she said I would just get her in trouble. Only you. No one else will even say two sentences to me about it." Susan Brinsky was the wildest girl at school. It was well known that she went all the way with boys, so well known, in fact, that she herself bragged about it.

"You already asked one person without involving me." I suppose I was hurt that she had confided this enormous streak of daring to someone before me. "Ask someone else. Ask Kim Smith. Ask René Tyler."

"None of them will have anything to do with me and you know why." She scrambled out the heavy doors at the end of the hall behind me. She always had trouble holding them, and I had to stop and help her.

"No, I don't. Why won't they have anything to do with you?"

"You know why. Because I'm religious. You know what I heard René say about me by the football field this morning?"

I didn't answer.

"She said I was a Jesus Freak without the cool clothes."

I didn't answer.

"They laughed their heads off at me. They knew I heard. They meant for me to hear. No one likes me!"

"Jesus, Cass," I sighed.

"I wish you wouldn't say that," she scolded.

I lowered my eyebrows at her.

"Never mind," she said.

I tried not to listen to her panting breath as she tried to match my long strides. I didn't understand that something had already happened that was too powerful for her to manage. How could I have known that? She used to tell me that God would never give you more trouble than you could handle. It was in these last days of high school that Cassandra realized that if God wouldn't do it someone else would.

My family lived in a narrow, light blue, two-story shotgun house, trimmed in white. It had been built in the mid-eighteen hundreds. Our front porch had a wide set of brick steps and whitewashed banisters leading to a broad wooden porch. Two pillars reached up and supported the balcony, which jutted out from my parents' bedroom on the second floor. No one ever sat up there because we weren't sure it was safe. To the left of the stairs was a small white iron table flanked by two white rocking chairs. To the left was a hanging swing.

My mother sometimes nagged my father to move to the suburbs or across the river, to someplace quieter, with better streets. Daddy said he'd lived in New Orleans all his life and he was going to live in New Orleans all his life no matter who had better streets.

Cassandra sat in the swing and kicked off on a post to start rocking. I tossed my books on the small iron table and leaned over the railing. Suddenly Cassandra leaned forward and scraped her feet on the porch to stop the swing. She had to extend one hip off the seat in order to reach. The swing went off center for a second, the other end arcing around halfway before she could get it to stop.

"I don't know what God thinks about me, but I have to have one night without the fear of hell fire. One night. Even if I have to be sick drunk to just plain block it out and forget it." Cassandra scooted back and the swing creaked. I looked over my shoulder at her. "Maybe I'm kidding myself, but I've got to get out of here." She tapped her skull with her fingernails. "You've never had to deal with it. There's no way you could understand."

The giant leaves of the taro plants we affectionately called elephant ears rustled near our heads. Huge mosquito hawks bounced lethargically against the screen door. I looked out at the street. I didn't want to go with her. I didn't like drinking. I didn't even like staying up late. She didn't know what she was getting herself into. That much I knew for sure.

"Please come with me. If you don't come with me I might not make it back home." Her eyes filled with tears. She turned her head away and wiped her eyes with her fingertips. "You know, I can't preach against something I've never done, so its time I try something, you know?"

"No, I don't know," I said.

"I'm scared of doing it, but I'm afraid if I don't I'll be like this forever, just scared and nothing and trapped and empty."

I knew that she believed that if she died without repenting of her sins that she would go to hell. A long time later I figured out that she probably wanted me to go so I could keep her from killing herself. Killing herself would be a sin she couldn't repent from but living her life was a living hell.

My parents invited Cassandra's family to join us for dinner at Antoine's Restaurant after graduation. Mama made the reservations far in advance. Mrs. Orgeron wore a flowered chiffon dress with butterfly sleeves and a matching hat. She glared at my parents as they ordered their bottle of wine. When my father poured a glass for me to toast our graduation she became visibly disapproving.

Cassandra lowered her eyes hopefully when Dad offered to fill her glass, but her mother swatted her arm and said, "We don't drink."

I thought of the row of whiskey flacons across the bookshelf in Mr. Orgeron's den. Interior Designers who purchased antiques from him or had him seek out special pieces for their clients gave him gifts of Scotch and whiskey at every holiday.

Cassandra looked beautiful in her white graduation dress with her cheeks glowing like translucent juice from fresh raspberries. Mr. Orgeron said, "Let the girl have a glass." He ordered a bottle of Chardonnay for himself and Cassandra. Cassandra was too humiliated to share it.

Eugene Orgeron, who was used to drinking alone, drank the whole bottle himself. Mrs. Orgeron's attempts to catch his eye were as obvious as his blatant avoidance of her. He barely touched his food, but Frances Orgeron made sure none of it went to waste. Then she let her drunk and soon to be drunker husband drive her family home.

My father, Dan Breaux sighed with relief that the event had ended as he settled into the driver's seat. He looked handsome in his black suit. His hair was thinning up front, and he'd grown a bit of a paunch but he was still young looking and tan. He had been embarrassed as a baby faced youth and had grown a mustache as soon as he left home. Now, cleanly shaven, that baby face was helping him retain his youth.

My mother, Jackie, was a strong looking woman, not beautiful, but satisfying to see. She was a person people trusted simply because she looked so competent. When I was feeling needy as a child, I sometimes just looked at the side of her face as she cooked or drove the car and knew that one day I would inherit her silent confidence, her unruffled mien. Tonight she wore a black sleeveless dress and pearls and could have been a Senator's wife. I loved her deeply, and so did my father. We knew of her sessions of sadness, but at times like this they didn't seem so bad.

TWO

The Wrong Way Out

I changed from my white satin graduation dress and patent leather pumps into a brown knit body suit under hip hugger jeans, and a belt three inches wide. I slipped under my covers in case my father was sleepless and came in to say goodnight on his way to the kitchen for a glass of milk filled with crumbled soda crackers.

I heard her rustling through the bushes. Even though I expected her, the sound of her knock on my window made my heart slam and turned my stomach as if a stranger in a dark mask was there instead of Cassandra Dee. I knelt on the pink blanket folded across the end of my bed and raised the window. The harder Cassandra tried to be careful the more noise she made. I loosened the screen hooks on the heavy wooden frame and leaned out to help Cassandra heft it to the ground. I slid to the ground. We couldn't get the screen back in place, and decided to try again after I crawled back in at the end of the night.

We crept across the lawn and didn't dare speak. A light was still burning at Miss Lizzie's house across the street. She had told my mother she sometimes had trouble sleeping. I knew she would call my parents if she saw me sneaking off like this. She was sweet, but she was also nosy. I urged Cassandra to run. When we were sure we were safe we looked at each other and giggled out loud.

"The streetcar stops running at 10," Cassandra said. She pulled the mascara from her crocheted shoulder bag and began to darken her lashes.

"It's eleven now." I reached for the mascara. Neither of us wore much makeup but she had gotten a make up kit for graduation.

"So," I asked, "Do we wait for the bus?"

"We walk until something better happens," she told me.

The mosquitoes peppered our bare arms and we swished and shooed them from each other with our hands. Cassandra had gotten me to buy her a pair of jeans. Cassandra was not allowed to wear jeans. She wore them with a wispy cotton blouse. She was tiny, but she walked with determination. We hustled past the houses of long time neighbors.

The humidity was so heavy we couldn't keep up a crisp pace for long. The streets were still glistening from the late afternoon rain. My new platform shoes rubbed on my heels. Every now and then a car would drive by, its tires buzzing in the silence. A few drivers slowed looking at us and when they did we stepped up our pace so we would look like we knew what we were doing.

"Do you think this is safe?" I was nervous and tired. I wanted to go back and forget this. "Do you think this is a good idea?" I looked at Cassandra. Her pale frosted lipstick was smudged and I reached over to fix it, rubbing her tiny lips with my fingertips.

"It's an adventure, Kate," she said.

We pressed forward for several more blocks. I had serious regrets that we hadn't done more planning. I was scared.

"Cassandra, where are we even going? Do you have any idea?"

"Stop fussing," she said and smiled up at me. "We have to have something to tell people we did on graduation night, don't we?"

We slowed our pace and ended up standing on a corner not far from Napoleon Avenue. A blue Chevrolet full of boys sped by honking the horn.

"Hey, Baby! Where ya' headed?"

"Not where you're going," I mumbled.

They rounded the corner and Cassandra and I giggled. We started to cross the street and they were coming back from the other direction. I recognized a boy from our school leaning out of the back seat. Buddy Boudreaux. Bouday, they called him. Boo Day. They pulled to the curb a few feet away from us.

"What are you two goody two shoes doing out past your bed time?" He leaned out the window. Someone inside handed him a beer and he waved it at us before downing the whole thing in one long chug-a-lug. "Bottoms up!"

"Grow up!" I shouted as they drove away again.

"Kate, don't be rude! They might give us a ride!" Cassandra scolded me.

"You want to ride with that pimple posse?"

"They're kind of cute. Besides, do you have any better ideas?"

"Lord, Cassandra." I rolled my eyes and started to cross the street. Suddenly the car burst into reverse.

"Hey!" I jumped back onto the curb just a second away from being flattened.

"How about a ride?" said Cassandra. I prodded her with my elbow and hissed her name under my breath. She grabbed my arm and looked past me at the carload of boys. "Will you give us a ride?"

"Where ya' goin', Jesus Freaks?" Bouday taunted. "Isn't it a little late for church?" The driver was a dark haired boy I didn't know.

Cassandra shouted, "I am going anywhere I can to get rid of my good reputation!"

Hoots from the car. "You've come to the right place, Sweetheart!"

"Cassandra, stop it," I pulled on her arm, trying to get her to walk away with me, back in the direction of home.

"You can come with me or you can go home. Either way I am going to have a good time tonight," Cassandra let go of my arm we stood looking at each other. I was breathing heavily. Her eyes were determined. Love bugs mated in the spotlight of the street lamp and I felt streams of sweat trickle down between my breasts.

"Fine. Have it your way," I said. I opened the back door of the car. "Move over!"

Bouday hopped out and held the door as I crawled in. I leaned as tightly against the opposite door as I could, holding on to the handle for all I was worth.

The driver leered out the window at Cassandra. "I never said you could have a ride," he said, grinning.

"Please?" Cassandra put her hands up as if in prayer.

"You'll have to pay for it."

"Whatcha got in mind?" She was grinning as she crawled across his lap to sit in the middle with the gearshift between her knees.

Lord, Cassandra," I said to myself, my heart pounding, my cheeks red and burning.

The Chevy was old and decrepit. It squealed as we rounded corners too fast, and it smelled of stale cigarettes and sandwiches left on the dashboard since last summer. And fish. It smelled a lot like fish.

The driver's name was Danny Boudreaux. He was Bouday's cousin. Bouday was trying to press his leg against mine. I don't remember the other boy's name, the boy who crawled over the seat to the back when Cassandra got in. He inserted himself between me and the window forcing me to move to the center of the seat.

Danny, it turned out, lived across and down the river in Venice, way down the Mississippi almost in the Gulf of Mexico. It was as far as you could go without falling in the ocean. People there were shrimpers or orchard keepers or worked in the oil fields. His family had one of the larger orange groves in Plaquemines Parish, but that didn't make them wealthy. They were still farmers and farmers live by the whims of nature. Wealth in Plaquemines came from political maneuvers the Boudreaux family simply didn't have the savvy for. Hurricanes and flash floods and freezes regularly stole a year's crops. When that happened the Boudreaux family would head out onto the water to bring in nets full of shrimp or crawfish to sell out of ice chests from the back of their flatbed truck. Those years their bodies smelled of fish, and there wasn't anything anyone could do about it. Ivory Liquid and even lye just teased the smell of sea flesh until it could be strengthened again the next day. The Lord must have really favored the odor of fish.

Danny's car remembered the smell of the crabs that had been sold out of its trunk for at least a decade, but Cassandra didn't notice. As I clung to the door of the back seat Cassandra drank a beer, a luke warm Miller Beer she shared with Danny. We stopped along the breakers at the Lake Front. Everyone got out except Danny and Cassandra.

"Come on, Cass," I pleaded.

"You go on. We're going to talk," said Cassandra. Danny nuzzled her neck.

I followed the other two boys down the breakers. I was mad. I felt betrayed. I felt foolish for coming along on an outing I didn't want to have. I kept looking over my shoulder at the shifting figures silhouetted by the street light in the front seat of that rancid old car.

We walked a while, the boys swilling beer and trying to engage me in conversation above the din of the waves. For all their swagger they were still high school boys. Pretty soon they gave up trying to talk to me and walked side by side a few feet ahead, sullenly drinking and cursing and occasionally tossing pebbles into the waters of Lake Ponchartrain. I stopped walking and stared out onto the lake. My father told me that it was the largest man made body of water... where? In Louisiana? In the world? Lights flickered faintly from across the broad body of water. Water splashed against the breakers. Spray moistened my face and melted into the wetness of the air that enveloped us.

The noise of the waves was so loud the boys didn't notice at first that I had stopped walking behind them. I turned and headed back toward the car. They caught up with me a ways back up the breakers. Bouday tapped me on the shoulder. "Hey! What's up?"

"Let's go back," I said. They didn't argue. Bouday shrugged and they both followed me. They tossed their empty amber bottles into the water, flinging them far, far overhead, their arms pushing out so hard their track shoes left the earth for a moment, as if to follow the bottles into the sky. The bottles turned end over end, making disappointing, hopeless splashes at the end of their arcs. One of them caught a reflection from the lights of Ichabod's Restaurant at the end of the pier. I thought of tomorrow morning when the bottles would be back at the breakers, intact but for their washed off labels, bumping helplessly against the cement breakers again and again.

When we reached the car Cassandra and Danny were in the back seat. Cassandra pulled her blouse together when she saw us. Her lipstick was smudged and she had a passion mark on the side of her neck.

Danny stood up outside the car to zip his pants. He grinned and raised one eyebrow at the other boys who whooped with glee, punching each other's arms, avoiding contact with my eyes.

Cassandra scrambled back into the front seat. I slid into the car and held onto the door and made the other boys crawl in from the other side. Cassandra didn't look over her shoulder at me even once during the whole long, hot drive home, or even after we stepped from the car and scuttled back the same way we came. She stared after the moon and didn't say a word. She didn't help me climb back in the window. My father found the screen against the wall the next morning while he was mowing the lawn and came inside to wake me.

"It must have fallen," I said, confused from sleep, blushing darkly against my pillow.

"It was against the wall like someone put it there on purpose. Did you hear anything last night? Anyone outside?"

"No, Daddy."

"I'm gonna get bars for these windows," he said.

Good, I thought. Bars to keep me in where I belong.

Cassandra didn't tell me for a long time that she didn't go to bed alone that night after she got home. Now I wonder if maybe I could have saved her if I had been standing outside her window when she discovered her father waiting in her room. If only I had gone to her window instead of having her come to mine, if only I had known.

Sex with Danny to cover for Daddy.

That night I tasted a beer offered by Bouday, trying to get in the spirit, but I gave it right back. The boys in the car decided that it was I who was straight laced, but I didn't care. I hated everything about that evening, even myself. The boys and Cassandra made me sick. The smell of fish will always remind me of that night. I can't walk through the French Market where they sell fish without remembering that night and everything that followed. When I gave up meat I never missed fish. I hadn't enjoyed it since that night.

Cassandra called the next day saying she was so sick she thought she was going to die, saying that she hoped she did die, that she deserved to die. I sat down on the floor in the hall where our phone was and put my head between my knees. She talked and talked about her hangover, as if it was something I could dilute, as if making me understand how she felt would take the sickness away. Finally, after it seemed like I'd been listening into that phone for hours, for days, she said good-by. I went to bed and slept all afternoon. If I felt grimy and dirty and disgusted, what must she have felt?

My mother came into my room, felt my forehead with her cool hand and asked if I felt all right. When I lied and said I was fine she opened my curtains so that the sun brightened my pink room. "It must be all the excitement yesterday." She always said that sunlight gave people energy.

The sun lay across my body as heavy as a cat but it didn't help.

Three

The Trouble With Friends

It wasn't hard to figure out that there was something really wrong with Cassandra, something I couldn't help her with, even if I had been older and wiser. We were kids who lived on the same street. We just happened to be together. I didn't ask her for trouble, but after growing up with her all these years she was about to give me more trouble than any person ever needed. Enough for my whole lifetime.

It seemed to me then that Cassandra turned into a big load of trouble just over night. Now I know she was handed trouble the day she was born, and warded it off as long as she could. The Lord's armor had a big bull's eye painted on it right over Cassandra's heart. If only I had grown up in a different city, in Pittsburgh or Seattle or even just up in Shreveport. If only I had grown up even a mile away, this wouldn't have been my problem. But I grew up on Jefferson Street in New Orleans two doors down from Cassandra Dee Orgeron and my whole life would be affected by that simple unintended fact.

Cassandra called Danny Boudreaux the day after they had sex in the back seat of that old fish car. She told me, and I decided that I'd had enough of Cassandra Dee Orgeron and I was going to bide my time until I could get rid of her without making it look like I had. I quit calling her, but she called me so often she didn't seem to notice that I never initiated anything. I listened but didn't say much. She talked so much that it didn't matter. I thought that trouble was something you should leave alone. You shouldn't ask for it, lure it, beg for it. But I listened with confused fascination. I didn't have the passion she had. I observed hers with alien wonder.

My mother asked what was wrong between us, but this time I couldn't tell her. My father would box my shoulder playfully and ask, "Where's your little side kick, Katie?" I would shrug and say, "At church, I guess, or something."

Danny Boudreaux called Cassandra the day after she called him. The next thing I knew they had a date for the next weekend without the entourage. Just the two of them alone.

"Maybe I am not a very good friend, Cassandra," I said, "But I would be an even worse friend if I didn't tell you what I can see that you must not be able to see or you wouldn't be going out with him."

"What you talking about?"

"He's only after one thing."

I could hear her breathing stop as if she were about to speak, but for once she said nothing.

"You can't keep going out with him and messing around like that. You can't." I rolled up the corners of the phone book pages around a pencil. It was dark and hot in the hallway. I laid down with my head in the doorway to the living room, trying to catch some of the air from the floor fan. We had window unit air conditioners in most of the rooms, but the hallway stayed hot. My mother passed through and stepped over me carrying a mountain of clean folded white towels. I could smell the powdery scent as she passed. I wanted to wipe my face with one but she would have scolded me. She was getting irritable and I hoped she wasn't getting ready to get sad, too.

"Why not?" Cassandra sounded preoccupied.

"What about your religion? Have you just forgotten all about that?" I could have hit myself for bringing that up, but it was the most provocative piece of ammunition I could think of at the moment.

"No. I guess I feel pretty bad about that. I just need him to like me."

"Boys don't like the girls that give them what they want. Everyone knows that."

"I guess they do, too. I guess he's seeing' me again, isn't he?" Her accent was rich and thick and lazy.

"What if you have a baby? Or what if somebody finds out?"

"I guess I'll worry about that myself."

"At least make him wear a rubber." I was reciting the information we got in Health class.

"A lot of good that will do."

"What is that supposed to mean?"

"Nothing'. It means nothing. I gotta go."

I didn't hear from Cassandra again for two days, until after the date. I thought about her the whole time. I thought about calling. I thought I should call, but I couldn't break my inertia. I spent my time painting in my room and gazing out into the hall trying to imagine what I would say if I were to call her. The more I thought, the more I felt like sleeping, and that is usually what I would end up doing. I'd sleep in my room which smelled of turpentine with the window opened wide and the sun stretched out across me. I'd wake up in the dark evening with a headache and a weight in my gut.

The phone rang one day when I was lying there in a sick to my stomach place between awake and asleep. I hadn't cleaned my brushes before I laid down. I jabbed them into the jar of turpentine as I went for the phone. I stood leaning on the door frame to my room, stretching the phone cord to it's limit, examining the still life I was painting of my shoes lying on my flowered purple skirt. I wanted to hear what she said, but I didn't want to hear it too well. I wanted to paint her face and not have to listen to her words.

She said she thought she was falling in love with him. She said he told her he felt the same. They were going to elope as soon as they could get a place to live. Her voice tumbled like ice in crystal.

"After two dates you decided to get married?"

"It was his idea. He really wants to, Kate. I can't believe it. I'm so happy!"

I sighed. "Wow."

I think I was too sleep intoxicated to understand. I was so tired those days. I thought of going back to sleep as soon as she hung up. My pink bedspread was wrinkled up where I had been laying on it. My mother made me make the bed every day even though I spent most of the day in the thing and it didn't seem to make much sense. The matching pink chiffon curtains fluttered in the breeze. The afternoon rain had just stopped and it smelled distinct and fresh coming into my chemical scented room. I pressed my face against the screen and breathed in deeply.

"Would you go out with us Friday?"

"Just the three of us? Oh, that would be fun!"

"I just want you to get to know Danny better. You are my best friend and he'll be my husband soon so it would be nice if you could be friends, too."

I flopped onto my bed. Laying on my back I walked my feet up the wall paper, one rose at a time. "It would be a little awkward for me, really, Cassandra."

"We could bring his cousin."

"If you're talking about Bouday, don't even think it. Maybe you could just bring Danny over here for a while. We could sit out on the porch, or something."

They came and sat together on the glider on the front porch while I brought them tall jelly glasses of tea. Mom came out later with some Fig Newtons before retreating to her bedroom. Cassandra ate nearly all of the cookies. Danny was quiet. I couldn't look into his face at all. I kept thinking of him zipping his pants with that nasty grin on his face.

"We want you to come with us to hear this music. Danny found this place down in the Quarter and he wants to take us. I want you to go with us."

I looked at Danny. He glanced at me, then stood up and walked to the railing. He leaned over and yawned. He wore a black KISS tee shirt which stretched over the definite muscles lining his back. His jaw flexed in his cheek.

"You just go on. I wouldn't have much fun being a third wheel."

Cassandra fidgeted with the top button on her white blouse, then wrapped her thick hair around her index finger the way she used to do in grade school. She looked like a little girl. I hadn't really seen how little she was in a long time. All the times I sat right beside her I had forgotten that she was so little. Too little to get married. Little enough to break. Right now it didn't endear her to me. Right now it made me sick.

"I really want you to," said Cassandra, with a little hurt whine in her voice. "Isn't that enough?"

"Does your Mother know you're going out?"

Cassandra laughed loudly and Danny and I both looked at her. She stood up and swung her purse around her self, back and forth, slapping against her thighs on this side and that. I wanted to tell her she looked seven years old. I wanted to shake her. Slap her.

"She met Danny," Cassandra sang. "She was in seventh heaven that I finally met a boy."

"I thought she wanted you to marry a preacher," I said.

Cassandra glared at me. "There weren't a whole lot of preachers knocking on the door. Besides, what preacher would want me?" Soiled, spoiled Cassandra.

Danny stood up. He looked at Cassandra like he was just waking up. "I'll bet just about any boy would die to have you." He wasn't leering now. He seemed completely serious. These were the first words he had spoken since 'hello'. I squinted my eyes so I could look at him without turning away. He was handsome in his way. Strong arms. His skin was the deep ruddy skin of people whose work kept them out of doors. He was gazing at Cassandra with his eyes bent in soft crescents, and I saw all at once that he had moved beyond that first night's conquest. He wanted her. Maybe he loved her.

There was so much to learn about Danny. I would later know that he had his own set of hurts. He carried a great load of shame and feelings of guilt on his young shoulders and there wasn't anything he could do about it. He was a lot like Cassandra in that respect. The only thing he could do was run away. As long as he ran by himself some invisible line kept drawing him back. So he found someone to run with him. If they both ran fast enough and far enough, and if they both pulled hard enough, maybe that line would break. That was all Danny could hope for.

Cassandra's face was as red as the gingham checks on her skirt, and her smile at him was just as wide open as the sky. She would pretend that all that lay before them was romance and maybe the routine of blissful ordinariness. She could imagine that being like everyone else was a big adventure of which she could never grow tired. Danny held out his hand to her and they stood there looking at each other until I said I would go get my purse. I could have been inside the house for a week and they would have still been standing there smiling at each other like idiots who had just fallen to Earth.

What did I know? I couldn't help wondering where that other Danny went. That one who had notched my tiny friend in the same back seat where I would soon be holding tight onto the handle, even though tonight I would be sitting in the back seat all alone. Danny was certainly different from the boy I met on graduation night. But he was floating on a wave that would take him helplessly up and down and up again until it found the darkest, rockiest shore upon which to hurl him.

I heard myself offering to paint their portrait together as a wedding gift. I wondered who Danny would turn out to be once he was captured.

"That would be cool," Cassandra said. Danny eyed me suspiciously. Then his hair fell over his eyes and he turned away. I was frightened by a cold wind.

The music we heard that night was loud and angry. The smoke was so thick that it was at times hard to see. Danny bought us beers. I wanted to go home so badly that I drank even though I detested the taste. Cassandra danced in front of the band with Danny's hands on her shoulders.

The next day, dressed all in black, Cassandra told me she wanted to be a poet. She read me a poem she had written.

Ants,

working hard
Hard working ants.
Could I be like them?
Do the dance of the ants?
Me,
Working hard,
Hard working me.

> *Would I be as admired as the ants?*
> *Would anyone take notice of*
> *Hard working me?*

I told her it was good and suppressed an urge to roll my eyes. She said she wanted to be a poet. I nodded. To be a poet would mean she was something of her own, at least.

"Is the wedding still on?"

"Yes. We haven't found a place, but it will have to be soon." Cassandra sat on the edge of my bed and swished my new round sable paint brush back and forth across her chin. I was afraid she would rough up the bristles before I got to use it. I must have been clutching the air because she suddenly looked at it and handed it to me. Absentmindedly I brushed it back and forth on my chin and it felt good, sweet, sensual.

"Why will it *have* to be soon?"

Cassandra pulled a pack of cigarettes out of her purse.

"What are you doing?"

"I started last night." She shook a cigarette out of the pack.

"You can't smoke in here!" I said. My parents were in the living room watching television. Dad kept getting up to fuss with the antenna. The set was new and he couldn't leave it alone. It was just across the hall.

"I just want to show you something."

"Lord," I said. I closed the door and sat down on the bed next to her. I kept my back to the door so that we could hide the cigarettes if my mom should walk in.

"Have you ever seen one of these?"

It was a small white hand rolled cigarette. She held it cupped in her palm like a tiny treasure.

I couldn't believe it. "Pot!"

"Smell it."

They told us in Health Class that it smelled like burned rope, like oregano. It smelled like straw on fire.

"You got this from Danny? Geez, Cass, you're getting in deeper and deeper!"

"I'm not going to get caught. Here." She handed it to me. "We smoked some last night and it was the best thing in the world!"

"You smoked it?" I spoke so loudly that Cassandra clamped her hand across my mouth.

"Shhh! Yes, and it's nothing. I mean, it's something, but it's something good."

"What are you thinking about, Cassandra? Aren't you afraid?"

"Wait 'til you try it. You'll see. It's great."

"What do you mean until I try it?" I grabbed my pillow and clutched it to my chest. "I am not trying it."

"Danny gave me this for us because I wanted you to try it. Tonight we'll sneak out. I promise, you'll wonder why you waited so long."

"I'm not smoking that."

The grass was wet behind Cassandra's father's tool shed where we sat handing the tiny joint back and forth. It burned my throat and nostrils and smelled strong, earthy. Cassandra instructed me to inhale the smoke and hold it inside my lungs for as long as I could. I coughed and coughed and so did she. We kept smoking, though, until we began laughing. It was a long time before we could stop. The laughs ended up in our nostrils, where we tried to keep them from escaping and creeping over the sills and through the open windows of her parents' bedroom.

We talked for long periods of time but when we came to what might have been the end of each anecdote we couldn't remember what we had been talking about. Everything we said seemed so wise at first, then tapered off into senselessness. When she would ask me questions I didn't know what she meant. I understood the words but I just didn't know what relevance they had. I giggled and looked up at the stars. I think Cassandra was laughing too.

Cassandra's head was next to mine; our bodies angled outward from each other. She began to talk about Danny kissing her and caressing her, and my heart began to ache. My nostrils moistened. I thought the stone growing in my chest would suffocate me. I wanted to reach over and hold Cassandra in my arms and make her safe from whatever was making her run toward Danny this way. A wisp of her hair lay near me on the grass and I picked it up and held it without really knowing what I was doing, feeling how silky and fine it was in my fingers. She began to cry. Not tears of joy like a young girl in love. Sad, heavy tears. Her sobs, though barely audible, came from her gut, from her soul, and they entered me like the heavy grief of death. I rolled over and wrapped her in my arms, lying there on the wet grass with pampas fronds waving above us. She pressed her head against my shoulder and wept.

When I asked her what was hurting her soul so badly she only said, "Everything will be fine now. Everything will be all right."

It seemed that every breath of the wind was the hush of fabric moving against itself. Every bird which moved in it's sleep was as loud as twigs breaking under a voyeur's foot. Cassandra said it was because of the marijuana. It can make you paranoid, she said.

In one changing moment, all I wanted was to be at home in my bed. I was terrified as I raced, stumbling home, unsteady on my feet, not remembering what I needed to be doing, not sure how to be silent. All I knew was that I would surely be discovered and that there would be serious retribution for my crime. I turned to look at Cassandra but couldn't return to her.

Cassandra looked after me as I fled, sitting up now, leaning on her hands. I turned back to look at her and I thought I saw the shadow of a man beside her among the trees. My skin rushed in waves from my face to my spine and back as I struggled to get inside my house. I trapped a scream still alive in my throat and thought I would vomit. Somehow I managed; somehow I got into my bed without my mother coming in to see if I was well. Without my father seeing if I was safe. Every time I began to fall asleep I remembered seeing the man-like shadow and wondered until dawn if it was real.

Cassandra said it was my imagination, that she had gone in to bed. I thought of how her hair had wrapped around my fingers and how she had clung to me. I wanted to ask her many things but I didn't know how. I was too afraid to know.

Four

Escape

We were clumsy at escaping from our houses late at night. Because I could no longer climb out the window there were close calls. Somehow we never got caught. As he had promised the night of graduation my father had installed burglar bars over our windows to keep peeping toms from creeping in. The elephant ears growing next to our back porch were as big as coffee table tops and once I had to hide under them for nearly an hour while my father rummaged around the kitchen for a midnight snack, never suspecting he was interrupting my attempt at breaking back in. He might have thought of me sleeping peacefully in my room. Another night he might have glanced in at me as I slept. My gentle daddy.

Danny continued to see Cassandra. Cassandra was delirious with gratitude. She urged Danny to marry her right away, but he said he began to drag his feet and said he wanted to wait until he graduated from high school. I couldn't imagine him caring whether he graduated or not. Cassandra began to complain that Danny was pulling away from her. I told her she was pressing him too hard. She didn't hear me. Didn't want to. Wouldn't. As soon as she would seem almost willing to believe that her knight in shining armor was deserting her, he would be back, urging her forward, dragging her away.

The three of us went to clubs together. Danny would wait in his Chevy at the corner while Cassandra and I sneaked out of our houses, then we'd go and listen to music and get stoned. I don't know why I went. I never wanted to be there. I kept thinking something was going to happen that I shouldn't miss. And I didn't know how to say no to Cassandra. I am not sure why Cassandra invited me. Perhaps I was her safety net. Her place to fall if everything should crash to earth around her.

Cassandra complained that Danny wasn't romantic with her any more. I had decided, for my own peace of mind, not to think about it. I felt responsible for her by simply knowing what little I knew and I didn't want the responsibility. I would have been happy if my parents had supported me until I was thirty. I didn't want to support anyone else, emotionally or otherwise. And yet I felt trapped in this complicated web. Somewhere on the edge. Not being eaten, but wasting away in wait. The more I tried not to think about it the more it was all that was on my mind.

I painted their wedding portrait. Danny's image took far too long because he grew restless sitting and being examined. He would let his hair fall across his eyes and wouldn't move it when I asked him to. He glared at me, his lip lifted in a hint of a sneer. Cassandra scolded me, "You've made him look too angry!" But that was how he looked when he looked at me.

One night I was driving Cassandra home in my father's old Buick. Danny wanted to stay at the club when Cassandra wanted to go home and they had argued. This night I had borrowed my father's car. Finally Cassandra and I left without him.

She lit a joint. I took it from her and inhaled deeply.

"It makes things just grow and glow and… wait …" Cassandra rummaged around in her large black crocheted hand bag for a fountain pen and a notebook. I was used to her ridiculous and melancholy poetry after they had a fight. She once said to me, "Isn't it great that we both are artists now?" Feeling good that day, I answered that it was.

They were fighting more and more often. She began to write in her notebook. Occasionally she would pause, holding the end of the pen to her lips, then she would scribble some more.

I drove steadily, but I was annoyed and fought the urge to press the gas pedal to the floor and tear through the streets. I didn't want to hear a poem.

"Listen to this," Cassandra said. She took a deep drag from the joint before beginning to read.

> *I sit in smoke*
> *Dreaming*
> *Hoping*
> *Growing like a butterfly…*
> *I grow*
> *I glow*
> *I wait for you*
> *To smash me*
> *Bash me*
> *Clash with me…"*

I interrupted. "What did you all fight about?"
Cass laughed through her nose. "He's a jack ass."
"Maybe you should break up with him."
"Can't."
"Why not? He's trouble."

"Right. Trouble." Cassandra stuck her head out the window and spat out smoke.

"Yeah, trouble."

"Well."

"You have to get a hold of yourself. What's life going to be like with him? You want this for the rest of your life? It's not going to change, you know. It will get worse."

Cassandra crossed her arms over her chest. "God, you've gotten holy lately. I'm starting to think you're headed for the convent. You never date anyone, and now you're trying to stop me from having a life."

"I try to pretend everything's okay. You are my friend, Cass. I love you. I just worry about you. I mean, you were this Jesus Freak, you know? You were at church every five minutes and now you sneak out and go clubbing and get high. What is going to happen if you get caught?"

"It would be a sojourn for my art."

"Caught for your art?" I sighed. "Cassandra, I don't think your Dad would feel that way if you got pregnant and he found out."

"I don't care what that old bastard thinks."

"You're being ridiculous." I fumbled with a cigarette and lighter. Cassandra leaned over to help me. She's the one who got me started smoking. It took me 20 years to quit.

"No, I guess if I'm pregnant I'll have help from my husband."

"Right. What husband? You just called Danny a jack ass and you insinuate that you're still going to marry him? Are you out of your mind?"

"I'm not going to marry him."

"Well, that's a relief," I said as I pulled up to a stop sign.

"I already did. I guess now I'm a jack ass, too."

I couldn't speak. I pulled to a stop at a red light.

"Say something. At least close your mouth. A love bug's going to fly in there." Cassandra sat wrapping a strand of her perspiration damp hair around her finger. She had circles under her eyes I hadn't noticed before.

"Why didn't you tell me?" I spoke softly.

The light changed to green and to yellow and to red again.

"I always thought I would be your Maid of Honor. You told me you wanted me to wear lavender. You wanted ten Bride's Maids." I hated the idea of wearing a big fluffy lavender gown for even one night, but it became my dream right then. I rested my hands on the steering wheel, still stopped at the intersection. Two cars drove around us in the other lane, honking their horns in the speckled night light.

"We did it last week and I started to tell you about a million times, but I just didn't know how." Cassandra was sitting so low down in the seat now that passersby must have thought I was alone. Her knees were beneath the dashboard, spread wide apart, her black denim skirt scooped between them like a hammock. "I think it would be worse to disappoint you than to disappoint my parents. They never thought I was worth a damn anyway. I always wanted you to think the best of me."

I pushed the gas pedal and we rolled along St. Charles, turned left before the Mississippi River bridge on ramp and turned right again on Magazine. It was dark and dark skinned people waited for something under flickering street lights, peering into some transparent future.

"You know what?" Cassandra leaned her head against the back of the seat and looked over at me. "My life is fucked up completely now."

I pulled over next to the curb in front of the Tic Tac Laundromat. The building faced the corner, its corner cut off to make an entrance way. It had a placard bearing its name hanging from the balcony above.

"Why did you do it?" I asked, not looking at my friend. My small, lost friend. I didn't reach to hug her. I didn't pretend to cry. There was no school girlish melodrama to play out between us. This was real and it was hard.

"I'm pregnant," she said.

My head fell back against the seat. The car didn't have head rests, so I lay there looking up at the water stains on the headliner. I felt betrayed, bereaved, cheated. It was a confusing emotion since what I wanted to feel, what I thought I should feel, was compassion.

"Yes. Pregnant. With child. Cassandra has a bun in the oven."

"What are you going to do?"

"Well, my friend, I thought about killing myself…"

"You wouldn't even think that," I begged. I breathed deeply to check the tears that were threatening to come. "You wouldn't do that would you?"

"No, it seems that I wouldn't. I couldn't think of a way that wouldn't hurt really bad." Cassandra laughed at the pathetic joke. She seemed old. No longer seven or seventeen, but seventy-seven. Ninety-seven. "Then I thought of having an abortion, but chickened out on that, too."

"An abortion?" I asked. "You thought of having an abortion?"

"When did you get so naive?" Her words snapped like a whip. The distance spread between us. "God, you're stupid." Cassandra saw my face pale.

She slapped her thigh and threw her head forward. She sat there, elbows on her knees and breathed heavily. "Jesus, I am sorry, Katie. I guess it's just the way I act when my life is over." Leaning back, she inhaled deeply and rubbed her face roughly with the palm of her hand.

We sat in complete silence. She breathed deeply and audibly.

I smoked quietly for a while. We moved only to swat at mosquitoes and swish away love bugs joined from behind in a helpless reproductive trap.

My nostrils tingled and I dabbed at tears. "Why am I the only one crying?"

Cassandra sighed. "I have cried so much I don't think I can do it any-more. I have cried all week. I have cried twenty-four hours a day. I have cried and puked. Cried and puked. Cried and puked."

"How do you know you are pregnant? Maybe you're just late. Maybe you're sick."

"You know, I don't know what's wrong with me, but I hadn't even noticed that I had missed two months. I thought I was nauseated because I had the flu and it just wouldn't go away. Remember when I had the flu? When I went to the doctor he knew right away. Did a little blood test and, sure enough! He ain't a doctor for nothing. I had to beg him not to call my parents."

"Did you tell them?" I whispered the question. The thought was too obscene to say aloud. I knew Cassandra's father. He had a raging temper. But Mrs. Orgeron was the one I thought Cassandra would have to look out for.

"Do you think I would be going home tonight if they knew I was pregnant out of wedlock?" She smoked a while. "No, Danny is going to get us an apartment. Then I'll move over there and write them a letter or something, after giving them a month or two to miss me."

"But he wants to finish high school first, right?"

"Not any more, I guess. He only wants to because he's scared of this whole mess. I sure wish I could get out of it. If I were him I'd run away fast as I could."

"No you wouldn't."

"I would. I really would."

"You can make like you were already married when you got pregnant."

"I can't imagine them believing it. I imagine I can kiss my family good-by. No great loss. Hell, it's what I've always wanted!"

"No you haven't!"

"Yes, I have. I was just too scared to admit it. Hell and all that. I hate them. I hate them both."

"Look, you could have them give you a wedding and pretend the baby came early."

"Yeah. Mm-hm. Mother would want to plan for six months invite everyone in our whole church. How would I explain having to go into the other room to give birth during the ceremony?" She rubbed her eyes with the heel of the hand holding her smoldering cigarette.

"No, Kate, this way it's done. They can pitch a fit if they want, and I imagine they will outdo themselves on this fiasco. Mom will get Reverend Billings to arrange a prayer meeting for me. But I am legally married. Went to the Justice of the Peace on Monday.

"It was this bare little office with rotten old linoleum. I nearly broke my neck when a piece of tile came up right under me. They had a plain green metal desk, and this weird little bald guy did the ceremony and a fat secretary witnessed it, looking down her big, fat nose the whole time."

"What if your parents try to annul it?"

"Well, then they'll have a hell of a time explaining Little Junior to Brother Billings, won't they? Besides, our church isn't the annulling kind. You get married for good and always."

I pondered Cassandra's decision, and debated with myself the options. I was appalled by the thought of an abortion, but knew that would have meant a chance for her to have a life fit to live as long as no one found out. It would have given her a chance of survival.

Cassandra told me Danny had found a doctor who would perform the abortion for three hundred dollars. That was so much money in those days. They sold everything they could, even the Fish Mobile. Danny borrowed a car and drove her to a place down to the Delta Women's clinic. I knew the place. It seemed so open and vulnerable. Cassandra said it was clean and tidy and the women behind the counters smiled gently. But it felt, she said, like she was on TV and everyone knew her whole life's secrets.

A counselor called them back to a small white office and asked if they knew what to expect. She showed them materials and described the procedure step by step. She told them they could get up and leave if they weren't completely sure. That was when Danny started to cry. He had started to pace, then returned to the chair. He sniffed for a while before Cassandra realized what was going on. But the counselor knew. She had seen tough guys break down before. Cassandra put an arm around him and he pretended he was just suffering from allergies. The counselor suggested that they make an appointment and talk to her later because this was not something, she told them, they would want to make a mistake about.

That morning, walking to their car, Danny had surprised Cassandra and proposed that they marry immediately, and she had gratefully agreed.

Danny had one option Cassandra didn't have, and that was to desert the baby and the baby's mother. By some magical chance he chose not to do that. I didn't understand it then, but now I think that Danny was groping for the fairy tale ending, too. The loving family, the little home. Things neither he nor his bride ever had. Chivalry was still taken at face value in those days and so Cassandra gratefully and passionately said, "I do." After all, what alternative was there?

But Danny was mercurial and if he was strong and decisive in one moment he was confused and overwhelmed in the next, or angry and spiteful. Cassandra's knight in shining armor was a child with less to offer than she could offer herself. But all she could see was a little light shining through the door and she had to go through.

There were things about Danny's life that we didn't know yet. Things that Cassandra could imagine but had not guessed, and things that were beyond my deepest fears.

I thought it might have been wise for Cassandra to go away for a while. Because neither innocence nor goodness insures immunity, I had heard occasionally of girls who would go away for several months and come back soft bodied and weary. It would be said that they had been away visiting relatives, maybe helping an ill grandmother, or attending school. Sometimes the truth would be told, in these liberal seventies, that she had a baby she'd placed for adoption. Those who returned would sit on their parents' porches sadly drinking iced tea, aware only of their mothers' fierce silences.

But that was the old way. Now Cassandra was married. I was beginning to see that women's lives were burdensome things.

The contrast between what Cassandra had been and what she had become was stark as I laid in my pink, ruffled bed that night. I clutched my pillow between my thighs. I felt isolated and deserted. I resented Danny as much as ever, but would never tell Cassandra. What good would telling do?

Five

A Baby

They rented a Spartan cube of an apartment. It was barely furnished, and had only a small window air conditioning unit that worked only some of the time. Cassandra was growing thick of waist, her small stature unable to disguise for long the growing belly holding the little baby. I spent many evenings there with Cassandra. Danny worked sometimes and went out partying alone sometimes and Cassandra didn't like to stay there by herself. She trembled at the strange noises, the voices she heard through her walls, the fear that her father would find her.

One night, in a generous mood, Danny asked me to take them to hear a new musician. He didn't have money to help put gas in my car. He didn't know the band, but he could buy marijuana there. He was going with or without us, he told Cassandra. She wept and pleaded.

"You stay home, then," he said. "It's not like I really want to drag you around all night anyway." Cassandra slapped him. He laughed at her.

I berated Danny often about exposing Cassandra to marijuana smoke while she was carrying his baby. I complained that it couldn't be good for the baby but Cassandra didn't stop smoking either. She claimed it calmed her queasy stomach. She did stop drinking but that was mainly because she threw up easily and alcohol seemed to upset her stomach worst of all.

This time I refused to drive them. Cassandra didn't even want to go. Danny left on foot, and I stayed behind until I could persuade Cassandra to go to bed. I stayed until she stopped weeping, then I tiptoed out and went home.

Danny occasionally stayed out all night. He would later claim he got too drunk to get home and spent the night with a friend or to have missed his ride but I assumed it was another woman. Or women. How easily he had gotten Cassandra. How impulsively they fled into marriage. How hard would it be to get someone fresh? Cassandra became hysterical when he didn't enter the door at precisely the promised moment. That happened every time he went out. Cassandra was trapped in a minuscule upstairs apartment off the back driveway of a larger home. It had a narrow flight of stairs with iron railings that ended with a small metal grating at the top. The building they lived in was painted mint green, one of the faded pastel colors you would see in New Orleans' older districts and the windows and doors were trimmed in black. Below their apartment was another apartment where an older couple lived.

Theirs was a studio apartment. It had one main room that wasn't large. In a corner there was a bathroom blocked out into the living area. The rest of that wall of the main room was a kitchenette. They had a table they had found discarded in the alley and two chairs my father gave them from our garage. A mattress they laid on the floor against one long wall of the living room was both the bed and the sofa. There was a pair of narrow windows that let in the morning light on the wall opposite the mattress, above the one threadbare chair. There was a small window over the kitchen sink which brought in the wicked west afternoon sun, but only in a narrow patch. I bought Cassandra a set of yellow ruffled curtains to block it. Their clothes hung from a rod across one end of the little bathroom. Cassandra complained that they were always a little damp. I gave her several paintings to hang on the yellowed walls.

Cassandra and I scoured second hand stores for furniture and clothes. We became adept at spotting things in the trash that could be repaired. We got a small rickety dresser, some curtain rods and a bassinet. I found a poster from a Betty Davis movie. Cassandra found a plant, still living but barely, and nursed it back to health.

Even though the apartment was coming to life little by little, Cassandra still had nothing for company but a radio and my visits. Her pregnancy was quite far along by now and she still had not called her parents. They called our house once, but my mother told them we hadn't seen much of Cassandra in a while.

Cassandra kept the radio on all the time. Danny found a job at the gas station two blocks away so he was gone all day as well as all night, but Cassandra was house bound. She sat in the cubical making curtains from burlap and looked out the window on the eternity that seemed to grow before her.

One night late in her pregnancy I painted her portrait. She had to lean way back in the second hand wing backed chair. She propped her feet up on the fabric covered foot stool my mother taught us to make from large fruit juice cans. The elongated perspective exaggerated the proportions of her body that was draped in a light cotton night gown. Her breasts crept around her sides and beneath her arms, her belly pointed upward like a mountain someone might pray to. The pregnancy seemed to give her substance and strength.

It was the evening of that day before the rain broke through the sticky heat like fragile balloons on the concrete sidewalks. Danny had not left yet when Cassandra felt the first contractions, but she didn't tell me this until later. She hadn't seen a doctor in several weeks because money had been scarce and it was uncomfortable to ride in the bus, and she didn't know what to expect when the child began to come.

She had no phone and she began to walk to my house only when it seemed certain that the contractions weren't going to stop. She didn't know how long it might take for the baby to come and she told me later how she had feared that it would fall out as she walked up Jefferson seven blocks to my house.

It was late in the evening and I was painting in my bedroom, touching up the "Cassandra Waits" portrait, when I heard the knock on the front door. I listened absently while my mother answered it. I was examining the contrast of light and dark on a lace curtain I was using as a backdrop for a still life. I was getting the white too dull and the grays were clouded and muddy, not the mauve I had intended.

Suddenly Mother shouted for me to come.

"What is wrong?" I asked. I stuck my head out into the hall.

Cassandra's face was flushed, and she crept over and sat on the edge of the couch.

"I think the baby is coming." She looked at the wall gritting her teeth. "I think the baby is coming," she said again, not sure we had heard her.

"Lord, Cassie, where's Danny? How did you get here?"

"I don't know. I walked. I'm scared. It hurts." She looked up at my mother, who paused for an almost imperceptible moment.

My mother didn't like being around pregnant women. She had lost a little baby when I was just two years old. His picture still hung on our hallway wall as if he had just gone away to nursery school rather than being gone forever. Joey's eyes, in the picture, are focused on the spot where the photographer must have held a bouncing toy he wanted. He is laughing and striving forward, even though he is too small, and always would be, to go anywhere by himself. The way his eyes are focused looks like he was looking past us to something so interesting that we could not hold his interest. I have no memories of Joey other than his little crib next to my parents' bed. Mama has too many memories. She would never have another child and she would hate looking at Joey's photograph so much that she would keep the lights off in the hallway all of the time. My father wouldn't let her take the photograph down. "It's all we have left of our little boy," he would say.

"You have to get her to the hospital," Mama said to me.

Just then a contraction came and Cassandra grabbed a handful of the afghan we kept on the couch. She whimpered like a cold puppy.

"Cassandra," said my mother, "Who is your doctor?"

"Dr. Griffin," she whispered. We couldn't understand her. We had to ask her to repeat it until she finally screamed, "Dr. Griffin! Dr. Griffin!"

"Can you walk, now?" said Mother. I stood behind her, letting her take care of things, take care of us. My mother reached out and placed her hand on Cassandra's forehead as if checking for fever. It was my mother. My mother.

"Yeah. It only hurts for a minute at a time, but it hurts bad, real bad."

"Come on, then." Mother supported Cassandra as she stood up, and at the same time said, "Kate you call the doctor as fast as you can and let's take her to Charity." Charity Hospital.

"You're coming, Mama?"

"I'm coming," she said to me. "We'll get you there," she said to Cassandra.

Mother took Cassandra's arm and led her down the steps at the side of the house. Cassandra bent over in a sudden and severe contraction. She moaned and grabbed Mother's arm. I watched in wonder out the window, clutching the phone, afraid of making a mistake. I knew I could never be a mother. How can you ever be sure enough and strong enough to be a mother? My mother would have been asking herself the same thing, I now imagine.

Mother held Cassandra's waist with her strong arm. "We have to hurry. Come on."

Cassandra couldn't respond. She leaned against the railing. Just then a gush of water spouted forth from under her cotton dress.

Mother sat her in the back seat of our car, wet as she was. I thought she had peed in her pants. I didn't know that her water had broken and the baby was ready to come. Dad was always so particular about his car interior and now a girl was spilling wet mother fluids all over it. But he wasn't home. He was working late. Mother ran back into the kitchen and grabbed some towels from the dryer. She handed them to me and took the phone from my hand.

"You drive. I'll sit with her in back. If we can get her out to the hospital they'll take care of her," she told me. "Let's put these on the seat under her if we can. There might be time, but maybe not, so hurry on up. Drive to the Emergency entrance. Now, come on."

"But Mama," I began to cry. I was terrified. I looked out at the car under the car port where Cassandra was straining and holding onto the seat.

Mother refused to meet my eyes and pushed me out the door. "Don't you worry, Kate. Don't worry. Birthing is natural. It's only living that's hard."

I got into the car, flustered and feeling incompetent. "I wish you had told your mother. I wish she could be here with you," I said.

"A lot of help she would be..." Another contraction.

"Are you okay?" I asked.

"No. I am not. I can't do this."

"You're fine," my mother said. "We'll get you taken care of."

"Don't call my mother." Cassandra was firm and succinct.

I maneuvered around a pickup truck carrying an enormous load of tree branches. It seemed these unwieldy vehicles waited around every narrow corner in the congested uptown streets. If you were in a hurry there was always a beaten down truck full of something overflowing to pull into your path on the two lane, car lined streets on which you could not pass.

"Don't you think you're going to want your mother, Dear?" My mother stroked her hair back from her face. Mother was finding her place.

"I don't need her," said Cassandra as the next pain took over her voice.

"What are we going to do, Mama? Danny isn't even home. What are we going to do?"

"In just a little while Cassandra's going to have a baby. We'll worry about the rest when the rest comes."

Another pain interrupted us, and it was followed almost before Cassandra could catch her breath by another, more powerful contraction. We could talk no more as the pains followed one upon the other. Cassandra was sweating profusely and crying in the few seconds she had between contractions.

"I can't do this any more," she cried.

"Here we are, Cass, we're here." I parked the car in the emergency parking lot. It was full and I ran across the lot. Inside I called for help at the desk and an orderly was shocked into service. He wheeled a wheel chair out the door.

My mother helped Cassie into the chair and Cassie screamed that she couldn't sit down. The baby was coming.

We reached the door and an old man in overalls holding a towel to a bloody nose held it open for us. The nurse at the desk looked at us across the room full of people awaiting emergency care, and sighed audibly.

"Come and fill out these papers," she said to my mother.

"Cass, you'll do better at that."

"We don't have time," I shrieked. It seemed my hysterical voice was the only sound in the world, and I only wanted to scream louder so that the nurse would move as quickly as my heart.

"How long has this been going on?" asked the nurse.

"I don't know. A long time," I replied.

"I'm asking the mother," she said. I looked at my mother. Mother pointed at Cassandra.

The nurse pushed Cassandra's wheel chair to the wall. Cassandra was crumbling under brutal waves of pain.

"Why didn't you get her here sooner?" she asked, looking at my mother. Mama shrugged. She took a step backward.

"Aren't you this girl's mother?" demanded the nurse.

"No, we're friends," I said.

The nurse bent over and asked Cassandra loudly, right into her face, "How long?" as if she couldn't hear, as if labor made one deaf.

But for all her working senses Cassandra was unable to answer, and the nurse adjusted her chair against the wall. Cassandra's contraction let up for a moment and she leaned her head over and cried.

Fifteen minutes more and I saw my mother returning. At the moment I saw her the desk nurse called me. "That little friend of yours meant business," she said.

"She did?"

"She had a little girl."

"A girl!"

"She'll be in the nursery in a little while. You can go up there and wait."

"A girl, Mama!"

"I heard," she said sadly. She was starting to get tears in her eyes.

"You called her?"

Mama nodded.

"What?"

"You don't want to know."

"Yes, I do."

"I should have listened to Cassandra." We took the elevator up to the fourth floor and sat in plastic chairs waiting for Cassandra's baby girl to be brought to her crib in the window.

I called the station where Danny worked, hoping maybe he was there. The phone rang and rang and there was no answer. When we had seen the baby I drove Mama home and she went quietly into her room. She didn't say good night to me and she stayed in her room the next morning.

Six

Finding Danny

The next morning I drove to Cassandra and Danny's apartment. I sprinted up the metal steps taking two at a time to the second story apartment. I banged loudly on the door.

"Danny! Wake up! I have to talk to you!"

I heard movement inside. Finally I heard the door rattle and open and Danny was standing there in street clothes he had obviously slept in. His hair was unwashed and his beard was a dingy shadow. I could smell his sweat.

"Where the hell have you been?"

"What's it to you?" Danny leaned against the door and rubbed his eyes.

"Do you know where Cassandra is?" I stood hands on hips, adrenaline beginning to flow.

"She's not with you?" Danny looked down to the parking lot.

"No, she's not with me. She's in the hospital," I said. I put my hands on my hips and glared at him.

"The hospital? What happened? What's she doing there?" He asked. Then becoming fully awake, "Oh, God! The baby! Did she have the baby?"

I stood looking at him. "You knew she was going to have that baby any time. How could you leave her like that?"

"Shut up and take me to the hospital," said Danny. He reached for a pack of cigarettes and a set of keys off the scarred linoleum table and held open the door for me to pass through.

I ignored him. "You can't keep doing this to her."

"Don't tell me how to live my life," Danny said, looking bored.

"I took her to have her baby last night. My mom and I did. She walked all the way to my house in labor because you weren't around to help."

I raced down the stairs. He followed, but I beat him to the car. He put his hands on the door handle and tried to open the door. I slammed the car into reverse and backed up ten feet.

I yelled out the window at him, "I only came here because she asked me to. You can figure out your own way to get to the hospital."

Cassandra stayed in the hospital for several days. The baby was jaundiced and they wanted to keep her until that was resolved. Then Cassandra got a fever. She was brought the baby on a schedule so strict that her breasts ached. Often the nurses had already fed the baby formula in the nursery and the child wouldn't eat, so she got little relief. She refused the medication the nurses offered her to make her milk dry up because she thought it would be cheaper to breast feed her baby once she got home.

I visited the baby every day and gazed at her through the glass. Cassandra named her Melinda pending Danny's approval. The nurses would not allow me to hold the child. I might infect her with something, they told me. I came bearing gifts of all kinds, from layette items to teddy bears, spending almost all my pay check from TG&Y on the little baby with her tuft of hair as black as night. Cassandra had a few other friends who came to admire the child and leave small tokens like pacifiers and booties. It was three days before Danny came.

When he did come I was there. I looked away from him. Hating him, hating him.

Cassandra was in a ward of other new mothers. There were six beds with their heads against the walls and their feet toward the center of the room forming an aisle. Patient charts hung from the feet of the beds. Each bed had a curtain track around the ceiling from which beige privacy curtains hung.

The women all received their infant for feeding on the same schedule, and the rest of the time visited with guests, sat talking to each other or tried to sleep. One woman in the far corner had borne a still born baby. She wept into her pillow during feeding hours and most of the other times as well. I didn't understand why they left her in there with all those other happy new mothers. My mother couldn't come to visit. She sent flowers and an apology instead.

"Where have you been, Hon'?" Cassandra asked when Danny appeared in the doorway. She held out her arms to embrace him. He seemed embarrassed, and gave her a quick peck on the cheek. The women on either side of Cassandra in the maternity ward cast sideways glances at this belated husband and raised their eyebrows toward each other. I closed the curtain around myself and Cassandra's family.

"Kate wouldn't bring me," Danny said, as he kicked rhythmically at the leg of the bed.

"Don't you dare blame me," I hissed. I wished I could sear him, brand him with my eyes. Make a mark so people could see what he was, what he had done, and what he had not done.

"I had personal problems."

"What problems, Danny," asked Cassandra in a coddling voice. She caressed his arm and he pulled back and crossed his arms over his chest.

"I can't talk about this with her in here." He fiddled with the IV bag. I wanted to slap his hand.

Cassandra looked at me and I looked at Danny.

"Look," said Danny, confronting me. "What is your problem? I never did anything to you. I just asked you for a ride to see my wife and baby in the hospital."

"If you were ever around when you were needed maybe I would think you deserved my help, but you don't seem to ever be short of a ride to go out partying," I hissed in a half whisper.

"I never seen you turn down a smoke either, Goody."

"Please don't fight," Cassandra said. "I just had a baby. We're supposed to be happy. Did you see the baby, Danny? She is beautiful, isn't she? Kate, could you leave us alone? Just for a minute? We need to talk."

"Fine," I said. I flipped the curtain behind me to show them my disgust. I stopped in my tracks as I realized everyone in the room was looking at me. Against my own will I stood inside the door to the ward listening. Listening along with everyone else in the room, to every word I could catch.

"I can't stand that bitch," said Danny. Loud enough for everyone in the ward to hear.

"Danny, don't," said Cassandra.

"Yeah, so what," Danny said.

"What was that all about?"

"I don't know. She came over all worked up when the baby was born and wouldn't bring me back over here. I don't know what her problem is."

"Sometimes she gets moody," agreed Cassandra. I gritted my teeth but didn't move from the room.

"I don't like you seeing her." I could see Danny's silhouette through the curtain.

"Danny, Honey, we've been friends forever," Cassandra said, "I don't know what I would do without her. She practically delivered the baby. The emergency room was all busy that night and… "

"I don't like her. I'm your husband. I don't want you seeing her. End of story." "But, Danny," Cassandra said.

"Cass, she's trying to run our life. You can have her or you can have me." Cassandra was silent.

"Look, Cassie," Danny said. "I got some bad news the other day." Cassandra whispered, "What?"

"My dad died of a heart attack. I got a call at work yesterday."

"Aw, Danny. I'm really sorry."

"Don't be. He was a bastard. But my sister's alone over there in Venice."

Danny's sister, Helen, was sixteen years old. She had lived with their father in an old stilt house on the edge of Venice, Louisiana. Their mother had died when Helen and Danny were small.

"Helen found Dad dead in the bathtub two days ago and has been alone ever since. Helen didn't even have the sense to call me herself. The neighbors called."

I was staring at the flecks of color in the gray tiled flooring. I looked up and noticed all the women in the room staring at me. A few turned away when I looked at them. I slitted my eyes at the ones who still stared.

"She needs help with the house," Danny continued. "We gotta go down there for a while and get things settled. We could live in the house and we'll have the old man's car to use."

"I'm not getting out of here for a while yet. What about your job?"

"I can get another job."

"Maybe we should think this over. You go down there and check things out, help out a while, then…"

"Look. I got a new baby to feed and a wife, and maybe it's just what we need. We'll have a place; I'll get a job at the refinery. Did you ever think of that?"

Cassandra stammered, "I'm sorry. I just meant..."

"I'll decide what we'll do. I'm your husband and I guess you'll do what I say."

"I didn't mean anything by it."

"I am going on over there tomorrow and I'll stay for the funeral."

"But what about me and the baby?"

"I'll try and come get you when they let you out of here. If I can get my dad's car."

"What about the stuff in the apartment?"

"I already got rid of most of it. Tried to sell it out front to get some money, but the asshole landlord got pissed. Ended up giving it to one of those charity places. They brought a truck."

"But Danny. My things! Did you give away my clothes! The baby stuff! You can't just give them away!"

"I didn't give your clothes away. The rent is almost due and I don't want to have to pay up. Send Kate over for your stuff tonight. You still got your clothes and the baby stuff, but I got rid of everything else. I'm leaving tomorrow morning and she can't get in after that."

"Then what is she supposed to do with the stuff? How could you do this, Danny?" Cassandra's voice got very high.

"She can find a corner to throw it in at her house 'til you can get it, can't she?"

"Danny, we have a new baby. Wait until we get out of here to move. We can decide what to do then, when I'm home."

"It's too late. I told the landlord we're leaving already. You'll just come over to Venice as soon as you get out of here."

"Why don't you ask Kate? She's gonna have your stuff anyway."

I slipped out the door and went to the nursery. I was livid. I could barely walk a straight line. In a minute Danny came down the hall behind me and stopped near where I leaned against the window frame looking at the infants. I recognized his sauntering walk. My heart beat quickened and I took a deep breath to calm myself.

He stopped a few feet away with his hands in his pockets. I looked up and stared him in the eye wanting to spit. He looked through the window and raked at his hair. A row of tiny beds lined the wall near the window, each containing a swaddled baby either sleeping or in some degree of unattended distress as a plump nurse tended one after the other down the row in no particular hurry. A red squalling infant wrapped tightly in a tiny pink flannel blanket lay helplessly against the edge of her bassinet in front of the window.

"That the one?" Danny asked.

"Mm." I reached into my purse and got a cigarette. I held it in my fingers rolling it back and forth, unlit. I still remember that. It's funny how you remember such details when the world is changing.

Danny stepped closer. "It's little."

"Yep," I said, my teeth clenched.

Danny gazed at the baby silently. He was barely twenty, and his beard was thin and immature across his chin. He had a few black heads on his nose and his black, uncombed hair flopped lazily across his forehead. He was thin, and his skin, though anemic from time spent in the bars, bore a tell tale tan line across his upper arm from working in the sun. He fancied himself worldly but he was really just a farm kid, a deep south Cajun country boy.

"Kind of red," he said after a while.

I looked tenderly at the baby and forgot my anger for a moment. "She is beautiful." If he had been anyone else, I would have told him about every day of this infant's life, but that was my knowledge. I wasn't giving any of it up to Danny.

"She isn't too happy is she? Shouldn't they come and do something to her?"

"They're on a schedule."

"Schedule, my ass," said Danny. He pounded on the window to get the nurse's attention. The nurse scolded him in muted words he couldn't understand through the window and held her finger to her lips. A few more babies began to fuss. He pointed at his daughter. The nurse reached over and turned her onto her tummy with her face away from the window and the child seemed to calm down a little.

I walked around Danny and knocked softly on the nursery door. The nurse stuck her head out.

"This is the Boudreaux baby's father. Could you hold her up?"

The nurse's face suddenly softened.

"Oh! The Daddy! You'll have to be quiet so not to disturb the others, but stand by the window and I'll get yours. You will have to put out your cigarette, Miss. No smoking in here." I looked at the unlit cigarette in my fingers.

The nurse lifted the child like a puppy under her shoulders and rump and held her up. The baby squalled.

"She's mad," I said.

"She doesn't look mad. She looks scared." Danny looked silently at the wailing child as the nurse held her aloft.

I looked at the baby. The corridor was cool and I shivered. I wanted to hold that child, to bind her to my breast, to turn her away from her father like from a bitter wind. But he was right. She was afraid. Danny knew what fear was like. Knew it in his genes. Saw it in his child. The poor little thing had good reasons to be scared.

Chapters or other Divisions(required)

Please copy and paste this page as many times as necessary based on your number of chapters before you begin to input

Seven

Delivering Cassandra

Cassandra lay on her side in the hospital bed. I was sitting in a plastic chair next to the bed. I shifted as uncomfortably as if it were my body that had born the child.

"Cassandra, I will go get your things. I will put them in my garage. I will do whatever I can for you, but I won't take you to Venice. I don't feel right about this. Danny needs to come back here after the funeral and tend to his family. If he wants you to go to Venice, and if you really want to go, he needs to come get you."

"But he has to take care of his sister. He can't just leave a sixteen year old kid over there alone."

I leaned my forehead into my hands and rubbed my eyes. "Why doesn't he bring her with him to get you? Besides, how long will it take him to get you? She can stay alone a day, can't she? You and I were both baby-sitting when we were twelve."

Cassandra changed the subject, groping; "If he won't come and get me there's no way for me to feed myself and the baby. I don't even have an apartment to go home to."

"What makes you think you're going to have food over there?" I stood and faced the curtain and examined the weave of the fabric. "You going to live on oranges and shrimp?" Light filtered through the cloth at intervals where the weave was looser. If I squinted it seemed like the sun was right behind it. Blinding. I closed my eyes. Strange oblique patterns developed and collided under my closed eyelids. I imagined the other women listening. We had become a tragic soap opera.

I whispered, "Cassie, let him stay there alone. Don't go."

She turned away from me.

"Maybe this would be a good way to see if he really cares about you," I continued. "See if he comes back to get you." I picked at the hem of my sleeve. A long thread came loose and the hem hung free.

"And what if he won't? Where will I be? I have to go whether or not he comes to get me. I don't have anywhere else to go! How much will he think I care about him if I won't support him when he's grieving?"

"Grieving. Right. You told me he didn't even like his dad."

"Lord, Kate! Who likes his dad? Do you like yours? Do I like mine? But we would still be upset if they died."

"I like my dad. I love him, in fact." I picked a leaf off a carnation in a vase on Cassandra's table and bit it.

"Well then, you're the strange one. He's just under a lot of pressure right now. I mean we had a baby and now his dad is dead and his sister has no one to take care of her. That's a lot for anyone to manage."

"Maybe," I admitted. I wanted to go outside and smoke until my lungs burned. I began to pace the three feet available inside the closed curtain.

"We'll just find a relative for Helen to live with, then save some money. He'll finish school. You'll see. We'll be fine."

"I have a bad feeling, Cassandra."

"You know what?" asked Cassandra, perking up. "I think you are just jealous! I mean here's this guy taking away your best friend and you feel left out. Well, bless your heart, Honey! I wish I would have realized sooner. I'm sorry about all this, but we'll be back before you know it. I promise you."

Before my eyes Cassandra had turned back into the little church girl I knew such a short time ago. I wished I was talking to the hard headed girl who cursed at me when she found out she was pregnant. She would see how insane this was.

"I'm certainly not jealous. I will miss you. But I'm also worried that something is going to happen. It doesn't take ESP to see that this is a rocky road. Danny hasn't been reliable, and I just don't trust him."

"Women's intuition is just an old wives tale. Nothing bad will happen. I promise. Please take me, Kate. I have no one else to turn to." Cassandra began to cry. "I'm going to take a bus over there if you won't drive me. I'm going."

I bit my fingernails for a moment. "Fine, Cassie, fine, then. I'll take you. You just let me know."

"You need to find someone and get married, Kate."

"I can't see myself married. Your marriage is all the trouble I need."

My father checked the oil in the car before we drove away and went over the directions with me. He gave me some money in case I had car trouble, and asked if I had change in case I needed to call from a pay phone.

Cassandra and I pulled into the driveway before the afternoon rain came. We'd gotten lost just once on the dirt roads because there were no street signs. The oyster shell gravel crunched as we walked up the driveway to the house. To the north of the house were the acres of orange trees. To the south lay the family garden of tomatoes, okra and corn, and beyond that was a hen house.

The house stood three feet from the ground on a dead forest of cypress pilings that had been driven into the ground to hold the house out of the water that washed through so often from the Gulf Of Mexico. The place had once been painted red, but everything about it was faded and little of the original paint remained. A flight of wooden steps in front and in back lead to a narrow plank porch that surrounded the entire house above the ground.

My father had helped me load Cassandra's things into the car. He told me this was crazy. I told him I agreed. My mother told me sometimes women have to do hard things. Dad said, "Yeah, men have it made with women doing all the hard stuff." Mom shoved him. She had intended to be playful. She just seemed sad.

Cassandra held the baby against her as she knocked on the door. There was no answer, so she walked to the edge of the porch and called out into the yard. I stood back, quietly holding a sack of clothing and a suitcase.

"Hello?" She sang out, "Is anybody home?"

A shuffle came from inside the house. The creased venetian blinds slapped and the door opened halfway. A teenaged girl peeked out. Her eyes, though free of makeup, had black circles beneath them and her hair was uncombed. She wore a loose yellow dress, dirty from wear and threadbare. She was several months pregnant, and, as if to make the insult unbearable, barefoot.

"Are you Helen?" Cassandra shifted the weight of the baby to her left hand and extended her right toward the opening in the screen.

"Uh-huh." She stared at her visitors with a blank expression.

Cassandra and I exchanged a glance. Cassandra withdrew her empty hand. She looked weak and tired.

"Well," stammered Cassandra, "I am your new sister-in-law, Cassandra. I'm Danny's wife."

Helen just looked at her.

"Is Danny here?"

The girl didn't say anything for several seconds. I was starting to wonder if we had the right house when she said, "Yeah. You got a car?"

I raised my eyebrows when Cassandra looked at me, surprised. "Yes, Kate has a car. Can we come in?" Cassandra tipped the baby so that Helen could see her.

The girl eyed the baby curiously. "I don't know."

The door closed.

"Well!" said Cassandra. I began to pace, wanting to leave.

Suddenly the door flew open and Danny swept Cassandra into his arms, almost crushing the baby who let out a tremendous squeal and began to cry.

"Oh, you surprised her!" said Cassandra. "She wasn't expecting such a warm welcome!" Cassandra kissed Danny's cheek as he looked at her.

"I wish you would have called first. We ain't really ready for you yet," he said. He noticed me. "What are you doing here?"

"Well, someone had to bring her! You didn't even call first, Cassandra?" I sighed loudly. "I can help out while Cassandra gets unpacked, but I won't be staying, so don't worry about me." I said to Danny, as calmly as I could manage.

Danny stepped back and looked disoriented. He shook his head. He had been asleep. "Oh. Of course. I don't know what I was thinking. I forgot Cassandra and the baby were staying."

"Well, I'll be living here with you, silly. I brought the bassinet in the car," said Cassandra.

I could tell Danny was drunk, but I held my tongue. Danny held the door open and I started to follow Cassandra in. The screen door slapped it's jamb a few times with me on the outside. I entered after a moment. It took my eyes a while to adjust to the dim light. Helen was standing at the opposite end of the shot gun living room, beside a narrow doorway that led to the kitchen. The place was a mess. Newspapers and clothing were strewn about, dirty dishes lay on every level surface. The paint had yellowed from years of cigarette smoke, and the house smelled of mildew and rot. An odor of stale grease permeated everything. It was hot. A noisy water cooler gurgled in the first window and a window unit air conditioner struggled in the distance.

To the right of the main room were two bedrooms that appeared to be haphazard additions to the original structure. The doors were of different sizes. The first one was partially open. A small desk lamp was on the bed side stand. The bed clothes were disheveled and a smudged jelly glass of tea with ice still in it sat half empty on a stack of magazines on the bedside table. There were clothes scattered around on the floor and a baseball game was playing on the radio.

"When is the funeral, Danny?" Cassandra asked.

"We switched it to tomorrow."

"Why?"

"Funeral home said nobody would come if we did it when the game was on."

"Geez," I said. Everyone ignored me.

Danny led Cassandra to the second bedroom. He opened the door carefully and peeked inside as if he didn't know what he would find. It was the cleanest of the rooms I had seen, with a stained mattress stripped of linens and a bureau free of clutter. There were no curtains in the windows, just a tattered pull shade. Danny rummaged though drawer after drawer for sheets and lay them on the bed.

"You been sleeping without sheets, Honey?" Cassandra shifted the baby's weight to the other arm.

Danny looked around him. "No, no." He seemed embarrassed. "Helen must of just took them off to wash. This was Daddy's room."

I doubted that Helen had ever washed anything. I wandered to the bedroom door, my flesh tingling under Helen's odd stare.

"Can I do anything to help?" I asked.

"Sure," said Cassandra quietly from behind me. "Help me make this bed while Danny gets the stuff out of the car."

Danny slipped through the door. I closed the door behind him making the pretense of needing the room to make the bed in the tiny room.

"That girl is strange, Cass," I whispered.

"Shhh! She'll hear you."

"Are you definitely going to stay here?"

"Of course, Silly. This is my family. I'll help them pull together and we'll be fine."

"Nobody could pull that hard, Cass. This is more than you bargained for," I said as she pleated a corner of the yellowed sheet. Dust and age powdered our nostrils as I shook out another sheet to lay on top of the first. We both sneezed. Cassandra giggled.

Danny entered with an armload of baggage and said, "What are you two gossiping about?"

"Oh, just girl talk," said Cassandra. She giggled again and placed the baby in the center of the bed on top of a wilted blue and green quilt she had found in a drawer.

When Danny left the room again I said, "I can't believe you are acting like there is nothing wrong. There is something definitely not right here. Something feels weird."

"What could be more wrong than a little girl pregnant out of wedlock and grieving for her father? Of course there's something wrong, but they will get over it, and I intend to help by being as cheerful and doing as much as I can."

"You just had a baby. You can't take care of them. You need someone to take care of you."

"You are welcome to stay and sleep on the couch if you are so worried about us."

I leaned close to Cassandra and whispered. "Cassandra, this bedroom has obviously not been used in a while. Where is Danny sleeping?"

Cassandra grimaced. "Do you suppose their father died in this bed? I'll bet he couldn't stand the thought." She picked up the baby and backed up backwards until she was up against the wall. "I'll bet Danny's sleeping out on the couch. I'll bet it's too hard for him to sleep in here," she said.

"I think it would be too hard for me to sleep in here, and he wasn't even my father," I answered. "But at least it's cleaner than everything else in here."

Cassandra went into the living room and asked Danny if he would be okay sleeping with her and the baby in the back bedroom. He agreed with no apparent discomfort, which was not much of a relief. I considered sleeping on the couch overnight, afraid to leave Cassie alone here with them, but when I sat on it I discovered that it was greasy and lumpy and had a spring covered with a crumpled cushion. I knew the place must be crawling with huge southern roaches. I debated my options. The floor? Sharing a bed with Helen? Neither was the least bit appealing. I busied myself with a mountain of dishes, crusted and stinking in the sink.

Helen remained silent and watched each move made by either of us women with intense scrutiny, but when Danny moved she concentrated on a crossword puzzle from the paper. While Cassandra went into the bedroom to nurse the baby I tried to engage Helen in conversation.

"Helen. That's a pretty name."

No answer. Helen stared at me over her crossword.

"I've always liked that name. Like Helen of Troy. Is that who you were named for?"

"I don't know." Helen's hair was so dirty I could smell it. She was somewhere in the last part of her pregnancy, and it was quite obvious. She had spindly thin arms and legs covered with mosquito bites that she scratched fiendishly, leaving bloody scabs.

"You know, I have some cream which would make those feel better. Would you like to try it?"

Danny came in from the back yard about then and said, "She doesn't talk much."

I smiled at Helen, who seemed nervous. "I'll get it from the car."

"Just leave her alone. She doesn't like strangers." I looked toward the closed back bedroom door wondering if I could convince Cassandra to leave with me. All I could think of was getting away from this dreadful, stinking place as fast as I could, and taking Cassandra and Melinda with me.

Cassandra must have heard us from the bedroom through the thin and cracking walls. She must have clutched the suckling baby close to her and squeezed her eyes tight. I can imagine her doing that although I was in the other room. She must have sensed, too, that something wasn't right. Something in her must have been saying that something was wrong, like surging movie music trying to warn her. But then maybe she had learned to ignore that kind of premonition a long time ago.

All she could do was to try to work things out. What choice did she have? She made me promise not to call her parents again. She never wanted them to find her. She told me driving over that she hoped they thought she was dead, and she hoped they hurt something terrible. They hadn't looked for her when she disappeared. They hadn't come to the hospital even after my mother called. They would never find her now. Not as long as I kept my mouth shut.

"We're going to make things different, Melinda," she whispered to the drowsing baby that afternoon, "I'm telling you. You won't hate your Mommy and Daddy. I'll make sure of that. I am going to cuddle you and read to you and make you a princess. I promise you that. I promise you that."

I wish I could have painted them in that moment, that one hopeful moment. Maybe I could have seen what was going to happen next in time to stop it. I painted them later at home, from memory. The baby's face a blur. Cassandra etched in my mind like a scar. "Cassandra and Child" was a good painting. I hated making it.

Darkness fell too soon and I reluctantly asked Cassandra if I should stay. I was tired and wanted to go home but at the same time felt uncomfortable leaving her there alone.

"You could sleep with Helen in her bed, I guess."

"I guess not. Have you noticed how dirty she is? I'll bet she has lice."

"She is a mess. She would be so pretty…" Cassandra looked out a window although all there was to see was a light up on a pole across the road.

"Look, I think I'll go back to town and come back in the morning."

"You don't have to do that. Gee. I'd feel terrible. It's too far."

"I would feel better," I said, finally deciding. "In fact, I would feel better if you would come with me, too."

"Kate, I don't know what you are so worried about. We need to get the funeral out of the way, and then I'll get to cleaning this place. God. I never wanted a maid as much as I want one today." She sighed deeply. "Kate?"

"Yes?"

"Will you come to the funeral tomorrow?"

"No."

"Please?"

"No, Cassandra. That's more than I can do. Aren't you guys supposed to be at a wake or something?" It is a southern tradition to hold a wake the night before the funeral. The family sits with the deceased and takes callers offering their sympathy.

"Danny doesn't want to go, but the body's over at Ransom's if you want to see him."

"What would I want to see him for?"

"I don't know," Cassandra said. "Do you think Helen wants to go?"

"I don't know."

"I don't know if Danny would let her, anyway. He's ashamed about her being pregnant."

"Who is the father? Does she have a boyfriend or something?"

"Danny said she wouldn't tell him. Their dad made her quit school when she started showing. I guess it was a school boy."

"Too bad."

"Yeah."

"If she'd had a mother I bet this never would have happened," I said. It wasn't long before I realized that mothers couldn't stop bad things from happening. All they did was soften the blow, and it took a pretty damned good mother to do that. Cassandra's mother didn't do anything to save her.

"Yeah. I'm going to make sure Melinda never has to go through anything like this. You can bet on that."

I hissed, "Then what are you doing here?" I looked dramatically around the wretched house.

"Lord, Kate," sighed Cassandra. "Don't you see? A socially correct home doesn't mean kids will grow up all right. Look at me. My family was so Christian, and look at me. And look at Danny. He's here for his sister. His family. That's good for something. He's going to change. Trust me."

Cassandra's hair was damp around her pretty face. I wanted to hug her, but I knew I wasn't strong enough. I walked out into the bug infested night.

Eight

Unexpected Company

The car was enveloped in a cloud of love bugs. Several got inside the car with me. I lit a cigarette and waved the match at them. Love bugs are soft bodied and black with a red spot between their shoulders. They mate, end to end, while flying. While copulating these bugs are helpless and vulnerable, but they are many in number. I noticed that there were some bags behind the seat. I would bring them to Cassandra tomorrow when I returned. I guided the car through the yard listening to the hollow crunch of the oyster shell gravel and headed for home. I turned the radio loud to keep myself awake and tried to sing. But I was too worried to sing.

The car smelled odd. I opened the windows to air it out. Too close to the ocean, I thought. More salty than at home near the river. Too much in the mouth of the sea. The air smelled stale and sour. The heat pressed the odor in on me. I guessed it was the bags Cassandra had left in my car. I would bring them to her tomorrow. I hoped there was no spoiling food in them. I thought of stopping to check, but I just wanted to get home. Once I was rolling I was able to ignore it.

It was after eleven when I arrived at home. I reached over the seat to grab my hand bag. I laid my hand on warm flesh that suddenly pulled away from me. I screamed. I shouted for my father, pressed my back against the door, scrambling to open it and see who was there at the same time.

"It's me, Helen." Helen cowered in the foot well behind the driver's seat. I held my palm to my chest.

Helen saw the armed man running toward us and dropped down behind the seat again. I got out of the car and hit my dad with the door. He was wielding his twenty-two. He yelled. Helen started to whimper.

"What's going on?" shouted Dad. "Is he in the car?"

"It's not a man. Its okay," I panted.

"Then what are you screaming about, Girl?" Dad lowered the gun but remained tense.

Helen peeked up over the seat again.

"Helen, what are you doing here?" I nearly shouted at her. "My Lord, you nearly gave me a heart attack!" I opened the back door. Helen whimpered and clasped her face in her dirty hands.

"I am sorry, Dad. She startled me. I didn't know she was in there. She was hiding!"

"You know her?" Dad peered into the car as if we had a wild animal trapped in there.

"Danny's sister, Helen. What were you doing in there, Helen? Come on out."

Helen dropped her head to her chest. She was filthy. Her hair hung like weeds around her head. She was what I smelled while I was driving.

I looked to my father and held my hands out, palms up, begging for advice.

"Come on out, Little Lady," Daddy said.

Dad gave me a questioning look as Helen crawled out of the car hauling three crumpled paper grocery sacks.

"What's all this?" I asked.

"My stuff."

"What did you bring?"

"Everything I could carry."

We went inside the house. Dad woke Mom up and she came out looking befuddled. She pulled her house coat tight around her throat although it was a hot night.

"Kate, go call and let them know where she is so they won't worry," said Daddy.

"No," barked Helen.

"What do you mean, no?" asked my mother. Mother was never very good about being awakened at night. I put my purse on the table and some of its contents tumbled out. Helen stared at them in fascination. Ink pen, lipstick, notepad, compact. She didn't take her eyes off the shiny compact.

"We have to call someone," my mother said.

"He'll come and get me," Helen said without taking her eyes off my makeup.

"Who will? Danny?" Mom sat down at the table with us, stirring way too much sugar into her tea.

The dark brown eyes lifted suddenly. "Yeah," said Helen, softly.

"What would be wrong with that?" I asked.

"I want to stay here," she said, looking again at the make up. I saw my parents look at each other with alarm.

"Well," I offered, "I could tell him you are staying here with me tonight and then…"

"I don't want him to know where I am," she insisted.

I put my hands on my hips. "I don't understand this," I said. "This whole day I have felt like something was wrong and now I know there is." I leaned across the table in front of Helen. "Tell me what is wrong," The table limped over onto its short leg as I leaned on it. A tube of lipstick rolled toward Helen and she caught it in her grimy hand.

"I don't want to live there any more. I don't want to see Danny anymore."

My father pulled out a chair and sat down at the table across from Helen. "Where do you want to go?"

Helen pulled back from him, pushing her chair out from the table. "Don't matter," she said. She slid a dirty foot out of a generously holed sneaker that had no laces. She snaked her arm around her leg and over her bulging abdomen and began to pick at a blister on her shin. The foot was black with dirt, and callused. Helen's ankles seemed swollen.

"Don't do that. It'll get infected," said my mom. I think it was a reflexive comment because in a minute she grimaced and went to stand against the counter by the sink. She still clutched her robe to her throat, and looked alarmed.

Helen looked at me and put her foot down on top of her opposite knee, but she didn't leave it alone. It itched. It looked like fire ant blisters.

"What do you want us to do?" I threw my hands up in exasperation.

Helen lowered her chin. A moment passed, slowly. "Can you keep me a while?"

"God," I moaned.

Mom shook her head violently from side to side at my father making her big pink curlers dance behind Helen's head.

"There's not enough room," said Dad.

"Please don't make me go back," Helen begged.

"Why not? You have to at least tell us why," I said. "You're asking to live here so you have to say why."

Helen buried her head in her hands.

"You have to tell us why or there's nothing we can do to help you," I said.

"I don't have no other way." Helen's eyes were empty when she looked up again. A chill ran up my spine. Mother walked around and looked at Helen's face. Then she came and sat down at the end of the table.

"What is going on over there?" I asked. I reached for her hand, but decided to rest my hand on the table just next to where hers still held her shin. "Don't you see that my friend is over there? Is something going to happen to her?"

"I guess it could." Helen shrugged and picked at a scab. I took her hand in mine, then.

"What could happen? What?"

"In the bed," she said.

"In the bed?"

"What does she mean?" my father asked my mother. As if my mother could know. He rose and went to stand near the back door behind my mother's chair. The kitchen was small. He touched my mothers shoulder as he moved behind her. She looked up at him, questioning.

Helen began to squirm and stood up. She turned around. She backed herself up to the wall next to the doorway to the living room, looking from Mom to me and back. She slid down the wall until she was sitting on her haunches and wrapped her arms around her knees. She looked at my father. She was afraid.

"He might do things to her in the bed." It took all of her courage to say those words. We could see her straining to say them.

"But, Helen," said my mother, "Danny and Cassandra are married. It's okay."

"Not him. Not Danny."

"Who then?" said my mother.

"Daddy. It's his house, you know. He can do whatever he wants in his own house. He always says so."

"I crossed the vinyl kitchen floor with its pale yellow squares with peach flowers in the corners and crouched down next to Helen. "Helen, your Daddy can't hurt anyone. Don't you remember?"

She shook her head just a little bit. She looked into my eyes. She seemed bewildered.

I hesitated and looked at my mother for help. She looked away and reached for my father's hand.

"Helen," I said, "Your daddy died. He's dead. Don't you remember?"

"He's really dead?"

"Yes that's why Danny and Cassandra came to your house, to help you since your father died."

"Who killed him?" I stopped for a second and looked at my father. His expression didn't change. He was mystified.

"Nobody killed him. Don't you remember? You found him in the bathtub. He had a heart attack."

"Daddy drank a whole lot."

"Do you suppose that killed him instead of his heart?"

"It maybe did."

My father shuffled his feet and leaned against the back door.

Mama tilted her head. She had an idea. "Did your Daddy hurt you?" she asked, without looking at Helen.

"He says it don't hurt. He says it's fun." Helen shivered. I waited for mother to ask more questions but she was silent.

"What does he do?" I asked.

"Mostly the bottom game."

"What's the bottom game?" Mother's face turned white when I asked.

"The one where he gets on me and sticks hisself in me."

I was so innocent myself. In spite of knowing Cassandra, in spite of smoking pot, in spite of staying out all night and pretending I was so grown up. It made no sense. He was her father. She was his child.

"Helen, Daddies don't do that to their daughters," I said. My father abruptly lowered his head, brushed past us into the living room and down the hall. We heard the gentle click of the bedroom door closing.

"Daddy says all daddies do that so their girls'll be ready when it's time to get married."

I made an involuntary sound deep in my throat and Helen whimpered. She buried her face between her knees shivered like a cold puppy.

"He was lyin', wasn't he?" Her chin quivered and her shoulders began to shake.

My mother finally moved. She slowly came to sit on the other side of Helen on the floor.

"They don't all do that, Helen." Mother covered the callused little hands with one of her strong ones. I smelled the Jergen's Lotion. "And yours isn't going to do that to you again," she said. "You'll stay here until we figure out what to do. We'll get it figured out."

I leaned my head back against the wall and breathed deeply against the emotion in my throat.

"Daddy's waiting for me in that house, you know? Even though he's dead. He's in every room and I can't get away from him."

"Of course, Helen, you don't have to go back. You stay here and we'll figure it out." My mother crooned to her like to a baby. She put her arm around Helen's little shoulders that tensed and then released. She didn't cringe away from the smell. If you're a mother you can't be put off by a little thing like the smell of fear.

I wanted to drive back right then to that evil house and make Cassandra come with me. I wanted to, but I knew she would do only what she wanted to do, and she wanted to be with Danny.

I showed Helen where to take a bath, and she came out looking little better than when she had gone in. She hadn't done anything to her hair. I asked if she would like to have her hair braided. She shyly nodded, and

I said I would have to wash her hair first. I leaned her over the sink and she nearly fell asleep with Prell in her hair.

When her hair was clean I filled the bath tub with warm water and some old Mr. Bubble bath bubbles I found under the bathroom sink and told her to sit in it while I worked on her hair.

Her hair was so matted that I had to cut out some of the tangles. When it was finally, finally braided, the shorn part still showed in the back. She would have to have her long hair cut off, I knew.

When I handed her a mirror and showed her the braid down her back in the medicine cabinet mirror she said, "I never saw my hair be so pretty." I told her to sit in the bubble bath until we fixed her a place to sleep. My mother put a cot in my room, nestled between the dresser and the window.

I gave her one of my mother's old nightgowns. It managed to fit around Helen's abdomen, but just barely. She said it was beautiful.

I took her clothes to be washed and asked her what she had to wear tomorrow.

"The pregnant dress is all that fits."

"Just one dress?"

"I got more for after the baby." She pointed at the row of paper sacks along the wall.

"We'll figure out something for you to wear," I sighed. I was so tired.

"I always wear my yellow dress. You'll give it back won't you?"

"Oh, of course. But you should have more things."

"I don't have money. Dad said since I'm only going to be pregnant a while there's no use in lots of pregnant clothes."

"We'll think of something."

I thought about the lipstick she had grabbed on the kitchen table. She had dropped it when she moved and sat on the floor. I went and got it from the place where it landed near the cabinets and applied some lipstick to Helen's dry, cracked lips. She looked into the mirror and beamed. I told her she could have the little gold Avon sample tube. She held it like a treasure. I rarely ever saw her without lipstick again. She loved make up and that was for ever after her one extravagance just for herself.

When the sun finally broke through the curtains the next morning I was already awake. Helen stirred in her sleep. I had a stiff neck and a headache. I got up and dragged the telephone from the hall into the living room as far as it would go. It rang six times before I heard Danny say hello.

"Danny, let me talk to Cassandra."

"She's sleeping."

"I need to talk to her."

"What time is it?"

"Six, I guess. Let me talk to her."

There was silence, then shuffling on the phone line.

Danny blurted, "Hey, you got Helen with you?"

I hesitated, then admitted I did.

"Okay. Just bring her back, or do you want me to come and get her?"

"No, she's fine. She can stay here a while."

"What are you gonna do with her?"

"She needs some things. Clothes. And she needs to see a doctor."

"What for? She sick?"

His lack of awareness sickened me.

"The baby," I said.

"She don't need a doctor for that. She's strong enough."

"My mother thinks she should." Passing the buck.

"She don't need it. There's no insurance on her."

"I don't guess you would think she did need one. I want you to send me some money to get her come more clothes."

"I don't have none to send. Just bring her back and I'll take care of her."

"She asked if she could stay here and we said she could. She doesn't want to go back."

The quick snap of a match being lit and his long inhale. "Don't she want to come to the funeral?"

"I don't know. When is it?" My skin lifted in goose flesh.

"Tomorrow at two," said Danny.

"I'll ask her. Look, Danny?"

"Hm."

"How's Cassandra?"

"She's okay. Sleeping. Tired."

"Well, let her sleep. Tell her I'll talk to her later."

"Yeah." He hung up.

I laid down on the couch and turned my back to the room, pressing my face into the rough fabric. Helen stepped quietly into the room and sat in the rocking chair. I could hear her soft footsteps and her light breathing. I listened to how lightly she stepped for such a big pregnant girl. I waited to see if she would leave.

I turned as she rose from the chair, in time to see her standing in the hallway, the light from my bedroom window filtering through the nylon nightgown. I wanted to paint her in just that way, but when I heard my parents begin to stir in their room I rushed Helen back inside my room.

"You can see straight though that gown in the light." I brought her the yellow dress, wrinkled from the dryer. Most of the wrinkles disappeared across her spreading stomach. I wanted to touch her tummy. I wondered if she could feel her baby the way Cassandra sometimes let me feel hers when she was pregnant. I knew that wasn't going to ever happen to my body but it fascinated me just the same.

I drove Cassandra to the Salvation Army that morning and we found a few dresses she could wear until the baby came. I apologized for not getting anything new, but I was spending my dime store pay and there wasn't much of it, plus a few dollars my mother gave me to help her out.

She said they were the nicest clothes she ever had. I didn't have any trouble believing that. She said she wanted to wear them even after the baby came and she was thin again. I told her we would work out something for then. I felt uncomfortable making promises I didn't know I could keep. I tried to be vague.

"I'm a hard worker," was all she said.

She complained about getting her hair cut that afternoon, but Marilyn, the beauty operator my mother and I always saw, and I finally managed to convince her there was nothing to do about the short spot but make it match. We promised it would grow out. Helen's face showed concern until two hours later when she emerged from the dryer and curlers all flipped and teased. She could hardly remove her eyes from the mirror.

"I'm as pretty as you," she said to me. She was prettier. I could barely believe how different she looked myself.

"I feel like a princess," she said, beaming.

"Well, I guess everyone should get to feel like a princess sometimes," I said.

"You must feel this way all the time," she told me.

"No, I just feel regular."

"That must feel pretty good," Helen said.

On the way home in the car I asked Helen if she wanted to go to the funeral.

"You take me?"

"Aw, Helen, I really didn't know your dad. Danny will come get you if you let him know in time."

"No," she said firmly. "If he comes I won't go."

"You don't need to do that, Helen."

"I would. If I have to go back and live in that house I'll kill myself."

"Helen, that's really scary. We think enough of you to take you in, so you could at least think enough of us to not kill yourself."

"You just gotta understand." Her knuckles were white on her clenched fists. "I can't go back there. It is too hard back there. I don't want to see that house ever again and I can't go back never."

I drove in silence for a moment, mulling it over. "So you don't really want to go to the funeral?"

"I just got to make sure he's really dead."

"If Danny takes you I will come and get you after."

"Danny never would let me leave again. He always listens to Daddy. Does what he says."

My face tingled with heat. "You mean, Danny…"

Helen picked up on my meaning. "Danny never done the bottom game, but he might. He looks just like my daddy. I hate him to even look at me. Makes me sick."

"So if I don't go, you won't go?"

"I want to see he's dead, but I can't take a chance of getting stuck there with Danny. I got to know you will be there."

"You think they would try to make you stay? Because if they would there might not be much I could do about it."

"I got a knife."

I was incredulous. "You would stab them?"

"Whatever I have to do."

I shook my head hard as if this bizarre conversation were a dream I couldn't get out of. "What about your baby?"

Helen put her hands against her belly. As I was checking an intersection to cross I noticed her chin was quivering. As I turned right on Magazine she choked back tears. I drove up along Magazine until we reached my street, turned again, drove up into our driveway and stopped the car.

"We should ask my mom and dad what to do. I don't know what to do."

"Do you tell them everything?"

"Not everything, but this is pretty serious. I don't know what to do. I'm not sure they will let me go once they know what is happening."

"Maybe they will take me," Helen whispered.

"Maybe. I don't know." I tapped the steering wheel self consciously.

"It's for the baby. If it was just me I could go on and manage some way, but the baby doesn't got a chance if I don't get out of there, see?"

"But if you kill yourself the baby will die, too."

"I know," Helen fought with her tears for a moment. "It's better to be dead than to live that way, though. I can't let my baby live like that and I ain't going to live that way no more either. I'd even rather have it dead than…"

"But your daddy is dead now. Things will be different."

"They might not." Helen wiped her nose on her sleeve and looked up at me. "It's too big of a chance." The lipstick she had applied moments before was crooked and smudged on her sleeve.

"I didn't tell you everything yet." She reached forward and pressed both her palms against the dashboard, as if she might fall to the floor if she didn't support herself.

"Last year I had another baby." She spoke so softly I had to lean toward her to hear. "Soon as she was born Daddy took her from me and gave her to somebody who came and got her. They gave him money for her. I tried to get them to give her back, but they just took her away in their car. I tried to chase them, but I fell and I was bleeding and fainted, I guess. When I woke up I was still in the grass outside and it was dark and there was blood coming out of me…I went inside and he did it to me before I ever got to my bed. He said if I could get us a baby ever year it wouldn't matter if the oranges didn't come in. He said we'd be rich offa my babies." She held her stomach and rocked back and forth.

"I didn't stop bleeding for a long time," Helen continued, he voice heavy. "I thought I was going to die. I got real sick and Daddy finally got a doctor who said I'd have to tell my boyfriend to leave me alone 'til I got better. But I never had a boyfriend. I told him so, and he just laughed. Said I couldn't fool him that easy."

Helen heaved as if she would vomit. I sat still.

"I never did find out where my baby went," she said. I asked ever'-body I saw and they just said I was crazy askin' about it. Some of 'em didn't even believe I ever had a baby. Then I got so sick with the fever I couldn't get up no more and even Daddy couldn't make me work, all I could do was lay. I almost died, I think. I wanted to die. I felt almost happy that I was so sick 'cause I coulda got out of there that way if I'd died. Seems like I was sick a long time. Daddy left me alone for a while then. But one day he brought a man to do it to me and the next thing I knew I was getting another baby. She rubbed her belly and it shifted.

"This one's mine," she said.

I waited for her to go on, but she never did.

I wiped at tears with my fingertips. I coughed several times to clear my throat. "Are you sure you want to go to the funeral? I mean, I would understand if you didn't. I bet Danny would, too."

"I just want to see that old bastard dead to make sure."

I asked my mother if she would take us, but I could see by the look in her eyes that she was sinking into her own sadness. I begged her. She could be so strong and then sink so low. She said I should handle it myself. She said that I was the one who brought Helen home and this was something I needed to see through. She said that I was an adult now and I could deal with anything I set my mind to.

I didn't tell her all Helen had told me. I knew that would just sink her faster. I thought Mother should have helped just because she was my mother, just because she cared about me. I knew my father would-n't let me take her if he knew all Helen had told me. I was scared to go, and I knew it beyond my means to manage, but I was also a kid, and my curiosity got the best of me. I wanted to see the guy dead, too, after what I had heard the last two days. I decided to go. I decided that I could be in control.

It seemed, that morning, as if I went to this funeral that somehow I would find out this was all made up. That's what I wanted. I wanted Helen's tragedies to be lies so I could blame her for the trouble they were causing me. She was there; She was concrete; I could see her flesh and I could hate her for telling me such dreadful lies. Her father was dead. I would never hear his side. I couldn't fathom the things she told me he did at the opening of the Mississippi River into the Gulf of Mexico.

Nine

Helen Says Goodby

We had to leave immediately to get there in time. I told Helen what dress to put on, and rearranged her hair after she mussed it. The funeral was at two o'clock. Two is the time the southern Louisiana rains begin, but it had rained off and on almost all that particular day. The ride down from New Orleans was punctuated by the characteristic spot showers that reminded me of cartoon clouds that followed around that bad luck character in "L'il Abner" in the Sunday Times Picayune. You could drive down Belle Chasse Highway on dry pavement when up ahead a small dark cloud would appear. Beneath it the concrete would be wet, you could see the wet darkness of it ahead, a mirage of a flooded highway. The car would go beneath the cloud and the fat rain drops would splat, splat against the windshield like giant palmetto bugs, three inch long cockroaches, then it would all be behind you. It was a little joke nature played. Now it's raining, now it's not.

The rain must have come hard that day down south in Venice because the funeral home grounds were marshy and the rising water in the canal lining the highway looked like a few million gallons of cafe au lait poured to overflowing. We were early and I asked Helen if she would like to go have coffee somewhere before we went inside. She looked at me as if I had offered her a dead frog.

Few cars were parked in front of the funeral home. I didn't think she would want to talk to anyone. I didn't really understand why she wanted to go, but I was caught up in the anomaly. All my grandparents had died by the time I was small. Until that weekend I hadn't really given much thought to people I knew dying and being dead and gone forever. So I asked her if she wanted coffee. I didn't know that when you need to see someone dead a cup of coffee isn't going to do anything but waste time.

We got out of the car at the cemetery entrance between the mausoleum and the funeral chapel. Helen walked ahead of me toward the door, her feet slapping the wet concrete walkway in flat Salvation Army shoes that didn't fit well. I followed her inside, past the yard of crumbling planks of concrete that held the dead under. So close to the water that if the dead aren't cemented down, the ground water will suck them out and carry them down the river. Sometimes two hundred year old relatives would end up being dug up on neighbor's farms and gardens after the shifting ground separated them from their rightful burying places.

Danny was standing in the foyer in the wind from the air conditioner. He wore a pale green suit, the only one he had. It fit poorly under the arms. Beneath it he wore a black turtle necked sweater.

Danny took Helen's arm in his hand and she pulled it way. He straightened and looked at her.

"You look good," he said through clenched teeth.

"Where is he?" Helen's little eyes darted around the place anxiously. She looked around, searching.

"He's inside," whispered Danny. He pointed at a set of double doors behind him.

Helen glared at Danny, full of ferocity.

"Where is he?" she demanded. "Is he really dead?"

"Well, Helen, of course he's dead," murmured Danny, embarrassed. "You know that. You're the one that found him."

"Then why are you whispering?"

"That's just what you do, Helen," Danny replied. "It's weird being loud around dead people." But Helen was already finding her way into the chapel slamming open the double doors and striding to the front of the chapel where the coffin lay. Danny and I helplessly followed her, drawn by her curious force. The casket was buried under one large spray of red carnations as the organist played an unfamiliar dirge. The casket was closed. Helen walked from top to bottom, examining the box. Then she tried to pry it open with her fingertips.

"Jesus, Helen," hissed Danny. "Just stop acting like some damned hick. There isn't going to be an open casket. He looked too bad."

Helen hit the casket with both her fists and leaned against it, her head bowed over it, breathing hard. The spray of flowers shifted and started to fall. I caught it and straightened it.

"Don't cry, Helen," said Danny. "I know it's hard, but you gotta be strong." He awkwardly stroked her back.

Helen's head shot up like a snake at his touch, her eyes bored into Danny's face. "If you think I'm crying over this bastard you're as stupid as I always thought you was."

"Helen, there are people here to pay their respects," said Danny, still whispering. "Try to act half civil, please?"

An elderly woman came into the chapel followed by three younger women and three men. They filed into one of the pews and sat watching with interest.

"Half civil? Is that how I'm supposed to act?" Helen's voice was full of venom. She could have bit his nose right off his face and it wouldn't have surprised me a bit. "Is half civil the way you was acting when you pretended you didn't know what Daddy was doing to me? Is half civil how you was acting when he sold my baby?"

Danny shifted inside his jacket. "Jesus, Helen, I was just a kid. I was just a kid."

"It was last year, you son of a bitch. You're just as much of a bastard as Daddy." Helen was breathing hard and loudly. Her shoulders lifted and fell beneath her navy blue calico Salvation Army maternity smock. "I'm not gonna let you push me around like he did. Nobody's going to do that no more, you hear me?"

Danny was growing defensive. I was afraid he would erupt. The people sitting in the back of the chapel were motionless, taking everything in. I later learned that they were Helen and Danny's aunt and six cousins. The older woman's face was leathery and stern. Her hair was a mass of wiry gray tendrils trapped in a barrette at the nape of the sun scalded neck. She was nodding almost imperceptibly.

The Funeral Director appeared from the front of the chapel.

"Is there something you need?" he murmured.

"I want this box opened," said Helen.

"Are you a family member, ma'am?" He was portly, his pale face was flushed and he smelled of whiskey. "We have been instructed by next of kin," looking to Danny for agreement, "that the casket will remain closed."

"I want you to open it now," said Helen. The director took stock of this small pregnant and very young woman demanding that he break with protocol.

The director's gaze shifted to Danny as he asked her, "Are you a relative?"

In a voice as low and dangerous as thunder Helen said, "He was my daddy."

"The coffin was opened briefly last evening for the wake. Were you unable to attend?" The director was working hard to maintain the upper hand. "We have a schedule to keep for the sake of the other mourners today." The man looked solemnly at Helen, then turned to Danny for approval.

Helen stepped up to the man's be-jowled face. "Don't you be looking at him. My name is Helen Boudreaux and he was my daddy and I want the goddamn box open and I want it open now."

"Sir," said the director dangerously deferring to Danny. Danny paled. He raked his fingers through his hair.

"I don't see what it would hurt to open it a few minutes if it would calm her down," said Danny. "She's gonna make a scene if you don't, looks like." Danny looked around the room self consciously. Danny had never been in charge of any formal event in his young life, especially not one as grim as this. He was a little boy thrust into command and he knew he was not up to the task.

So much, so suddenly, had become his charge. His young wife, his new baby, the affairs of his dead father and traumatized sister were all his charges now. I saw him wither beneath the weight of it. I felt sympathy for him then and it surprised me.

I sat down on the front pew. I had never seen a dead body before and I thought I would need to be sitting down.

The director beckoned another man dressed in funereal black, this one looking much, I guessed, like the dead people he worked with. He was tall, thin and slow moving, but like his boss, his face was flushed pink. His eyelids were red and drooping. I thought I would have to be drunk to have this job, too.

The men stood at opposite ends of the casket. The assistant pushed the carnations to the foot of the coffin and the director opened the part that covered the dead man's upper body. They stood aside with their hands folded in front of them.

Old Michel Boudreaux's skin must have been tougher than a saddle. His eyes and mouth were creased with lines as deep as the Mississippi, but with more tributaries. He had the system of squint lines typical of someone who had smoked for years and years. Even his hands, folded across his chest in a corny and maudlin way were yellowed and scarred from the hard work and the sun. He was swollen from his time beneath the water in his bathtub. I found myself rising to look at this monster, to see what evil looked like.

Helen's father was wearing a suit much too small for him. It wrapped him in such a way that I thought, underneath the out of style coat, perhaps his pants were not fastened. I imagined that the suit had been cut up the back to allow it to close in the front. Or maybe they had chosen this suit from a stash of clothing they kept for the dead. Mr. Boudreaux probably had not had a need for a suit in many years, maybe since he wed Danny and Helen's mother, the woman who died when they were young, that union where the trouble began. Helen was raised to take her mother's place. He certainly didn't need a suit for that.

I sat down again as Helen stepped up to the coffin and fixed her eyes on her father's dead face. She stared at him for a few seconds. I could only see her back, but it was taut and squared. I could nearly smell the rage. The passing time, minuscule as it was, grew electric. I rose, slowly, silently, from my seat, drawn by curiosity. I wanted to see what she was seeing, to see what was filling her with such fury that just the shape of her body proclaimed it.

The very second my knees locked beneath me Helen bent her head to the side, screwed up her lip, gagged like a cat with a fur ball and spat onto her daddy's dead face. The globule of thick sputum ran down the side of old Michel's nose, into the valley containing his eye, and slowly emptied into the tributary that led to the pool beside his mouth.

Helen relaxed into a satisfied smile, the wrath releasing into the air with her slowly exhaled breath until she seemed almost peaceful. Her shoulders softened. He was dead; she could rest.

She turned to me and said, "Can we go now?"

All of our eyes followed her back down the aisle. I gathered my wits and walked after her. I saw Helen's old aunt and her grown children still sitting at the back as we passed. The children sat with mouths open, gaping, eyes lurching from Helen to their dead uncle. The aunt looked at Helen straight in the eye, smiled and nodded.

Ten

Another Goodbye

Helen and I left the funeral home and went to dinner at May's Catfish House on I-90. She was hungry. I was not.

It began to rain again, so we sat drinking tea for an hour. May, the restaurant's name sake, kept bringing hush puppies, freshly fried to the Mama-to-be. If only she hadn't kept saying how proud the daddy must be. Helen ignored her and ate three red plastic baskets full of those cornbread balls, dipped one at a time in a puddle of catsup.

While Helen ate I thought about Cassandra and told Helen that we needed to stop by the house to check on them. Helen shook her head vigorously. She refused to look at me. Tears came to her eyes and she just ate faster.

With her mouth full she said, "I don't want to go there. Don't make me."

The rain let up. Maybe they were home by then. I was afraid of Danny's mood but I needed to see that Cassandra was okay. Helen argued with me and said she wouldn't go in the house.

"You can just sit in the car with the love bugs, then," I told her.

Cassandra had been nursing the baby out in the car behind the funeral home the whole time we were viewing the deceased, and missed the whole episode. I didn't know how Danny would be acting by now. For all I knew he could have taken off on a drunk and left Cassandra alone.

They were already shouting when we got there. The air was thick with moisture. My hair was sticking to my face. I could hear their caustic voices through the screen door. I knocked. No answer. I banged on the door loudly and kept at it until Cassandra came to undo the latch.

Danny's voice followed her. "I don't know why you lock that door. No one's interested in getting you."

"I just feel safer, that's all. Okay?" Cassandra looked at him hard for a moment, then turned and smiled weakly at me. She was already in her night gown, buttoning up the top button. Dried breast milk stained the front.

"Look who's here!" She said, trying to sound cordial. "I'm so glad you came by. I saw you when you two stopped by the funeral. Why didn't you stay? Where's Helen?"

"She doesn't want to come in," I whispered. I looked to see what Danny was doing.

"She pretty upset?"

"Well, sort of. She just doesn't want to come here."

Cassandra began to chatter busily. "Oh, Danny, go on out and get her to come in."

"I told you what she did," Danny said to Cassandra. "Man, she just laid a plug right on the old bastard." He leaned back his head and laughed, then took a swig from the can of beer he was holding.

I fidgeted with my keys. "Cassandra, you doing okay? I just wanted to say hello before we head back." "Helen's not staying?"

Cassandra looked past me out to the car. Helen was sitting low in the passenger's seat watching us. "Danny go get her."

"Kate brought her. Let Kate get her."

"No, we're letting her stay with us for a while. I guess it's too hard being here after her dad," I hesitated. "Well, you know."

"Yeah, sure." Cassandra looked over at Danny from under her bangs, "You don't suppose we could move back into town?"

"Why would we want to do that?"

"Since Helen doesn't even want to live out here. We came for her and…"

"We got a place of our own out here, paid for. What have we got in town?"

Cassandra's face sank. "There's just more for me to do in town." She looked at me apologetically. "I get kind of bored while he's at work, you know. Did I tell you he got a job at the new refinery in Alliance?"

"No," I said. "Good," I lied.

"You only need to be taking care of the baby and looking after this place. That's enough to do," said Danny with a sarcastic roll to his voice. "You sure don't need to be farting around with Kate all the time when we could be having a place of our own."

I lowered my voice. "Why don't you and the baby come with us for just a few days? My mom would like to see the baby. It would be…"

Danny stepped between us. "You just think you're going to steal my whole family, don't you?"

"I'm not stealing anything, Danny, it's just that Cassandra has been though a lot after just having a baby and she could use someone to take care of her for a while. Just for a rest. That's all. She'll be back soon as she's rested up."

"I'll be going to work this week and she's gotta take care of the hens and the garden. She don't need to be in town. We live here now."

"The hens? What does Cassandra know about hens? You can't be serious about keeping them."

"Of course we're keeping the hens. That's that much less food we have to buy." Danny turned around and sauntered into the kitchen. He leaned over the kitchen sink and looked out into the yard behind the house. He started tapping his beer can on the counter top.

I gathered my courage and brushed past Cassandra to follow him to the kitchen. Cassandra stayed by the front door, eyes weary, her hand clutching the door knob.

"Danny, let her stay with me just a couple of weeks. Or days. Just a couple days. That way you won't have to worry about her and the baby. It will be better…"

"She ain't going. Period. End of discussion." Danny moved away from me and opened the back door. He stood there looking outside. It was growing dark.

I walked back through the house, hearing each of my footsteps strain the rotten floor boards. Tears of frustration were building in my chest. Two steps before I reached the front door the floor creaked. The last three feet of flooring before the door felt soft. The house must have been flooded dozens of times living down here with the support stilts only three feet off the ground as they were.

I paused and looking straight ahead, not at Cassandra's exhausted posture, whispered, "Come with me. I mean it. Come with me. Just come. Don't explain it to him. Just please come with me."

"I can't, Kate."

"Please. Cassandra. What if he leaves you here alone like he did in the apartment? You can't walk from here to my place if you need help."

"We have a phone out here. It's going to be okay…"

Danny yelled from the kitchen, "Don't think you're going to change her mind. She's staying here. Period."

Silence. Danny's eyes eating through the back of my skull. My hair rising on the nape of my neck. Cassandra's eyes far away. The wind picking up. A shock of lightening. A drop of rain.

A deep breath. "I guess I'll be going, then."

"Yeah, sure. I'll be in touch." She turned her face away from me, averting her eyes as she held open the door for me to leave. She wrapped her arm around her stomach.

"That cat's on the hen house again, Cass," shouted Danny from the kitchen.

The screen door snapped shut at my back, flapping against the frame.

"Then go chase it away," she snarled. I thought her voice was too soft for him to hear. I thought she might have said it to make me feel better. I grimaced and walked slowly to the edge of the porch.

"I'm going to rest until Melinda wakes up," she called to her husband, louder this time.

I paused on the second step, eaves-dropping.

"Not 'til you get rid of that cat, you ain't. It'll kill that whole new batch of chicks before morning." Did Cassandra leave the front door open on purpose so that I could hear? Cassandra, who locked the door even though no one wanted her?

"Then chase it away," she yelled, disappearing into the darkness of that house. The bedroom door slammed. Loud footsteps. A bang on a door.

"The hen house is your job, Cassandra! I told you that!"

I stepped down another step, embarrassed.

Danny yelled, "If you want to be the lady of *my* house, you get off your lazy butt and take care of the goddamned cat!"

I heard the bedroom door crash open. Against my better judgment I turned and watched their silhouettes.

"Then I quit!" Cassandra screamed the words. "If someone who just had a baby can't rest in her own house, I don't need to be the lady of any house of yours! I'll pack up and go with Kate!" It was she who smashed the door open, toppling an end table and sending several dirty glasses flying. She was a small black form back lit in the doorway, leaning forward, raging. Fists tight knobs. Body trembling. I stepped down the last step sideways, and froze in the grass invaded oyster shell gravel at the bottom, watching.

Moments passed, or so it seemed, and I heard nothing more. I tore myself away and went to the car, looking back over my shoulder, aching to burst in and save her. Thinking I could. Not knowing. Helen's face was tense and white; her fists were knotted together.

"Let's go," she urged. "Please, let's go."

"He's drunk," I said.

"Let's go," begged Helen. "There's nothing you can do. Let's go."

"I can't leave her here."

"There's nothing to do about it. Let's go. Let's go before Danny sees us and comes after us. Please."

I started the engine. The car popped over the gravel as loudly as a thousand gunshots. I stopped it behind some bushes down the road a few feet and got out, leaving the motor running. I was stressed by Helen's desperate urging, let's go, let's go, and I started to turn back.

"You gotta wait, Helen," I said. "I have to see if she's okay."

I got out and crept up the driveway to the side of the house. The oyster shell gravel crunched and slipped beneath me, piercing my crepe soled shoes. I jogged up the weed lawn, hitching my cotton skirt up above my knees, crouching forward as if not being erect would make me less visible. I stopped and caught my breath beneath the water cooler sticking out of the first window. I stood with my hands on the porch catching my breath with my face beside the mildewed vents of the rattling machine. A spider web made my skin tingle, and I stood still, not brushing it away, keeping my presence secret. I crept the length of the house stood up before the next window, trying not to disturb the oyster shells and give myself away. The baby was squalling inside and Cassandra was cooing to it, loudly, frantically, trying to drown out Danny's shouts. The porch formed a barrier between me and the window and I could not peer inside.

"I have to feed the baby, I am tired as I can ever be, and I am not going to get dressed and chase away some cat that's probably already long gone. You're okay, Melinda, Baby. Everything's okay. Shhh. Shhhh."

"You don't have to get dressed. Just go out there and do it. Nobody's going to see you. Jeez, you'd think every guy on the river was just dying to ball you. Let me assure you, Babe, they ain't."

"You goddamned jack ass! Go do it yourself! I'm not doing it!" She screamed and the baby screamed and I wanted to scream, but I held it in. Taking a chance I lifted my torso up onto the porch beneath the horizontal rail. The noise of the water cooler covered my ascent. I lifted my leg and hoisted myself onto the porch.

I crawled upon my hands and knees and pressed my ear against the thin wall beneath the bedroom window. I could hear Cassandra's furious breathing through the rotten clapboard and crumbling asphalt shingles. The window was open just a few inches. Open the window, Cassandra, and crawl out to me.

"I am telling you that you *are* going to do it, so get out there and go do it before I have to *make* you do it!"

"Danny, you're making a great big deal out of nothing." That's the way, Cassandra. Make him listen to reason.

"Let me feed the baby and if there's still a cat out there in the morning I will go chase it away." Don't go for sarcasm, Cassandra. Play it safe.

I pressed myself against the wall, being invisible.

"You stupid bitch! The cat will be gone by morning and so will all the chicks!"

I could feel the tension filling up the house. I knew it couldn't hold much more.

"Then we won't have to worry about them any more, will we?" Could Cassandra scream that loudly? Could Cassandra's voice do that?

"You're getting the goddamn cat now, and don't argue with me, you understand?"

Goose bumps rose across my face and arms in the ninety five degree wet heat.

Seconds passed with no sounds from inside. So many seconds that my head started to clear and I tried to plan what to do next.

Slowly I turned around and rose to my feet, keeping my face against the brown shingles to see if I could hear more. The sandpaper roughness scraped my flesh. Rain sweated out of the sky, wetting my hair, making my clothes stick to me.

A crash. Thud. The baby's sudden piercing cry.

"Danny stop," pleaded Cassandra, her voice tiny and small again. "Danny, you're hurting me. Let me put the baby down and I'll go get the cat."

"You bet your ass you will."

Another crash and Cassandra's scream. "Stop," she cried. I heard her weeping and I didn't move. The baby screamed and broke my inertia and I scrambled to the back of the house to the kitchen window not knowing what I was going to do. A honeysuckle vine scraped my legs and caught at my skirt. Through the window and through the darkening kitchen I saw Cassandra dash across the living room and put the baby on the couch, nestling her behind a cushion. Melinda lay helplessly flailing her arms in terror as her parents battled. I ran back around the side of the house where the porch was narrow and peeked in the bedroom window. Cassandra was on the floor behind the bed, but Danny was pulling her up by the arm and the hair. She punched at him to ward him off, but couldn't make contact. He slapped at her hands, and then her face until she was exhausted and he could contain both her tiny wrists in one of his strong working hands. I stood transfixed in horror. As Danny pulled Cassandra out the bedroom door he turned and saw me at the window.

I raced to the back of the house, getting tangled in a honeysuckle vine that clambered up the stilts to the porch along the way. I reached the back door just as Danny pushed Cassandra out. She landed on the planks on her knees. She still didn't see me.

"Danny, don't you dare lock that door!" Cassandra was hysterical, racing to catch the door before he slammed it. She was too late. She pulled at the knob and screamed. Her knees and her left elbow were bleeding and she lifted her right ankle to rub it in her hands.

"Let in me in there! Let me in!"

"Go home with Kate," he screamed back.

"She's gone! I'm not going anywhere without my baby! You let me in!"

"Not until you get rid of that cat."

"You want me to get rid of the cat? I'll get rid of the cat!"

Cassandra lifted her nightgown to her knees, flung herself down the steps and ran barefoot and limping, arms flapping like the terrified chickens', toward the hen house yelling, "Ahhhhhhhh!" She fidgeted with the makeshift latch that was a rusted wire twisted around a stick. The gate swung open. She ran inside the little chicken yard, "Aaaaaah! Get away, Cat!"

A dirty brown tabby cat had seen her coming and scrambled down the back side of the tiny shed the hens lived in and disappeared into some brush, a yellow tuft of feathers clutched in its mouth. The chickens scrambled around their bare patch of yard, squawking chaotically. A black rooster mounted an oil barrel and attacked but Cassandra swatted him to the ground. He stumbled and flapped his wings trying to get to his feet.

I caught up to Cassandra and ran along behind her feeling Danny watching. "Cassandra, come with me," I pleaded. "We'll get the Police and come back for the baby!"

Cassandra swung around in rage. "What are you still doing here?" She shoved me hard. I staggered backward three or four steps. How could she be so strong? She was so little, so much littler than me.

"What do you think you're doing here?"

Cassandra ran past me and back up to the porch, wet to the knees now from the wet grass. She wore only pink nylon panties beneath the white cotton night gown that clung to her. Streams of red grew pink as they washed down from her knees in the increasing rain.

"Let me in, Danny!" She screamed through the back door. She beat it with closed fists.

I stood at the side of the porch. It was about waist high. "Maybe we can get the baby out through the window, Cass," I hissed, "The bedroom window is open."

"What?" Cassandra turned around disoriented. "What are you still doing here? Go away! Go home! I don't want you here! You shouldn't be seeing this!" She gestured with great sweeping movements. "I don't want you seeing this!"

"Hush," I begged, whispering. "I'll climb in the window and get her."

"What?" Cassandra glared at me like I was speaking complete gibberish.

"We'll get Melinda through the window," I whispered, loudly as I dared.

"You go. Get out of here! Go home!"

"You keep Danny busy. I'll get the baby and run out the front! Then you run to the car! By the road!" I pointed in the direction of the car. Cassandra looked. Her eyes narrowed.

I jumped onto the side of the porch and crept back to the bedroom window. I didn't know if Cassandra was going to do it. The baby was still crying, long terrified bawls like an angry cat's. If I could get the baby maybe Cassandra would come with me. I peered into the window.

In the dim light I could see that Danny was leaning over the baby on the couch, jabbing at her with a bottle.

"Come on and drink it, Little Girl. Come on and drink it for Daddy." Who was he to be so gentle? Who was he to leave Cassandra outside of his gentleness?

I sunk down on my haunches and waited, trying to quiet my breath. Leave the baby, I thought. Leave her alone, Danny, for just one minute and let me run away with her. I could hear Cassandra still calling to Danny from the back door. She was screaming to him.

I flattened myself against the house beside the window as Danny took the baby into the bedroom. They were so close I could hear his feet shuffle on the floor. He got a dresser drawer and put the baby inside on top of clean baby clothes. He took her into the kitchen. I crept around the back of the house again, waiting for some chance.

"I got rid of the cat, now let me in," Cassandra pleaded. "I have to take care of Melinda." She saw me at the corner and turned away from me.

"How do I know you got rid of it?"

"Look out there, Danny! Do you see a cat? I got rid of the cat. It's all gone. I saw the cat take off. Your precious chickens are okay. Safe and sound."

"Where is Kate?" Danny demanded.

A second too long before she spoke. "She took Helen home."

I slid off the porch into the honeysuckle.

"You lying bitch! I saw the bitch peeping tomming in our window and you can't tell me she's not still here."

"She was here but I made her leave." Cassandra's voice was defiant. "You heard me!"

"Like hell!"

"I did! Do you see any car?"

Danny appeared on the back porch without the baby, grabbed Cassandra's arm and dragged her to the edge of the porch. I sank down behind the honeysuckle, not daring to breathe.

By some miracle and the falling darkness, he didn't see me. He went back inside and left Cassandra on the porch. Almost immediately she began wailing at the top of her lungs.

"Why won't you let me see my baby? Please, Danny!"

I reached under the porch and grabbed a minnow bucket. Crawfish had been rotting in there for weeks and I dumped them releasing their vile odor. Cassandra came to the edge of the porch and screamed, "Get out of here! Go away! He'll never let me in if you're here!"

"Fine. I'm going!" I shouted.

I ran to the car, where Helen was huddled miserably. I started it and revved the engine. I drove around a bend to where I could not be seen from the house, letting him hear the tires on the gravel. I fought off Helen as she tried to hold me in the car, to make me keep on driving. I walked back up the road and crept back to the window, by now knowing where the porch boards would creak. But it was darkening fast, harder and harder to see.

I waited for the moment I heard the back door open and hoisted myself onto the window ledge. I got my upper torso inside. Suddenly Danny's hand was on the crown of my head. He shoved hard and I tripped backward. I crashed against the railing. It split and I fell from the porch three feet to the ground, splay legged in the oyster shells.

"Get out of here before I make you wish you never came."

"I already wish I never came," I screamed.

Again I went to the back of the house. Danny opened the door and tossed a shot gun at Cassandra. She caught it against her stomach and it knocked the wind out of her.

"You want to prove you got rid of the cat," Danny said, "you bring it to me! And while you're at it, bring me Kate, too!" He laughed before he slammed the door.

Cassandra lurched back and forth on the porch with the rifle cradled in her arms like a baby, patting it. From where I was hiding I could see that her ankle was thickening and turning blue but she seemed not to notice. She had forgotten about everything but getting to her baby.

Suddenly she stopped pacing right next to the edge of the porch. Without looking down at me she hissed, "Tell me if he's in the living room with the baby. If he is, I'll shoot the lock off and get inside. You grab the baby and run."

"Just shoot off the lock and hold him off with the gun."

"I would have to shoot him if I did that," she hissed.

"Jesus." Oh, Precious Jesus. "Does he have another gun?"

"That back locker is full of guns. You think he'd let me have one if he didn't? Danny can shoot a deer from a mile away. He could out shoot either one of us without even looking."

"Then we gotta out smart him. When I yell, 'Go', you shoot the lock."

"'Kay."

I crawled back around the house, under the porch. My heart was beating in my throat so hard I might have puked if there had been time. My ears could hear nothing but the shells cracking beneath my knees and the blood rushing back and forth from my brain to my heart. I hurt all over; I thought maybe my left hand was broken from the fall.

The rain was falling harder now. I got onto the porch and lifted myself to the window and as my eyes cleared the sill

SLAM! The window crashed down on my hands. I was caught hanging for an eternal moment before I realized that I was falling, unable to stay on the porch, then suddenly lying in the gravel again. In the next second I saw Danny's face laughing at me from inside the cracked pane. I pulled my hand toward my chest; I knew it was broken now.

I held Danny's gaze as I rose to my feet and yelled, "Go!" I was going to go inside and kill him with my bare, damaged hands.

Nothing happened. I stumbled around the corner to see why Cassandra hadn't fired. The pain in my hand was excruciating.

Cassandra was crying. "It didn't shoot! I don't know how to work it!"

"I think you pull back that thing and then pull the trigger," I hissed.

She tried it and shot a hole in the porch.

Danny appeared at the kitchen window.

"I don't want you to shoot the damned house up! I want you to shoot the goddamn cat!"

"I gotta figure it out, Dan! How do you work this thing? I never shot anything before!"

"Just cock it, aim, and squeeze the trigger, and BAM!"

"Help me, Dan!"

"Cassie, you're about as dumb as they get."

"I never shot a gun before! How well did *you* do the first time?"

Flirting with her tormentor.

Danny was quiet for a moment. He chuckled softly. "I shot a hole in Daddy's new Chevy pick up. He never let me live that down."

Melinda's cries were softer now; she was growing tired.

"Did you get in trouble?"

"Naw. We was out hunting with his gang and they made such a joke about it he never did get around to beating my ass." His voice wandered. "Those were the days," he said.

I dared hope just then. I dared to let myself believe things were cooling off, that Danny was softening and things were going to be okay. If I could just stay still until Cassandra was safely inside, they would make up and I would drive Helen home. I could come up with a plan at home and come back tomorrow when everything was saner. The pampas grass at the edge of the drive waved and rustled. A mosquito hawk bumped against the window. I thought about the long drive home in these wet, ruined clothes and looked up at the still dripping sky for signs of relief. There was a drifting ridge of gray clouds passing over the house followed by a chain of puffs. I thought of Helen and hoped she was no longer in the car. I hoped she had run far, far away. Time stood still.

"You just pull back there," said Danny. He was out on the porch, showing Cassandra the gun.

Click, click.

"Then you hold it like that. No, not like that. It'll give you a black eye when it kicks if you hold it by your face. It'll knock you clear off the porch."

I slapped a mosquito, forgetting. Danny stopped talking. "What's that?"

"I didn't hear anything," said Cassandra. Her voice was still tense, still on the edge. Sharp, sudden, pitched so high.

"Then you squeeze the trigger. Jesus, we gotta load it again."

"It doesn't have any more bullets?"

"You just shot the last one into the porch. Jesus! Look at the size of that hole."

"Oh, come on, Danny. Let's just don't fight any more."

"Who said we was fighting? I'm gonna get some more bullets out of the house."

"I'll just check the baby while you're doing that."

"Like hell you will. You wait out there."

The clouds grew black. I shivered. Sweat dripped into my eyes mingled with the rain. Acrid salt found my tongue. Wait, I thought. Wait. Wait. I heard Danny's footsteps through the house. Some distant rattling from deep inside.

"She's probably half starved and scared to death," pleaded Cassandra at the kitchen window. "She's still crying, Danny!" Melinda's cries were whimpers now, soft but to her mother's ears.

He opened the door. "I don't want you going in there to her until you get the cat and I ain't changing my mind."

"What purpose is this serving, Danny?" Cassandra tried to reason with him. "You trying to punish that little baby, too?"

"I'm teaching you how to live on a farm. You gotta take care of things when they gotta be took care of. When you learn that you can come in. Not sooner."

"Let me just get her and bring her out."

I got to my knees, to my feet; I crouched like a runner on my mark ignoring the pain in my hand. Just let her have the baby and we will run. We'll get to the car, we'll fly, and we'll never look back. Let her have the baby, Dan.

"How you gonna shoot a damn cat with the baby in your hands? You can't even shoot it when that's all you've got to do. You should of had it shot by now and started dinner."

"Start dinner? Dan, I can't start dinner 'til I nurse the baby. Let me have her. We'll worry about that cat later."

The door slammed shut. I peeked. Cassandra was alone on the porch. Her chest was heaving; she wove back and forth. I thought to run up and catch her should she fall. I thought she would fall for sure. She was still holding the gun. She lifted it to her shoulder, aimed it at the door knob.

She took a stance with her delicate feet a foot and a half apart. Blood wept down her legs. Her toes gripped the beaten planks of the porch where the old man Boudreaux had walked to his evil missions with his daughter, across which Helen had run, afraid to stay, nowhere to go… where Danny had closed his ears and mind and made small boats of aluminum foil and floated them in the old dog's dish.

Back she pulled, cocking the gun just like she'd been doing it all her life. You only had to show Cassandra once. Cassandra was a fast learner.

Raise up a child in the way he should go and when he is old he shall not depart from it.

BAM! Just like Danny said, Bam! I thought it was a lot of noise for an empty gun. It kicked her hard. Cassandra staggered back and back. As she groped for balance on the edge of the porch Danny's scream rang out loud and ancient as pain, fresh as life, high as terror, far away as time. Danny must have screamed forever in that minute of late afternoon down so far south in Louisiana that just about no one cared.

That is why in movies they show those things in slow motion. The things happen as fast as a flash of lightening. They happen fast, faster, they just happen all in one instant of time, but the action takes a day or a year or a lifetime. Terror is when time bursts with too much happening. Pounded into one moment is the tragedy of a lifetime and no lifetime can hold it, so it explodes.

Danny's scream was still alive, still soaring and diving as I bounded the edge of the porch, pried away what was left of the hardware so I could free the door. A vacuum sucked me up there and into that space between where Danny screamed and where Cassandra lay retching, knowing.

Danny's scream was still as it had always been, a high lost note stretching into eternity, when I crouched upon that bowed porch. I opened the door and lifted my bloody hands from it's fragmented panels. Blood, not Danny's blood. Blood filled the dresser drawer, blood still expanding among the soft flannel blankets and pink baby clothes.

Melinda's baby blood. All spilled. All wasted. All gone.

Police hovered around, looking sick and embarrassed. Cassandra wailed and tried to put the grotesque remains of the infant back in the drawer. A policeman peeled her fingers from the dresser drawer, holding her to him. I sat on the grass, trembling, mosquitoes biting me, my face bent over my injured hand.

Cassandra was covered with blood when she was taken to the hospital. It wasn't her blood. Not anymore. Her nerves were shot, one policeman said. It would take a while to get her straight. He'd never seen anything like this before. It was so horrible it had to be an accident. No one could plan this.

Danny was silent and white and still as ice, though I could have sworn I still heard his scream. It was over that scream that the police officers had me answer the questions. What are their names? Does he live here? Is he the father? Who did it? What happened? Is anyone else hurt?

Danny wasn't hurt. Not in his body. The blood was not his. The bullet passed through the drawer as he reached for the door and lodged in the kitchen table. For the report I said Danny wanted Cassandra to go scare off a cat and when she was coming back in it discharged.

Discharged. The police word. I said, "It just went off." The officers took note of a pile of rags I had used to try and clean Cassandra and I can only imagine they thought they were for cleaning that gun. Maybe they were. I don't remember where I got them. I just started wiping and wiping the blood. Cassandra had as much blood on her as Danny did. She was holding the little drawer when the police arrived, she was screaming. She couldn't pick up the broken baby, so she held the whole drawer. There was blood on everything. I was so thoroughly shocked that I didn't feel my hand. The next day I found out it was broken. Injured more and more when I used it although it was hurt so badly. I would never again be able to extend three of my fingers completely. I would suffer from wretched arthritis all of my life.

One officer, a bald man with a sturdy build and a shocked face had found Helen and talked to her so gently. He motioned to me and I followed him to my father's car and told him her name was Helen. I told him she had been waiting in the car for me the whole time and didn't see anything. She stared straight ahead and didn't say a word. She was shaking so hard. She didn't yet know that the baby was dead. She was too sad to cry.

Helen knew that this house was nothing but evil. She tried to tell me. And I could have gone away that night just as she wanted, run away from all that wickedness. But the baby might still have been dead. Yet Danny might not then have blamed me. He might not have turned my Cassandra against me. And all that was yet to come might not have been. Danny stood as silently as his scream had been loud and looked at me as the police asked him the questions to fill out their report. His eyes bore right through me and I knew from the start that he blamed me.

But he did not tell the police that he blamed me on that hideous night. He let my lie save him that night.

I wonder how I got through it. I was such a little girl. I thought of my mother and her shifts of control and of sadness. That night was when I realized that you don't intend to be the one in charge, the one who figures out what to do. You just do what you have no choice but to do. You manage because you have to.

"I'll clean up here, Danny," I heard myself say after the police had left. "You go to bed."

He obeyed, slowly, silently. I was afraid. I couldn't find a mop bucket so I emptied the kitchen trash can out in the heap that would be burned behind the chicken coop and scrubbed the floor and walls and table with a wad of steel wool I found rusting beneath the kitchen sink. I filled the trash can with ammonia and water and rinsed towel after towel of blood into it.

I was crying and gasping when Helen appeared in the doorway, trembling. She got a sponge from a drawer and knelt beside me in the maternity smock we'd found almost new at Salvation Army.

"You don't have to do this, Helen," I said.

"Neither do you," she whispered.

Eleven

Heat

I wanted to be cold. I wanted to shiver and wrap up in a big Parka and mukluks and pile on all the quilts there ever were and still be so cold I couldn't stop trembling. I wanted my teeth to crack together more loudly than my thoughts. Maybe cold could have shaken the horror out of me. It could have made my head clear and my eyes see. It could have frozen the inertia so I could chip it off and make it fall away in glassy crashes.

But there was no cold place. Every place burned with death and horror. There wasn't any escape, nowhere to turn. Hell. Everywhere I turned, never ending, stinking, rotting hell. I sweated out my putrid sorrow and found no relief. There was no drop of cool water, not a breeze, not a hopeful expression on any face. Just hell. Fire and brimstone, terror stricken, bloody, lost baby hell.

A Charity Hospital administrator called our house on a sweltering afternoon a week after Melinda died in her terror. He asked to speak to me. I was in my bed again, ready to give up. There was nothing else I had the power to do. I was floating in a ponderous Hades and had no control over anything. Things were done to me. I didn't make anything happen. I cradled my arm in it's cast like a lost baby and rocked it. I was handicapped and helpless.

But they called me. Why me? Why not some grown up person who wasn't melting in this unrelenting swelter? Someone whose body and mind were free to think of sweeping floors and buying new clothes and petting small dogs that come when they are called? Why wasn't my mother taking care of this call? What did I know? What could I do?

Cassandra had refused to give the hospital the names of her parents. They wanted to release her and she wanted me to take her home. I couldn't say yes or no. I just told them I would do whatever they said to do because I was too weak to refuse. But it was so hot I didn't know if I could.

I didn't know how I got from one day to the next. I bathed many times each day, until my skin wrinkled and began to peel. The water was always too hot. I poured all the ice I could make into the tub and my daddy scolded me when he drank his warm tea in the evening. My mother said I would catch a cold. Summer colds, she warned me, are the worst kind. I didn't want a summer cold on top of everything else, did I? I looked at her not understanding and I sweated.

My parents tolerated Helen's stay in our small house with no small amount of discomfort. They tolerated her living in our house with us but only because they were so worried about me. Our house was too small for there to be another woman there, another broken little girl with another baby that might be another big tragedy.

I told my mother that the hospital man said Cassandra needed to come live with us.

"There is no more room in this house," Mother told me. "Already we've lost the spare room to Helen and there are no more beds. Does she plan to sleep on the couch?"

My mother used to sew in a small back bedroom off the screened porch. Someone built the little room a great many years ago. The room looked out onto the backyard that was lined with oleander and taro and orange canna lilies. It overlooked the little house that held the lawn mower and the tools my father used to fix things when they broke so that we would know he loved us.

"They say she has no where to go." I rested my leaden body on the couch and fanned myself. My mother didn't check me for fever. She just stood up over me and shook. How could she have been shaking? It was so hot in the house. It was so hot everywhere. Mama was crying. Shaking from sadness.

"Haven't you talked to Mrs. Orgeron?"

"Didn't Cassandra say she didn't want me to tell them," I wondered.

"Don't be smart," my mother ordered. I didn't understand what she meant. She told me, "It seems to me they have a right to know. They lost a grandchild and their daughter needs their help. Cassandra's in no shape to make decisions about who to call right now."

"I think I promised her I wouldn't call them. I think I did. Remember what they did when you called them from the hospital?"

"Well, you'd better be figuring out what we're going to do. You've got to be strong now, Kate. You have to. You can't fall apart." But what choice did I have? Everything was falling apart in spite of me.

I tried to call Danny. It was the first idea I'd had in so long. I called him and there was no answer. I called and called. I called and just sat looking at the wall in the hall in the dark while the phone rang and rang and rang. I didn't know what I'd say to him if he ever did answer. I didn't know what I'd say.

In desperation, I called Mrs. Orgeron. I couldn't make myself remember the phone number and I had to look it up in the book. It seemed to take forever to find it. The pages got damp where I handled them with my damp, sweaty hands. I hated myself for giving in, but it was too hot to come up with another plan. There was so much weeping to do. I knew I should have thought of something else, but I wasn't even sure how to try something like that. Thinking up something. What would I have thought of?

Mrs. Oregon surprised me. She said Cassandra could come back. I thanked her and was relieved. She said she and Mr. Orgeron were missing her, needing her home. I didn't know. I wish I didn't know. I hope I didn't know. They would get her. They would take her home.

Mrs. Orgeron called her daughter The Prodigal from that day forth. Cassandra went to the home of her childhood too depressed and vacant to acknowledge my betrayal. Mrs. Orgeron wouldn't let me see her at first. I said I would go and get her from the hospital. She said I had done enough. Quite enough, she said. Mr. Orgeron went to get her with Mrs. Orgeron. They were smug when I watched them get into their car. I walked over to their house as they were leaving and I said I would go with them, and they turned their backs on me. They drove away like I was a weeping willow wilting in the heat. Blaming me.

My mother went over to the Orgeron's house with a loaf of banana nut bread. She told me that Cassandra looked so bad she had suggested to Mrs. Orgeron that she get counseling for the girl, even though my mother didn't really believe in psychologists for herself. Mrs. Orgeron didn't believe in psychology, either. She said Jesus would cure The Prodigal, just as He had brought her home.

I saw Miss Lizzie go to the Orgeron's house from time to time. She would carry a jar of something she had canned or an aluminum foil bundle of something she had baked. She would wave at us, and sometimes come up on the porch and talk a minute before she went on her way. Miss Lizzie saw right through me. She knew that I was falling apart and I could tell that she saw it. Seeing her made me cry and made me want to have her hold me like she did when I was a little girl and she baby sat for me. She would read me story after story at bedtime though my parents only read me one. She would rest her hand on my cheek when she was leaving, and somehow her hand would always feel cool.

I went to see Cassandra a few times. I don't know how I did it. Usually her mother wouldn't let me come in. She said that Cassandra was resting, or not up to it. But sometimes she let her guard down and let me talk to her. When I saw Cassandra she never spoke. She just looked at the wall or the lamp or whatever was in front of her. She never said hello to me, she never said good-by. She wore a sweater, but she never perspired.

Mrs. Orgeron said that the only time Cassandra spoke was when Danny called her. He called her every week, Mrs. Orgeron told me, and Cassandra would drag the phone into a corner and murmur into the phone, or just sit still and listen.

Her mother entertained us by quoting scriptures. She quoted parts of the Bible as if they were stories that had just happened to her yesterday but filled with ancient wisdom. I remember hearing her and looking up at her hopefully, wanting her to explain all of this tragedy. Maybe in a minute I would get it, I thought. Was she just telling a story or making a point? Did I know this language? I was sure I could understand if I just paid attention.

Cassandra's weight dropped until there was nothing at all between her skin and her bones. She just looked out of her hollow eyes without seeming to see anything. When I visited I had nothing to say. What would I speak of? Helen's pregnancy? The good old days?

We sat side by side, me sipping iced tea, just to stay a little too hot, Cassandra doing nothing but staring from tortured eyes to somewhere I couldn't go. It wasn't easy to convince Mrs. Orgeron, but I finally managed to get her to let me paint Cassandra that way, as I had painted her so many other ways so many times before. I painted her outside on their porch to keep the smell of turpentine out of their house.

I believed it comforted Cassandra for me to be there. She was less trouble for her mother. She didn't pull out her hair or bite her lips until they bled. I learned as I sat with her then not to strive to put a particular emotion in my paintings. I learned then that if I only painted what was there the emotion would come through all by itself.

There is an artist's saying. Paint what you see, not what you know. It means that if you look at a piece of fabric falling gently across a lap and what you see is paleness and blue, do not paint the stiff dark stripes that you know you would see if you held the cloth up before your eyes. To me as Cassandra's portrait painter it meant, if you only see sorrow, do not paint a tear.

After I finished that painting and stood back and saw what my painting said about Cassandra, I was sick and thought I might never be able to paint again. I would walk as far as the sidewalk leading up to that porch from where her mother had swept her inside when she was only six. I would just stand looking. If I had seen a curtain flutter in her window, if I had even seen her mother notice me as she swept the floor, I would have gone on up the way to her door and asked to go inside. But I didn't see anyone living in that house until the heat had begun to lighten and the wind had begun to cool.

Twelve

Helen Gets A Job

As Cassandra lived her lost life in the house two doors down, Helen bloomed. The death of the baby stilled her as it did us all, but she had hit the bottom and there was no place to go but up. Her life was as full of possibilities as Cassandra's was of hopelessness.

Helen would stop whatever she was doing when the baby moved, lay her hand upon her belly and let her smile spread. The baby she'd borne before was taken from her, but this one was hers. She was free of the thief who both gave her the first child and took it away. People were taking care of her for the first time ever in her life. For the first time ever in her little life she felt that the world held promise for her and for her child. I wondered if she ever thought about how this baby came to be, of the filthy rotten scum who was lead to her by her father, but if she did, she never said.

Helen probably didn't understand that to move in with people you barely knew was very disruptive. If she understood she couldn't afford to admit it. She helped with dinner and she learned to care for things.

She was eager to participate in family events. She wanted to be in our family. She watched everything we did, imitating us. She began to pay attention to her speech, learning that double negatives were positive but double positives were not negative. She learned how to hold a fork and to modify the sprawling way she sat so that we could not peer up her skirt. She learned to set the table, fork, plate, knife, spoon, glass at the point of the knife with it's blade facing the plate.

My mother was often silent when Helen was with us. The house too small for another woman to move into. Especially a child expecting another. There was one bathroom in the house and Helen spent much time in it. Of course the baby grew heavier each day and sent her scurrying to the bathroom, but she also had become very fond of baths. It was a pleasure so simple, yet one new and exotic to her. She had never been able to take the time for herself, to just take care of Helen. She would lie in the white porcelain tub until one of us insisted she come out so someone else could use it.

Helen ate enormous amounts of food. She was especially fond of the fried okra my mother taught her to serve with pork chops. My mother taught her that you must cook the okra and cook it some more until it no more had long wet strings of flesh. She could eat as much red beans and rice as we could fix. Mother was going to the grocery store three times a week for a while, then gradually she stopped. She made me do it.

The stress of having Helen live there was enough, but knowing she was going to multiply soon seemed to depress my mother further. She looked at the growing abdomen on Helen's young frame with deep sadness. When Helen and I talked about the new baby my mother's face grew tight. At first it was subtle, but then it was clear. My mother didn't want that baby in her house. It made her think, I imagined, of little Joey and the chance she never had to get to know him. Maybe she was afraid she would betray my brother if she loved another baby, even just a little bit.

Helen's skin was beginning to shine with the baths and the rich food and the hormones of pregnancy. She glowed. She gained weight as she should. We bought a bassinet at the Salvation Army and installed it in the corner of her room. I taught her to knit and she made a pile of irregularly sized booties and put them in the corner of her drawer full of dime store underwear in a dresser we had bought used from a neighbor. Miss Lizzie, my old baby-sitter, brought a stack of baby clothes that had belonged to her grandchildren. She said she had seen the pregnant young woman and thought she might be able to use them.

Lizzie Giraud didn't bat an eye when she asked my mother and me who Helen was to us and we stumbled over our words. She didn't ask why there was no young father living here, too. I could have said, "He's dead," had she asked straight out, but I knew Helen would have said, "No, he ain't dead." She might have even thrown in, "He's just a ol' bastard my daddy knew."

Miss Lizzie stayed for a glass of tea one day on her way over to see Cassandra and Cassandra's mother. Sometime during the afternoon she said, "There's lots of babies in this world with no daddies around. Lots of babies. Look around you. You never know whose daddy married whose mama. If they married or not wasn't the baby's idea. It's good to have a daddy if you have a good one, but if you don't, you can get by without one."

Helen was delighted with Miss Lizzie and her gifts. She would thumb through the tiny garments again and again, holding them up to her taut abdomen. Some were well worn and some were stained but her eyes saw linen and lace and it was enough. Some of them matched the tiny booties she had been knitting from my mother's yarn scraps and she laid them out in little sets with the outfits. I bought her a package of brand new white diapers every pay day until we thought she had enough, and Helen would lay them out with the shiny safety pins with plastic ducks on the catch. Bonnet, gown, diaper, booties. Knit hat, Sailor suit, diaper, diaper cover, booties. Again and again she arranged tiny outfits. We found one of my old baby dolls and both of us practiced pinning diapers without sticking ourselves or the doll. We laughed sometimes. I cried sometimes, alone in the bathroom, thinking of Melinda. Thinking of Cassandra.

One day Miss Lizzie brought over a brand new layette. She said it wouldn't be long now, and that baby would need something new to wear home from the hospital. Helen put down the tiny yellow shirt and looked at Lizzie.

"I'm not having this baby in a hospital."

"Well, I don't know," Miss Lizzie said. She looked at Mama, questioning. My mother shrugged. Lizzie looked at the lady of the house, but the lady of the house looked at me.

Lizzie asked Helen, "What does your doctor say?"

"We haven't been able to get her to go to a doctor," I said.

"Oh, Honey," Miss Lizzie crooned. "When I was a girl nobody went to a doctor for babies, but a lot of people didn't make it through the birth. You need to see a doctor and just see that everything is okay."

"I'd be scared having the baby in a hospital. I could just have the baby at home in the bathroom where I wouldn't make much of a mess."

"Oh, Honey! It's not the mess, Child! Nobody minds the mess. It's just that you could really get sick, have problems. The baby could die. So could you!"

Helen looked at her hands. "I'll be having the baby at home…here, I guess."

"At least we'll have to see a doctor to see you're okay. They can't make you go to the hospital if you don't want to. But they can help you if there's a problem you haven't noticed yet."

"Doctors cost money. I don't have any. I took too much from the Breaux's already."

Lizzie sat back. "I will help you pay for it. A loan, maybe. I have some money set aside. If you will come over after the baby comes and you're on your feet, and help me out around the house I will pay your doctor. You need to see your doctor and I won't hear no for an answer."

"I'm scared of doctors," whispered Helen. "I don't want no man touching me."

"I'll go, too, Honey. I'll go with you and you'll be fine. Maybe we can find a woman. I know a woman doctor."

Helen's hands stopped caressing the tiny yellow dress she was pressing to her belly. Her eyelids lifted. "You think you'd want to help me?"

"Well, you're going to help me, too. There's a lot around the house I just haven't been able to do as well as I used to."

"It'd be a job?"

"Sure. Until you get on your feet. I'll figure out the details on what I can afford and let you know, but I could use the help, and maybe you could, too."

"What will I do with the baby?"

"Bring it along while you're working. If it doesn't work out we'll know that later, but you look strong enough, and I couldn't live with myself if I didn't see to it you had a doctor."

Miss Lizzie and Helen went to the doctor the very next day, a young new female partner of the General Practitioner Lizzie had been seeing for thirty years. Old Dr. Hale lifted his eyebrows when Lizzie showed up with the young unwed mother.

"Are you sure you're up to doing charity like this, Miz Giraud? You're not as young as you used to be."

"She's going to work for me. It isn't charity."

"Well, Young Lady," he said, "You could have done a lot worse than to meet up with Miz Giraud. She must have taken in a dozen young ladies over the years."

"Naw. Only five. Five girls. Five young women who just needed a foot up."

"They all did fine, too, didn't they, Miz Giraud?"

"They did pretty good. Nobody ever goes through life without problems, but they all did pretty good. Got a letter from Maria last month. You remember her?"

"Little Mexican girl, wasn't she?"

"Tiny as you ever saw. Not even five feet, I'll bet. Had an eight pound baby when she was sixteen and next day you'd never know she'd been through such labor. She was up scrambling eggs before light. Used to put cheese and onions and peppers in them. I never got so fat as when Maria was living with me. She stayed almost a year. I found her sleeping in the park. Took her home right then. I was younger then."

Helen stayed with us for a little longer while she and Miss Lizzie visited the doctor and cleaned out a back room for her to use. Helen went to church with Miss Lizzie for two Sundays in a row. Miss Lizzie was a Methodist who used to be Catholic, but she didn't believe it mattered what you were as long as you did what was right. I watched them walk down the street from my bedroom window that first Sunday. Miss Lizzie walked with her head held high, a neat black straw hat nestled into her neat gray curls. Next to her was Helen, looking as curious as a child, but waddling beneath the weight of her heavy belly and broadening hips.

Helen talked about Miss Lizzie often after her outings with her. The first Sunday after she arrived home from church, she was beaming as she set the table, trying to remember how to lay the knives and forks and spoons next to the plates.

"Know what Miss Lizzie said on the way home from church?"

"What?" I asked.

"She said the reason why she never told me about them other girls she kept before me until Dr. Hale said something was that she didn't want me to think I wasn't special. She said she wanted me to know I was special and deserved nice things."

"She's a nice lady. I never knew about those other girls either. I thought they were just there to help her out."

"I think she's like a grandma would be if I had one."

"I used to have a grandma. My Dad's mother. I remember her a little."

"Was she always saying nice things and giving you stuff?"

"Yeah, I guess she was. I still have a jewelry box with a ballerina in it on my dresser. She gave me that."

"You showed me that. I wish Lizzie was really my grandma."

"I'll bet she would be glad to fill in."

"You think?"

"I think."

"I don't know what she messes with me for."

"Same reason I did, I guess."

"Why is that?"

I didn't say anything for a moment. I didn't know for sure. "First I didn't know what else to do. Then I felt sorry for you. Then I found out I liked you," I said. I didn't tell her it was because she didn't give me any choice. Helen was blooming before my eyes. She was becoming a friend.

Helen blushed. She filled the tumblers with ice cubes from the aluminum tray, spilling several onto the floor. She couldn't reach them over her round belly, so she kicked them under the cabinet. I gave her a look and reached under and got them, and tossed them into the sink. "I know why you'd feel sorry for me but why would you like me?"

I scraped the boiled cabbage, potatoes and ham we'd prepared into a large bowl while she poured tea into tumblers of ice. The tumblers were aluminum ones my parents had gotten when they married. The window was open and I could hear a pair of grackles arguing outside. A brownish youngster as big as its mother was pestering her to give it what she was gleaning from the lawn. The mother bird showed things to the baby, then swallowed. I thought she was being cruel, so I watched for a moment. Finally the mother took a tidbit and shoved it into the baby's mouth. The baby ate it, then picked up a mouthful from the ground on its own and ate that.

"It's hard to say." I put a loaf of white bread still in its Wonderbread wrapper on the table next to the dish of hard yellow butter. My mother was sitting in our glider in the backyard, silently rocking.

"It has something to do with you making it through all you've been through and being okay instead of falling apart. I don't know what I'd do if I found my daddy dead in the bathtub."

"Your daddy ain't a bastard."

"No, he isn't." I was listening for his car to pull up so I could call mother in for dinner. "He's always treated me great. So has she." I pointed toward mother with a large spoon. "I've had it pretty easy."

Helen looked out at my mother. Mother rocked softly in the aluminum lawn chair. She held her empty glass waiting for us to call her in. She watched a sparrow on the fence.

"Since you didn't have any other way," I continued, "you looked for someone to take you away from where you were, and eventually you found someone."

"That makes you and your folks someone to like, not me."

"But you're real strong, Helen. There are people who couldn't take all you've been through. Losing that baby, for example."

"I'd get her back if I could. She's always in my heart right here." Helen pressed her palm hard against her sternum. "Sometimes there's nothing to do but keep going. Life don't stop just because things ain't going good.

"I know I thought about killing myself for a little while if I would have found out Daddy wasn't dead or something, but that was only because dead was better than being with him. Now I don't have to worry about that no more. Any more. Now I can just work on getting us along, you know?"

"That attitude will take you a long way, Helen."

"You think?"

"I think."

Thirteen

Another Baby

Helen came home from Miss Lizzie's one afternoon as I was preparing supper. She lowered herself into the wing backed chair next to our picture window. She had moved her few things into Miss Lizzie's spare bedroom and had been sleeping there for a few nights. Miss Lizzie said it was silly for her to get up and come over in the morning when she could just stay there and let Mama have her sewing room back. Just like Lizzie could see through me, she could see through Mama and she knew the strain of having Helen live with us was too much.

Helen still helped with dinner at our house when I had to work evenings. She said she felt like she owed us, even though we told her she didn't owe us anything. We gave her money when we could to get things for the baby or a lipstick for herself.

"I'll help you with dinner in a minute. I need to sit down a minute. My stomach keeps squooshing up."

"What do you mean, squooshing up?" I asked. I watered a philodendron with the water I'd poured off the boiled new potatoes. It had been cooling on the counter top.

"It gets hard up then goes back down."

"Maybe the baby is turning over."

"It feels different."

"Does it hurt?"

"It don't hurt but it don't feel good." She leaned back and sighed. "Look there!" She snugged her dress back against her stomach. There I could see it as I looked down on her. Her stomach rose and fell.

"That was the baby's foot," she said in another minute.

"How do you know that?"

"I can tell. At night, especially, when I lay in bed, I can find her head and follow it around and sometimes there'll be her shoulder and her elbow and her bottom and her feet. That is a foot. There, feel it."

I put my fingers along the place below her ribs. There was a tiny hard triangular shape. It pulled back from my touch.

"Does that hurt?"

"Sometimes a foot gets up in my chest and that hurts some, but it's mostly sweet when I feel her little body in there."

"How come you keep calling it a her? You know it could be a he, don't you?"

"I'm just hoping it's a she."

"How come?"

"I guess I knew too many bad men."

"They're not all bad. Look at my Dad."

"I do. Mr. Breaux is the best man I ever knew. The way he put those burglar bars on the house just to make sure you're safe. My Daddy would have only done that to keep me in."

"That baby's going to need you whether it's a boy or a girl. You know."

"I know it is. I guess I'll start looking to your daddy more."

My dad was outside trimming the short hedge that separated our yard from the one next door. He wiped sweat from his brow with his handkerchief and rested with his hands on his knees.

I leaned out the storm door that had the big silver letter B on it and said, "You okay, Dad?"

"Just hot, Honey. You wanna get me some tea?"

"You all sure drink a lot of tea," said Helen.

I stopped and looked at her. I had never thought about it, but I agreed we surely did. After Dad drank the tea in one swig, he asked for more. I brought it to him and he drank it more slowly. His face was red even though he was now sitting in the porch swing. Helen had moved outside to the aluminum rocker she and I had painted pink.

"I believe I'll go in and lay down a bit and let the yard wait 'til it cools off," said Dad.

"You sure you're okay, Dad?"

"I'm fine. Just hot."

Helen said, "You want me to help with the yard after a while?"

"You?" Daddy laughed. "You have enough to do just carrying that baby all day and all night. You just sit here in the shade and drink tea, Young Lady. Don't you let me hear you did otherwise."

Dad went inside and I sat down in the swing. It creaked the way it always did. I wiped my face with the dishrag I'd been carrying around. I tied my shirt up in a knot around my waist. Helen pulled her dress up above her knees and unbuttoned three buttons from the top.

"You think anyone would mind if I took a bath to cool off?"

"Ask mom if she wants to go in first."

We went in and mother was lying on the couch fanning herself. I stood in the doorway and looked at mother. She sighed and picked up the Ladies Home Journal that came in the mail that morning. We could hear the water running in the bathroom and Helen singing, "The Old Wooden Cross" in a wavering soprano.

"I don't think the air conditioner is working right," Mama said. "You hot?" I nodded.

"Helen says her stomach keeps hardening up on her," I said.

"Lord," said Mother.

"What?"

"Lord," said Mother.

"Why are you saying, 'Lord,'" I asked.

"She might be starting labor." Mother fanned herself even harder.

"Labor," I said.

"Having the baby," my mother said.

"I know what it means. What do we do?"

"Does she hurt much?"

"Said it doesn't feel good."

"It's probably labor."

"Should I call the doctor?"

"Are the pains regular?"

"She doesn't have any pain. She said her stomach just squooshes up every now and then."

"Labor is always different, but you never do know. It sounds like labor. Get her to time the squooshes."

"Time the squooshes?"

"Yeah, start at the beginning of a squoosh, then time to see how long in between. If they get regular call the doctor."

"Shouldn't I call her now?"

"It wouldn't hurt, but it could take forever."

"I feel like I should call someone."

"Call Miss Lizzie."

Lizzie brought a stop watch and a tablet of paper that had begun to yellow around the edges. She made a chart and began to time the contractions. She made Helen put her shoes on and took her for a walk around the block.

"Should you be doing this? Shouldn't she be lying down?" I darted between the front door and the kitchen door, knowing the ham should be done by now, worrying about Helen.

"This is better," said Lizzie. "Doctors don't know everything about having babies."

"Helen's doctor is a woman."

"Yeah, but she never had a baby out of her own body. All she knows she learned in medical school from men. Going to a man to have a baby is like going to a priest for marriage counseling. Doesn't make any sense. Helen needs to keep up as long as she can to let the baby drop down. Walking helps keep her busy anyway."

"I'm not sure the baby's coming," said Helen. "It just squooshes. It don't hurt."

"It'll hurt soon enough, then you'll want nothing but getting it over with."

"I remember," said Helen.

"They say you'll forget," said Miss Lizzie, "But I could describe each of my five labors like they happened yesterday. You don't forget hurting like that."

"This don't feel like last time when the baby came."

"Every time is different."

Helen started to cry.

"What on Earth is it?" I asked, and wished at once I hadn't asked. There could be a thousand things wrong with Helen. Lord knows she had reasons enough to cry.

"Your Daddy wanted me to rest."

"Well, he didn't know you might be starting labor."

"But he wanted me to rest, see? He wanted *me* to rest."

"You're crying because my daddy wanted you to rest?"

"My daddy made me work 'til the baby was coming. I only could stop when I locked myself in the bathroom with a kitchen chair under the door knob. Your daddy said I was working hard enough. I think he likes me."

"Well, sure he does; we all like you." Lizzie nodded at me. "Women's' hearts get soft when they are expecting."

"Yeah, she sure does cry a lot over strange things." When she did cry it was always so unexpected. The week before I'd seen her weep over a baby robin that had fallen from its nest while learning to fly. The mother was flitting around it flapping her wings. It would fly a few feet and land. Sometimes it lay on its side for several moments before it tried again.

"What if it can't do it?" Helen asked.

"It will," I said.

"What if a cat gets it?"

"We could sit here and make sure it doesn't."

"We can't sit here forever."

"It will be fine."

"I wish we had a cage to put it in," Helen said.

"It's a wild bird," said my daddy, who was painting the banisters on the porch. "It couldn't live in a cage. It's better to let a cat get it."

Helen made a little sound in her throat. "I don't think I can stand it. Look at the mother. She doesn't know what to do. She's afraid for that baby."

"She's doing fine. She flaps her wings, then the baby flaps his and learns he can take off," said Dad. "She'll go get him some food if it takes too long."

"What if he goes out in the street and gets run over?"

"We'll stop him," I said.

"The mother bird will stop him," said my dad. "She will take care of him, just like her mom took care of her and her mom took care of her and so on and so on."

"What if her mother bird died?"

Daddy sighed, then laughed. "Birds have instinct. She will just know what to do."

"I wish I had instinct," said Helen.

"What's the matter?" I asked, watching the baby bird take a four foot flight from the hedge to the row of gardenias beside the porch.

"Cause I don't know how to be a mama. Nobody ever showed me. I never had a mama."

"What?" My dad took a long sweep with the paint brush. "A smart cookie like you? You will raise the finest baby in all the south. You can bet on that, Young Lady!"

"Your dad called me a Smart Cookie," she whispered to me later. She was grinning from ear to ear.

A day went by and then another. Lizzie took Helen home and hovered over her. It wasn't until the end of the second day that Helen started laboring in earnest. She didn't sleep much that first night. I sat with her a while in Lizzie's living room full of antiques and doilies looking out the picture window at the stars and the love bugs. I finally went home to bed and told Helen to call me if she needed me.

The next morning, I went over to Lizzie's house before heading off to work. Helen was pacing in the kitchen.

"I just can't get comfortable," she said. "sit this way and that and I'm full of ants."

She had occasional pains throughout that afternoon, but they didn't last long or come hard. Then, when I arrived home in the evening, she was in hard labor. Miss Lizzie called the doctor who reluctantly agreed to come if there was trouble although she really wanted her in the hospital.

We covered Helen's bed with a rubber sheet Miss Lizzie brought forth from a drawer, and then we covered that with the oldest sheets from the linen closet. Miss Lizzie made me wash my hands three times and I was glad just to have something to do. We tried reading to Helen but she snapped at us and waved us away. Miss Lizzie got a candle and lit it and put it on my dresser. She told Helen when the pain got its worst, look at the candle and the light would make her able to stand the pain. "It will still hurt," she said, "but you'll be able to stand it."

We walked Helen back and forth across the rug through the wee hours of the morning. We washed her face with cool rags and fanned her with newspapers. We set up the floor fan in the hallway and turned on the attic fan and the noises droned throughout the night.

I finally went to drink a glass of tea and sit on the couch a minute. When I woke, it was Lizzie nudging my arm. Light was streaming through the front window.

"It's a little girl," Lizzie said. I opened my eyes a bit, and she said, "Come see!"

Suddenly awake, I went to the room where Helen lay holding a wet little girl baby to her breast. The infant was naked against her suckling for all she was worth. Lizzie covered her with a small blanket.

"I finished," Helen yawned.

"You sure did," I whispered. "You got your girl, huh?"

"Yeah."

I reached out to caress the baby's sweet pointed head, the tawny puff of hair still wet. "What are you going to call her?"

"I wanted to name her for you," Helen drawled sleepily, "but I'm so glad to Lizzie. Miss Lizzie said her real name is Elizabeth. I want to call her Elizabeth Kate."

"You don't have to name her for me," I said.

"Don't you want her named for you?"

"Oh, yes, I love it, I just thought maybe there was a name you loved or something."

"It means more to name it for someone. If I name it for you it thanks your mama and daddy, too, 'cause you're theirs."

I tingled and blushed. I still get a chill when I remember it. "Thank you Helen. It's the nicest thing anyone ever did for me."

"Oh, your life is full of nice things. Maybe so many you just don't see it."

She handed the little girl to me when she was through nursing. I held her to my chest. She was chunkier than Melinda, and wiggled more. Her eyes were wide open, taking everything in. I thought of Melinda and somehow still felt happy this little new person was here.

After I gave the baby back to Helen and went out onto the porch and wept for all I was worth. Joy and sadness and hope. Lizzie came outside and wrapped her arms around me. I melted into her chest, helplessly. She whispered, "There, there, Sugar. It helps to cry," as she stroked my hair.

The next day Lizzie called the doctor out to check the baby and to see Helen. I sat on the porch swing while they were in her room. Lizzie stayed with her because Helen was still afraid of the touching, and afraid the doctor would take the baby away.

I had such mixed feelings. My childhood friend had only just lost her baby to the most horrible of accidents, and here was another life happening in my life. The new child had come from the most terrible of origins, yet her mother was trying to get past that, to make that baby a life she never could have dreamed of if her father hadn't died in a bath tub one day.

I was sitting there swinging, letting my thoughts go back and forth from joy to sorrow when I saw the gate move two doors down and across the street. I looked up and thought I'd see Mrs. Orgeron going out to the French Market to get her bread. I felt a shudder of dread and hoped she would go the other way. Above the hedge, instead of the upswept bouffant hairdo of Mrs. Orgeron, I saw the pale, gaunt face of Cassandra. She was thinner than ever and fragile looking. Her dark hair was in a pony tail, pinned back around her forehead. Her face was wan, her gait weary. She started toward my house, but looked across the hedges at me sitting across the street and began to walk my way. She seemed as old as a thousand lifetimes.

She slowly made her way down the sidewalk. She occasionally reached out to touch Mrs. Wheeler's wrought iron fence between our two narrow yards, as if to keep her balance. I searched through a lifetime of memories. Finally she crossed the street. I held my breath as if she were a wild kitten I hoped to lure to my caress. I moved to the side of Miss Lizzie's swing, remembering old times when she would sit with me across the street and rock. She stepped carefully up the four steps and across the three steps of wooden porch to the swing. I stopped rocking and let her on.

Long moments passed and nothing was said. The doctor stopped on her way out, followed by Miss Lizzie, and gave us advice for caring for Helen. Lizzie noticed Cassandra, but acted as though nothing out of the ordinary had come to pass. Cassandra stared straight ahead. We rocked slowly. She was fragile and I felt that I could easily break her. She was skittish and I knew that if I moved too fast or too much I would scare her away. I counted a hundred and eighteen links of chain. I watched a honey bee testing the honey suckle. The vine was making it's way behind some of the clap boards. I would have to tell Daddy so he could come over and trim it for Miss Lizzie.

Lizzie said that Helen and the baby were napping. Cassandra blinked. Don't scare her off, I thought. Just be still and quiet so she won't run. I looked into Miss Lizzie's brown eyes and she nodded and went inside.

Afternoon passed to evening. She seemed to relax. I finally told Cassandra that Danny's sister had her baby in Miss Lizzie's house. Her eyes shifted almost imperceptibly. She didn't speak. Lizzie brought out tea in a pitcher and two jelly glasses. We passed the afternoon sitting and rocking. When dusk came, Cassandra silently stood and went back home.

Fourteen

Helen Helps Herself

Helen wasn't getting much sleep when Elizabeth was new, but after the first week she tried to help with the house. She would get up and fix breakfast, but she fell asleep about midmorning just plain exhausted. The baby cried each hour for the breast, and Helen slept with Elizabeth nestled in next to her so she could just nudge her into position and lose as little sleep as possible.

I knew what the old experts said. It would spoil her or ruin her in some way for her to sleep with her mother. But I also knew that people were getting wiser about children. I also knew that Helen and Lizzie got more sleep that way. If they could get a little more sleep, it would be worth it. The baby was growing fatter by the day, and by her fifth week she was smiling.

Helen brought the baby over almost every evening after dinner. I was surprised one day to pass Helen nursing in the wing backed chair and notice that she was crying.

"What on earth," I said.

"It's nothing," said Helen. She rubbed her face on her shoulder.

"It is so something."

"Well." Helen sniffed and rubbed her eyes with her collar.

"Well?"

"I'm just scared."

"What of, Helen?"

Helen looked at me with big wet eyes. "Just this living." I sat on the edge of the couch. "First," she continued, "I was so happy 'cause I was going to get to keep my baby and my daddy was through bothering me." She sniffed Elizabeth's Johnson & Johnson Baby Shampoo hair.

"Then I got here and I was so relieved, you know?"

I nodded. I reached across and took Elizabeth's tiny foot in my fingertips, and it squirmed as she suckled.

"I met Miss Lizzie and she has just made me feel so regular, like I had a family and all."

"So what's the problem?"

"So I don't know what's going to happen now. Nothing else seems as beautiful as to look in her eyes. But I don't know what's going to happen to us."

"We'll take care of you," I promised. "Me and Mom and Dad and Miss Lizzie."

"Maybe you will and maybe you won't, but it ain't really yours to do. Maybe not right away, but it's going to come a time when I'm going to have to take care of us on my own. Even Miss Lizzie can't be here forever. People die."

She was right, of course.

"Then I guess we need to figure out how to teach you what you need to know to do that."

"I'm so ashamed, Kate. I can't even read. I barely ever went to school. I think I'm smart enough, I just always had to work. Daddy said it didn't matter about reading if the crops didn't come in, so I picked oranges and when I wasn't picking oranges I was doing some other farming. Feeding them damned chickens, chasing away the foxes from the pen, chasing away rabbits from the corn. Planting tomatoes. Chopping branches. I was pruning when I went in labor last time. I was up in a tree having baby pains."

When he arrived home afterwards, I told my father that Helen wanted to learn to read. He dug around in the attic a while and came up with some readers that had been his when he was a boy and one or two of mine. He said we would work with Helen after dinner every night. I balked, and he said not to worry. From that night on, he sat with Helen at the kitchen table while I washed dishes and swept the floor. Helen worried about me working while she sat at the table, but I told her she was working hard enough.

Helen grew happier and more confident working for Miss Lizzie each passing week. By the time the baby was a few months old she came home and proudly announced that Miss Lizzie said she was half way through paying her off and she would be working for money now. She would get a little money now, and every six months the payments to Miss Lizzie would go down and the money she could keep went up.

Helen wanted to pay Dad for her lessons but he wouldn't hear of it. Helen said it would be an insult if he wouldn't take her first real earned money. She wanted to earn her way and this was how she would start. Daddy put the money in an account for Elizabeth but he didn't tell Helen. He'd begun to dote on the little one like his own grandchild. It was dear to see. It tugged at my heart to know that I would never have a child for him to dote on.

I never felt maternal urges as Cassandra had. I think I was kind and loving, but for me, a feeling of suffocation always accompanied the idea of motherhood. I have always been selective about companionship, especially since all that transpired with Cassandra. I have friends that I cherish, but I want them to be independent of me. A child could not be that independent. A child would need me even when I was unable to provide what she needed just as my mother was often overwhelmed by me. What if I had a child who did not like me, or whom I did not like? Would we feel obligated to share our lives' passages together, or would we be able to let each other go?

It was Helen who decided that work was what my mother needed to get her back on her feet. She decided that she would make my mother get up and dress each morning. She asked me if it was okay.

"If you can figure her out, help yourself," I said. Even my own mother exhausted me. I loved her so much, but sometimes I could not bear to face her.

This nurturing was a new part of Helen. She saw it, too, I think. Here was one thing she knew about. If anyone had ever felt sad and hopeless, it was Helen. And to her most honorable credit, she had overcome it. She saw my mother sinking into her depression, and she wanted to pull her out, and she thought she knew how that could be done.

"Miz Breaux," she would say, "We can't get by without your help. You have to help us. We need you."

Mother would turn her back, or shrug her shoulders. The first week it was all Helen could do to get her up and dressed before she was lying back on the bed in her clothes. The second week she got her to the kitchen table. Soon, the egg Helen placed before her on a plate wasn't left to be thrown out to the neighbor's dog. At the end of a month Helen told Mama she expected her to clean the kitchen each day before I got home from work, and remarkably she did. Helen would say it in such a way that Mama didn't seem to notice that Helen was ordering her to tend to her own affairs. There wasn't much to be done in the afternoons, just a few snack dishes and glasses, but it was a responsibility Mother could handle and succeed at. Helen seemed to instinctively know that Mother's jobs needed to be ones she could finish successfully.

"I don't know what we would do without you," Helen told my mother, many times a day. I watched her and marveled.

It wasn't a miracle cure. It just got my mother started and took a burden from my shoulders. My father went to work each day, seeming to be oblivious to my mother's anguish, and seemed surprised each evening that she was still sad. I worked at my menial job, hating it, and coming home exhausted from the tedium that filled my days. In the evenings Helen would put Mother behind the stroller holding Elizabeth and coax her around the block. "Come on, Miz Breaux. Just a little bit further. Just one more block and we're home. Now! Thank you," Helen would say sincerely, "Thank you for walking with us. I hate to walk her all alone."

"You can't sit in your sadness," Helen said one morning when mother was picking at her food. "You got to get up and climb out of it. You put me up in your house and I'm not going to let the sadness take you. Not when I can see what to do to help it get better. After you climb out you can look back and see things clearer. When you're sitting down in it up to your neck it seems like that's all there is. But it ain't all there is. There's sun and birds and trees, and, well, this beautiful baby girl right here." Elizabeth grinned at her mother.

"I had my chances to be sucked up by sadness," Helen said, "but I found out I couldn't just lay down and die. If I was just laying there, bad things, they kept happening to me. I had to keep trying for something better so I climbed out of it even though my legs was heavy as lead. I fell back in about a hundred times. But then there was nothing to do but try some more. That or get hurt some more. You got a family that needs you and you're not going to sit in your sadness long as I got something to say about it. You got people who love you and you got to show them some love back. Don't you know having somebody love you makes you where you could do anything you have to?"

My mother frowned at her but she got dressed and she did what Helen told her to do, as if she was just waiting for someone to tell her what to do all this time.

I told her once, on Miss Lizzie's porch, that it amazed me how much she helped my mother considering how much she'd just been through.

Helen bounced Elizabeth on her knee and they both laughed. "It seems like by telling your mother I see what I need to do myself," she said. "I don't really think of what to do. Just seems like I know it."

Fifteen

Autumn Comes

Summer's long hot days slowly shrank and we put away our white shoes and pulled out the sweaters we wouldn't need until the end of December. There was always the hope that this summer's heat would break early, and New Orleans shoppers gazed with longing into the windows of D. H. Holmes Department Store at the mannequins wearing fluffy sweaters and thick down coats.

In the autumn's cooler evenings my dad would sit on the porch at the small wrought iron table with Helen and work on her reading. After she learned how to do that fairly well, she wanted to learn to add and subtract so she could figure out how much money she could afford to spend. Dad got her a checking account and helped her make a budget that she meticulously poured over each evening. Before six months had passed she had more money saved than I did, and that was after buying all the things she needed for Elizabeth. It never occurred to her to want more than she needed. All she'd ever done in her life was try to figure out how to get by.

Cassandra came to sit on the porch at my house most Saturday afternoons that fall. Helen said that sometimes she came on other days as well while I was still at work and sat by herself on the porch. Cassandra sat there for hours and we would just let her sit while I went to prepare dinner or finish some task I had started. She never came inside with me. Dad put an extension cord on the floor fan and set it on the porch facing her, worried that she would bake out there without so much as a glass of water from the kitchen to cool her. It was still hot in the afternoon. I appreciated that gesture but Cassandra didn't even seem to notice.

I took the opportunity to paint her then, sitting so still, like a mannequin in a still life. Of course, if I had posed her, I wouldn't have bent her shoulders so far down. I might not have left her legs just hanging there like willow whips, actually blowing in the occasional breezes. Maybe I would have painted her doing something besides staring at the distance and seeing not a thing. Her hair might have shone the way it used to. Her hands might have seemed to be in motion.

But as I had learned to do, I only painted her the way she was, the way I saw her. The Lost Cassandra. I only painted what I saw, and stayed away from what I knew.

Helen came over from Miss Lizzie's house even on Saturdays, to check on my mother. When Cassandra saw her heading across the street she would silently rise and go home. I only heard her say one word through that summer. I asked her if she wouldn't like to stay and see Helen's baby before she went.

Cassandra said, "No."

Miss Lizzie came one afternoon wanting to borrow some eggs for a cake she was baking for Helen's birthday. Helen knew her birthday from a family Bible she had found that her mother had written in. I sent for her birth certificate based on what we knew and found out that she didn't have one. We had to make up dates and use the names she knew to get the document made up.

When Miss Lizzie came up the walk, Cassandra rose feebly, as if to leave. Miss Lizzie gently took her shoulder and pushed her back down in the swing.

"I didn't come to chase you off, Miss Cassandra. You stay where you sit." Cassandra blinked nervously and did what she was told. "Helen's told me about you and you should know that the troubles of women aren't strangers to me. I've had babies die in my arms. My own babies. One of polio and one of influenza. It's not like what happened to you, but I can at least not judge you when you grieve. You don't need to run away from me."

I watched from inside the screen door. Cassandra put her hands over her mouth and I heard her make a tiny sad sound. Miss Lizzie sat beside her and wrapped her in her arms. "You let it spill out of you, Honey. You let it all out. I won't let you fall apart. I won't let it happen."

Miss Lizzie walked Cassandra to her gate when she went home that evening. She didn't finish baking Helen's until cake late in the night, but Helen didn't mind. She'd never had one before anyway. I brought home cone hats from Kressky's and we sang happy birthday. Helen beamed and laughed louder than anyone.

"This is as fine a day as any I ever had," she said, licking the chocolate frosting from her finger and offering another spoonful to Elizabeth.

Before Elizabeth was two years old and Helen was eighteen, my father took Helen down to the school administration building and asked what she would have to do to get a high school diploma. The woman at the reception desk said curtly that she would have to go to school. My father insisted on speaking to the Superintendent of Schools. The indomitable Mr. Green sat patronizingly with my father and Helen and told them that it would be a difficult task for a girl that old to get it done in any reasonable amount of time.

"Why on earth," he asked judgmentally, "wasn't she in school all along?"

"I had to work."

"School is the work of the young," patronized Mr. Green.

"That's not what my daddy thought," said Helen.

"Then this is not your father?"

"This is Mr. Breaux. He keeps me now."

My father laughed when he told me that part. He said Mr. Green's face drained and his eyes spread open.

"Her parents," replied my father, hastily, "are deceased. Helen is doing a remarkable job of raising a young daughter of her own and working as a domestic while learning to read and add as well. She's eighteen years old, legally an adult, and she's here to find out what to do to get a high school diploma."

Mr. Green spoke to Dad, "Where is her child's father?"

"I don't know," said Helen.

"You don't know where the father is?"

"She doesn't know where the father is," my father responded.

"How do you plan to go to school and care for a child?"

Dad got up and leaned over Mr. Green's desk. What I wouldn't give to have seen my mild mannered father do that. "It was not her fault she has a child," he said, "but she has one and she wants to give that child a life. I would think you would be interested in helping a young girl turn a difficult life around."

Mr. Green looked past my father, "How old are you, Helen?"

"Eighteen. Just turned."

"Eighteen. Most girls are graduating when they are seventeen and eighteen. Not just starting out."

"I want to get a diploma so I can get a job."

"You will have to go to night school."

"I can do that," said Helen.

"You can't bring the child with you."

"Why not?"

"Too distracting. It would disturb the other students."

Helen stood her ground. "What time is night school?"

"It starts at seven and ends at nine. Right now there are no other girls in the class. You would be the only one."

"I don't care. I'll be there," said Helen. I knew Helen well enough by then that if I had been there I could have told Mr. Green that if Helen says she'll be there, you can count on it.

Helen asked if I could keep Elizabeth while she went to school but she must have seen the reluctance on my face. I loved that baby girl, but she was a lot of work, and with my job, as menial as it was, I didn't want to take the responsibility. Although my mother was not as depressed as she had been she was still prone to spells of sadness. She took so much out of me.

My father didn't think he could do it alone. He was great walking Elizabeth up and down the street, but he turned her over to us "women-folk" when the diapers became soiled or feeding time came. He could rock her to sleep but he couldn't get her into her crib without waking her and he didn't like making her cry. I told him I would teach him, Helen did, too, but he refused. Said it wasn't something he was comfortable with.

Miss Lizzie came to the rescue as usual. She said she loved that baby like one of her own. Her daughter had moved away to Houston with her husband who worked in the oil field, and she usually only saw her and their three kids at Christmas. Her older son had married only the year before and was not yet a father, and the younger son, well, he may never marry, he said, and so Lizzie, as maternal than ever, invited the chance to spoil the young Elizabeth like one of her own. Elizabeth was content as always. She went on fussing at nap time and eating only what she chose as if no change had come about. Although she fussed when her mother left, she was quiet in another moment.

Helen came home exhausted at night from school. She was determined to finish schooling and not let it affect her work for Miss Lizzie. She hoarded her little salary like a squirrel, spending only what she absolutely had to, scouring the newspaper and grocery stores painstakingly for the lowest prices. She dragged herself wearily home each night and looked at little sleeping Elizabeth in her crib. If she wasn't quiet enough and Elizabeth saw her, it would take Helen until well after midnight to get her back to sleep.

Helen rose at five a.m. to study until seven when she would come over and check on my mother before her days began at Miss Lizzie's. I urged her to come over later in the mornings, or to not come at all, but she refused. Miss Lizzie rose early and Helen felt it was her responsibility to make sure there was fresh coffee for her at the start of the day, so she might as well get my mother up and moving, too. She said she would be letting herself down not to keep doing everything people needed her to do.

After two weeks, Miss Lizzie put her foot down. "You're not to do a thing for me before ten o'clock in the morning. In fact, you're not to leave this house before ten either."

"But what about Miz Breaux?"

"You can get her started later. She doesn't need to get up at six just because I do. You go over there at ten and check on her. A few hours difference in the morning isn't going to make or break her. It's time she started doing more on her own, anyway. You can call her on the phone, for heaven's sake."

Although we had rescued Helen, it was to Miss Lizzie she had bonded. Miss Lizzie was her real family in her heart, the grandmother she had never had. Miss Lizzie was delighted when Helen brought her things in paper grocery sacks. Miss Lizzie walked Elizabeth around and around in the front yard like it was a huge adventure.

The living room of Lizzie's house had an old carpet with huge pink flowers on it, and Baby Elizabeth crawled around the room touching the designs with her pudgy pink hands. Her very first word was "Flower". It sounded like, "Fawa!" She took to napping on the floor on one big flower near the couch, her tiny blue quilt snuggled around her.

Sixteen

Kate Gets Restless

I loved Elizabeth. We all did. She was temperamental and whiny, curious and beautiful. When I was away from her my arms ached for her, but in the aching I would remember Melinda's little body against me just days after her birth. I lay in my bed and cried for her and for Cassandra. When I was able to be selfish I cried for myself. Poor Kate. Carrying all these people's griefs. Nothing of her own.

I painted Cassandra in the porch swing again one afternoon when she came to see me. My mother came and fussed at me about getting a spot of blue paint on the freshly painted white porch. It annoyed me, but it also made me glad that she cared about things again. She still had sad days, lying on the couch watching television. If Helen came over while she was lying there she would scold me for not getting her busy.

"I can't tell her what to do. She's my mother."

Helen shook her head. "I never had a mother. I just know that when she's like that, you're the one in charge. You have to make her get up and do something when she's like that."

"She won't listen to me."

"When I was living here I just started cleaning whatever she was laying on. Vacuum the couch and if she moves to her bed, go in and say you have to change her sheets. Ask her if she'll take the sheets to the washer for you, and while she's there, would she put in the soap. Tell her the hamburger needs to be thawed out and we're about out of tea. When she says she needs to lie down, ask her if she can do just one more thing."

"I can't be that pushy with her. You don't understand mothers and daughters."

"No, I don't. I just understand doing what needs doing. You can do that. You see a glass in the living room, you ask her to take it to the kitchen. You see a cob web on the ceiling ask could she knock it down with the broom. When she's down you are the mother."

"What about when I'm at work? I can't be with her 24 hours a day."

"You can call her and ask her if there's any flour when you already know there's not. Tell her that you'll make dinner if she'll get what you need from the store."

"What if she says no? I can't leave work and come home to see that she does it."

"You're being a pain," Helen told me. "You just do what you can. Then you'll never have to blame yourself for what you didn't do. You do what you can," Helen stood staring at me with her hands on her hips. To her it was so clear. For me it was so backward. Mothers told daughters. Not the other way around.

Hard as it was, I did what Helen said. When my mother dropped onto the couch and stayed there too long, I nagged her, prodding her to help me, keeping her busy. It never felt right but it was something for me to do, a way to feel in control, a way to keep myself from ending up the same way. I wasn't a kid any more. Mother had prodded me through childhood. Now it looked like it was my turn to keep her going.

My father was pleased with the way things were going. He was greeted with a meal at night. He sat at the TV table with popcorn and root beer each evening like a king. It wasn't fair for him to sit relaxing all evening as I took care of mother and dinner and cleaning up afterwards, though. He watched "Gunsmoke" or "Bonanza" on TV and he liked the role of the television father. Bring me my pipe and my slippers, have dinner ready when I get home. He didn't smoke, and he didn't wear slippers, but I worked a long day, too. I on my feet from morning to night. Who brought me my slippers if I didn't get my own? Who made sure my meals were ready? Who changed the channel when I was through with a show?

As I took on more and more at home I had less and less time to paint. I was frustrated and one day after mother went to bed early I said so.

"I am tired when I get home, too, Dad."

"I know, Sweets. You do a great job around here."

"I need you to help me out more."

Dad gave me the same look Helen gave me when I explained why I couldn't make my mother do things. "I provide you with this house. I do the lawn work. I fix what's broken. I pay the bills."

"I wash dishes. I work all day at the dime store. I change sheets. I wash clothes. I scrub the toilet. I cook. I sweep. I vacuum. I buff the floor. I scour the tub. I take care of mother. I make sure she gets dressed in the morning and make sure she doesn't sleep all day. I clean out the refrigerator and the oven. I shop for groceries on my lunch hour and go without lunch once a week. I dust. I take the dry cleaning to the laundry. I starch your shirts. I go to the Quarter every week to buy the Italian bread you like. I make sure the towels are put away and when they wear out I go buy more. I take the bill payments to the places they need to go. I make sure there aren't any dust bunnies under your bed.

"I take the street car to work most days so I won't have to use up more gas than I need to. I keep the spider webs off the front porch. Last week I painted the porch swing and oiled it so it wouldn't squeak. I made myself a dress and two skirts the week before that. I made a house coat for mother so she wouldn't wear that old pink thing any more."

"You didn't scrub the tub this week," said Dad. "There was hair in it this morning."

"And guess what? I'm not going to scrub it."

"It needs it," said Daddy, peering at me over his glasses.

"Then do it yourself."

Dad slapped the coffee table. "Whatever happened to a man being the head of the household?"

"If the head of the household cares about the house he'll help with it. I can't go on like this. I'm the kid in this family and I do most of the work."

"You're an adult! Your mother helps."

"Only if I make her."

"So does Helen! Your Mama used to have to make you do things. The least you can do is do some of the same for her."

"She was my mother. I was a kid."

"You're an adult now."

"Then I guess I should move out and get my own place."

My Daddy slapped his knee with his newspaper. "Why should you do that when you can live here for free?"

"You call this free? Maybe I don't want to be a clerk eight hours a day and a maid eight more. Maybe I'm tired of doing everything. Maybe I want to paint in the evenings, or maybe just once in a while watch Gunsmoke with you."

"Just what are you expecting me to do?"

"If you'd just dry the dishes after dinner while I wash. Maybe get your clothes out to the washer. Pick up after yourself. Drop by the store after work. Pick up the dry cleaning on your lunch hour."

"I guess I should start wearing curlers in my hair, too."

"If you want I'll give you a Toni Home Permanent."

Dad laughed. I giggled. I sat on the arm of his chair and wrapped my arm around his neck. An Ivory Liquid commercial came on.

"Maybe I should try to get in a dish detergent commercial, too," Daddy said. "See how young my hands look?"

"They'll look even younger if you use Ivory," I told him.

"I'll try to give you a hand, Katie."

"I'd appreciate it, Dad."

We sat like that for a minute. I started to get up and Dad caught my hand.

"Your mother's okay?"

"She's better," I said.

"Only because you and Helen keep after her. I think she'd just sleep herself away if you didn't keep after her."

"She'll be okay Dad."

"I've always tried to keep her from dwelling on things, but she always has taken everything to heart."

"What things?"

"Oh, the things we live with. People dying. Hard things happening. Little Joey. She can't get over that."

"Maybe we should get her to talk about it," I said.

"No. It's not going to help to open up old wounds. We need to just keep her busy like you're doing. I'll do more. I'll try to help. I really need you to be here a while longer. I know you'll move out someday. Meet a young man. Settle down. But if you could stay 'til then…" Daddy's voice cracked and I clenched my teeth so I wouldn't cry.

"Okay, Daddy," I said weakly.

"Your mother is a strong woman, but women feel things so deep."

"I know, Dad."

I did believe that it was harder for women, but I didn't think that was what my father meant. I think men and women each believe their lives are harder, or even better, because neither really understands how the other lives in this world.

When my father read a news story about women wanting to be allowed into combat in the military he was incredulous!

"These crazy feminists! War is no place for women!" he cried.

"It's no place for men, either, is it, Daddy?"

"Men can handle things women can't. You couldn't understand that. You don't want to go into combat, do you?"

"No, but I doubt if I would want to if I was a man, either. It's not because I can't do it."

"You don't know," he told me.

What I knew was that women had to take care of excruciatingly difficult things. The tedious daily things. Making sure our loved ones stayed busy, cleaning up other people's messes. The extraordinary things. Watching people be born and watching them die and picking up the pieces of their brokenness.

I was just twenty-one and I had held a newborn baby and seen it killed. I had seen the baby's mother go through labor only to turn into a shell of agony instead of basking in the reward of watching a sweet small human being grow. I had taken in another woman and her child and cared for them, too. And now I had become my own mother's care giver. I was taking care of things other people started and I hadn't had a chance to start anything myself.

Seventeen

Elizabeth And Cassandra

Cassandra came over more often as the weather cooled. Sometimes I would be prodding my mother off the couch telling her to vacuum, or going out to shake the rugs and I would see her there, sitting in the porch swing. It was mysterious, almost creepy. She never knocked upon the door or announced her presence in any way. She just sat upon the swing.

At first Cassandra didn't look at me when I greeted her, but slowly she began to respond to me just a little. Eventually she allowed her eyes to rest on mine for a second. I would come out and give her a glass of tea, setting it on the porch railing. Sometimes she drank it all, other days she acted as if she didn't know it was there, and at the end of the afternoon, I would take away the warm glass to be washed with the dinner dishes.

My mother worried about Cassandra. I feared that it would worsen her depression but Helen said she needed to worry about someone besides herself for a change. Once in a while mother would take out some Oreos or a peanut butter sandwich. Cassandra didn't acknowledge the gifts as Mama put them beside her, but sometimes she ate them later. If Mama sat on the porch with her, or lingered too long watering the ferns hanging from the ceiling, Cassandra would slowly get up and go home. I was the only one she would tolerate being near her for very long.

I wondered about how things were going in the Orgeron house. I never went there any more; I just didn't have time. I barely sat on the porch with Cassandra. I asked her a few times how her mother was. How was her father? She stared out at the street when I did, sometimes shaking her head just a little bit. I was surprised that Mrs. Orgeron let her leave the house. I was glad to let Cassandra spend her days sitting on my porch. If that was all she needed from me, I could give that much.

Things kept on as they had been for some time. Dad began to help more at home. Not enough, but more than before and it kept me going. I found myself asking him to do the things he had already agreed to do again and again. I was the lady of the house and it wasn't a role I enjoyed. It was I who warded off the salesmen at the door… must they always come during dinner? It was I who called the plumber when the pipes broke in our old house. It was I who made out the grocery lists, who told Dad he was getting too fat and couldn't have any more bread pudding. I saw that the drapes were cleaned and the linens folded to fit the linen closet. I made my mother do her chores. Sometimes I even made her do them over again if they weren't done well enough. I was becoming a nag.

I was continually surprised that my parents did as I told them. Finally I realized that they weren't the grown-ups at all. It dawned on me that they never grew up. They were just little kids who had mysteriously grown old on the outside. I did my chores resenting the people who made it necessary because I still felt like a little kid, too, and wanted them to be taking care of me. My parents let me be in charge because they had been waiting for all those years for someone to tell them what needed to be done.

My father's parents had loaned my father money whenever he fell short until they died around the time I was born, and so for twenty years Dad had relied on Mom to take care of things. When mother lost ability to stay in charge it all came down to me. I realized that my mom and dad were just as little and scared inside as I felt most of the time. They had only been acting grown up all these years, just as I was only acting grown up now.

I sometimes stopped in at Miss Lizzie's after work. It delayed the inevitable responsibility waiting at home. I loved the little round Elizabeth girl who was now walking and putting Miss Lizzie's collectibles in danger. She made little dinners with old pots and pans Miss Lizzie reserved for her use. When I sat talking to Helen in the kitchen, Elizabeth would come in with a lid full of black and red checkers and ask me, "Cookie?" Helen would nod proudly, and I would take a tiny pretend bite of the lovely checker cookies Elizabeth offered. Sometimes that was enough, but other times Elizabeth would make me pretend to eat all the pretend cookies, and I did.

Elizabeth was a pretty little girl. Not a beauty, but she had the best of her mother mingled with the mysterious genetic contributions of some father. A nose that turned up in spite of her mother's Roman version. A round and short body in place of her mothers' long, lean one. Her hair was auburn, dark with red that shone in the light. Brighter and richer than Helen's. Helen said it was due to the better food Miss Lizzie made sure she ate. She had bowed legs which the doctor assured Helen and Miss Lizzie would straighten as she grew.

She was good as all children are good, but she was mischievous. She played in Miss Lizzie's bath powder and broke Helen's treasured lipsticks. She could climb like a monkey. Before she was two she had twice needed to be retrieved from the mantel over the stone fireplace, standing amid crystal candlesticks and photos of children she didn't know. She got up there proud as a princess, only to scream when she thought there was no way down but to fall.

On her second birthday she scaled the cyclone fence in the back yard when Helen left her for a moment to answer the phone. She was teasing the little toy poodle through the back window, making faces and barking back at it. The tiny dog was snarling angrily and it's owner, elderly Mrs. Johnson, was beside herself when Elizabeth was finally whisked away by an apologetic Helen.

The next time she climbed the fence a few weeks later, Elizabeth fell on her head cracking it open. Mrs. Johnson called Helen, crying, saying she was afraid she would get sued for the little girl getting hurt on her property. Miss Lizzie assured Mrs. Johnson that she was not going to be sued, then she drove Helen and Elizabeth to the hospital for stitches. The hair had to be shaven back from the left side of her head. It took three months before it was grown back in enough to cut all her copper hair off to the same length. Elizabeth cried more about the hair cut than about the injury. She kept the shorn lock of hair in a braid tied with green ribbons in a box in their room. She played with it so much, though, that it wasn't long until there were only a few strands left.

Helen had better luck with the lock she saved, mashed inside the big white Bible Miss Lizzie gave her for Christmas the year after she came to work for her. She put it between the picture of Jesus beckoning the little children to come unto him and the picture of Jesus and the Samaritan woman. She thought the paintings were beautiful and wished she could hang them on her wall and look at them as she fell asleep.

When Elizabeth was three I was standing on our porch talking to my father before work. It was winter and darker than usual as the days shortened, but it was still warm. I wanted Daddy to stop and get pork chops on his lunch hour and bring them home and he didn't want to waste his whole lunch hour running errands. I remember standing there with my hands on my hips when I saw out of the corner of my eye little Elizabeth in her underwear coming across the street. It was the Tuesday underwear from the days of the week set I had given her for her birthday. It was yellow with a tiny green bow at the top. That was all she wore and she strutted as proudly as could be across the street.

"Elizabeth!" I called. She looked at me without smiling, and crossed the street like it was serious business. She looked for cars, but a white Cadillac still had to slow for her, and the driver looked angrily at me and yelled, "Keep an eye on your kid, Lady!"

"I'm not her kid!" yelled Elizabeth pointing her little finger at me.

I dashed down the sidewalk to meet her coming toward our house. Between us was Cassandra's house. Cassandra opened the front door. She came down the walk and opened the gate just as Elizabeth passed. She reached out for Elizabeth's hand. Elizabeth looked at her for a moment and took it. The two of them walked slowly toward our house. When Cassandra reached me she smiled, then passed me and took Elizabeth up onto the porch. Elizabeth ran to my father.

"I wanted to tell you good-by for work, Uncle Bill!"

"Liz'beth," cooed Daddy, "you can't just come out here and cross the street all by yourself. Does you mother know you are here?"

"No, she was still sleeping, so I camed over here to tell good-by to you!"

"I'm glad you came, Missy, but you must never cross the street alone."

Cassandra looked at Elizabeth for a moment in Daddy's arms, then turned away and went back home.

"Cassandra," I called after her, "Would you have some breakfast?"

Cassandra turned around and looked at my house. "I'm a little hungry," she said.

"I have some eggs left, and there's coffee."

"Thank you," she said.

I called Helen and told her Elizabeth was eating with us. I took Elizabeth into my room for a moment to scold her.

"You didn't know Miss Cassandra." I pulled one of my tops over her head. "You were lucky she was someone we knew. You can't go with people you don't know even if they seem nice."

"But I know her! My mama tells me about her. She is my auntie who's been sad. Now she must be getting happier to talk to me."

It seemed that Cassandra was getting happier to talk to people because she started to talk. She asked me if I thought Helen would let her bring Elizabeth with her to our house for breakfast. I asked Helen. Helen said that Cassandra would have to ask for herself. Helen believed she needed to do it herself or she would never get well.

A week more passed and Cassandra still didn't ask Helen, but I saw her looking toward Miss Lizzie's house as she paused on the walk up to our porch. Then I saw her cross the street one morning. She stopped on the porch and turned toward the street. I thought she was going to give up, but the door opened.

Little Elizabeth answered it, this time she was in her Saturday panties. They were red and white. I heard her little voice, excited and high, but I couldn't hear what she said. Cassandra wrapped her arms around herself. Elizabeth disappeared and returned with Helen. Helen was wearing a long blue chenille bath robe. I bought it for her at the store so she would stop wearing the one with holes in it she had bought long ago at Goodwill. Helen's hair was up in curlers.

She spoke to Cassandra for a time and I could tell it was a while before Cassandra answered. Eventually all three went into the house. My phone rang a minute later.

"Cassandra is going to eat breakfast with us. I hope you don't mind."

"Would you like our left over biscuits?" I replied.

"Yes! Could you stay?"

"Only for a minute. I have to get to work."

Cassandra ate breakfast with the women on the street each morning after that. I saw her walking there each morning carrying her offering of the day: a pitcher of orange juice, a plate of muffins, a bowl of grits. She was coming back to life, little by little. I don't know for sure, but I'll bet Helen was telling her to get busy.

Eighteen

Cassandra Gets Tough

Cassandra came over one evening, much later than she usually came. It was dusk and Daddy and I were playing a game of Monopoly on the front porch. Mama was sitting nearby, embroidering a pillowcase. I saw Cassandra pause at the gate. I sat up and expected her to turn toward home, seeing us all together on the porch.

"Hello, Cassandra," said Daddy. "We haven't seen you in a while. How are you?"

Why couldn't he remember to stay quiet, I thought. He's going to scare her away.

"Fine." Cassandra lifted her narrow face and almost looked at Daddy when she spoke.

"Come join us," my mother said. "I'll bring some more tea." She put down her needlework and went into the house. To my surprise, Cassandra joined me on the swing.

"I always like to have the hat when I play," she said.

"It's the race car for me, or nothing," said Daddy. He winked at her.

Cassandra sipped tea for a while and watched my mother making tiny stitches in blue, spelling out "Elizabeth".

"Could I talk with you?" Cassandra whispered and I had to ask her to repeat herself.

"Sure."

"By ourselves?"

"Sure." I looked around to decide where to go.

"Let's just walk down the street a minute."

"Dad, you mind? We won't be long."

"Go on. I'll make sure a cat doesn't run off with your horsie." I swatted his knee as I passed and he swatted my behind with the fly swatter.

There was a faint breeze from up the street. It brought a touch of coolness. Cassandra and I walked down a few houses before she spoke.

"Miss Lizzie wants me to go to church with her and Helen and Elizabeth Sunday."

"She does?" I slapped at a mosquito. "You going?"

"I haven't told my mother."

"Oh. Do you want to go?"

"I'd like to," she said.

"Well, you're an adult. You can do what you want."

"No," whispered Cassandra. "Not really. You are an adult. I'm... just... nothing."

"You aren't nothing. Don't say that."

"I am nothing. Helen and Miss Lizzie say the same as you, 'You are somebody', but I don't feel like anybody." She spoke slowly and took deep breaths. "Anytime I start to feel like I am anything it hurts. I don't get to decide what happens to me. They do," she said, pointing at her house. "I don't get to decide when I'm going to bed or when I'm getting up, or who's going to touch me..."

Helen would have known what to say to that. Even then I realized how much Helen knew about what women feel. But Helen wasn't there and I remained silent.

"I just want to go to church where I want to and if I want to. I want to stop being the Prodigal daughter."

"Then I think you should go to church with Miss Lizzie," I said.

"How am I going to manage that? How can I even possibly do that?"

"Just go."

"How will I explain it to her?"

"Just get up, get dressed, and go to church with Miss Lizzie."

"That's what you could do."

"I'm not the one who wants to go to church with Miss Lizzie, but, yeah, that's what I could do. And that's what you could do, too, if you want to bad enough."

"She'll never let me."

"She can't stop you."

"She said I have to go to church if I want to live there. If not she'll send me back to the hospital. Tell them I'm not getting better."

"Go to church with Miss Lizzie. She'll be glad you're going to church!"

"You don't understand. To my mother, if it isn't *her* church, it doesn't count. You don't even want to hear what she says about you Catholics."

"Probably not," I agreed.

"I want you to be there when I tell her."

"Oh, Cassandra, I don't know."

"She can't be too mad with you there."

"I'm just a Catholic," I laughed, sorry my joke was so feeble. "What kind of influence do you think I'll have?"

"It would just make it easier for me if you were there."

"I don't know."

"I know it's a lot to ask, but I have to do this if I ever want to do anything of my own again. I feel like I'm drowning and if I don't do something I'm going to just die. It may not sound like a big deal to you, but just going to another church is the biggest deal in the world to me right now. It's like being locked in a closet all your life, then suddenly getting a trip to the park one day. Will I be safe? Will the sun hurt my eyes? Will I want to laugh? Will they let me swing on the swings?"

I looked up into the cypress tree we were passing under. A woodpecker tapped high in the branches. The air was damp and rich with the smell of Spanish moss and rich earth. We turned around and walked back. I listened to the tapping of Cassandra's shoes against the pavement. Like a little girl's compared to my long hammering stride. We walked side by side. In a moment I felt her slip her hand into mine.

Mrs. Orgeron was kneading bread in the kitchen. She pounded the dough, turned it around and folded it into itself over and over again.

"Why, Kate," she said. "It's been a while."

"Yes," I said. "How are you?"

"Fine," she said, eyeing me suspiciously. "Cassandra, make some lemonade for your company."

"We won't be here long, Mama," said Cassandra.

"What is it then? You spend all your time around the block instead of here helping your mother, now you're not even going to stay and visit?"

I leaned against the arched doorway separating the living room from the broad kitchen. The dark blue linoleum was shiny from recent scrubbing, but worn across the paths where people worked and walked. The back door stood open and I could see in the porch light the row of tomato plants Mrs. Orgeron always grew. They were shoulder tall and heavy with fruit almost red and almost ready.

"I just need to tell you something, Mama."

"What is it then?" Mrs. Orgeron continued to pound the dough as she spoke.

"Well, see, you know Miss Lizzie down the street?"

"Of course I do. I should have known you'd make friends with her soon enough. She's been taking in unwed mothers long as anyone can remember around here."

"I'm not an unwed mother."

Mrs. Orgeron plopped the twisted log of dough into an oblong pan and rubbed oil onto the surface with a bare hand. She slid it onto the counter next to another loaf and dipped into a huge mixing bowl for another glob of dough that she began to knead roughly.

"No," she said. "I suppose you're not."

Cassandra straightened her shoulders.

"I'm going to church with Miss Lizzie on Sunday."

"Well," said Mrs. Orgeron, looking over her shoulder. Her apron was tied across her middle, but she had wiped a floured hand across her bottom and the navy blue house dress she wore was powdered white. "You would have thought you were going to join the army you came in here so serious."

"You don't mind?"

"I think it's probably a good idea to visit other churches just so you get an idea that they're not all alike."

"Well, then, I'll tell Miss Lizzie," said Cassandra.

"Well, then," said Mrs. Orgeron, returning to her work.

Cassandra went to the Methodist Church that Sunday. Little Elizabeth clasped her hand as they walked down the street with Miss Lizzie and Helen ahead of them.

Cassandra didn't comment on it all week although she sat several afternoons on my porch just as she had been doing. When I went to visit Elizabeth that week Helen mentioned it.

"I told her to go tell her mother and she wanted me to go with her," said Helen.

"She did?"

"But I said, no, she has to do some things on her own."

"Well," I admitted, "I went with her."

"You did?"

"It seemed like if it would get her to do something I should try to help."

"I guess it didn't hurt because she says she's going to come again next week. She said she liked it lots better than her church."

"Oh, really. I wonder how Mrs. Orgeron will take that."

"You think she'll mind?"

"She might. She's pretty particular when it comes to church."

"But if it seems right to Cassandra she should just let her go, huh?"

"You'd think."

"It's hard when they don't give you any thoughts of your own."

"Who?"

"Parents. People that own you."

"Did you feel that way at your old house? Like somebody owned you?"

"Well, it was different for me. I had thoughts of my own, but they weren't what I should have had to been thinking about. I see these girls my age at church and they go to dances and proms and weddings. They talk about boys and clothes. They're just getting married and starting to have babies when they're twenty. Doing what they want instead of seeing how to stop other people from doing things to them they don't want done.

"All the time I just thought about staying alive, getting out of there, not going crazy. They weren't thoughts of my own, really. Just surviving. You, though. You get to think about whatever you want to think about. It's different when your parents are okay."

"I don't know, Helen. My Mama's depression for one thing."

"You don't know," said Helen, nodding, "that's true. Your Mama wasn't depressed when she needed to be your mama. She was there then. She didn't get depressed until you needed to be growing up anyway."

"You sure have some opinions, don't you?"

"I've earned them," she said.

"I think I do know a little about it. I think I'm finding out. My mother is doing better, but I still am in charge of the house. I still don't know when she will fall apart again. I go to work, I come home and I clean and cook until I fall dead asleep in bed. There's nothing for me that's mine. I don't think about men or dating or clothes. I just think about keeping the house going from one day to the next. I go to the store, I come home and take care of the house and the family."

"I guess it's women's lives, isn't it?" Helen asked. "Just getting from one day to the next. For men there's always the thought of doing a little better and a little better, making someone else do something so they can do a little better, but for us, we just try to get to another day."

I looked at Helen's hair falling across her forehead. She was still just a girl. Her arms were thin and her face still broke out with pimples some-times. She was leaning over a basket of laundry, folding, folding. Miss Lizzie had taken ill with a bad cold and Helen made her stay in bed. Elizabeth was scribbling in a coloring book at her feet, singing.

"We do for other people and they steal our thoughts and our bodies. It's not right," she said softly. "But you know, I'm getting better. Look what I've done in the last couple years. I am still living with Miss Lizzie, but I'm getting paid. I go to school. I take care of Elizabeth. I have a cou-ple of friends. Did you know I never had a friend before?"

"Never?"

"Never did until I met you and Cassandra and Miss Lizzie. I still go to bed so tired I could die, but I lie there thinking things are getting better and I'm doing okay, and maybe somehow Elizabeth will do okay, too."

"She will do okay. She's smart and beautiful."

"She is that, but she's also illegitimate."

"That isn't her fault," I said. "It isn't your fault either."

"It's a burden, though. Nobody cares whose fault it is. Lots of things you can't do anything about are a burden. I heard someone say at church that God won't let anything happen to you that you can't handle. That ain't true. It plain ain't true."

"You have people who don't care where you came from," I said. "You have people who think you're great. Me. Cassandra. Lizzie. Mama and Daddy."

"But are they the ones Elizabeth will want to marry and can't because she's illegitimate? Are they the ones that she will need to give her a job?"

"Things aren't like that any more."

"Maybe," said Helen. She swept the hair out of her eyes and turned to the sink to pare potatoes.

Cassandra didn't arrive to walk to church with Helen that Sunday. Helen insisted that Miss Lizzie stay home another day until she got better. Helen took Elizabeth, dressed in her lacy pink Sunday dress and black patent leather Mary Janes by the hand and they went to the door of Cassandra's house. There was no answer so they went on to church.

After church they dropped by the Orgeron's house again. Mrs. Orgeron answered the door.

"Well, hello," she said without moving to let them in.

"Hello, Mrs. Orgeron," said Helen. "My name is Helen Boudreaux. I am Lizzie Giraud's housekeeper."

"I know who you are."

I was sitting in Cassandra's bedroom. Cassandra had called me to come over when she stayed home sick from church that day. Her parents were gone to church and I told her I would come and stay with her, maybe do some sketches. I didn't add, only until your parents get home.

"What are you going to do with all those paintings of me," Cassandra had asked that day.

"I don't know. Sell them. Make a million bucks."

I was clearly unwelcome when Mr. and Mrs. Orgeron returned from church. "I thought you were sick," she had said to Cassandra, looking at me.

"I don't have to do anything for Kate to draw me. Just lie here looking sick. I wanted some company."

"Why can't you draw her when she's better?" Mrs. Orgeron turned on me with a sugary voice. "Let her get a few pounds on her."

"It's just practice," I mumbled.

Then there was Helen at the door. I heard her explaining to Mrs. Orgeron, "Well, Cassandra said she was going to go to church with us today and I just wanted to tell her we missed her. I was afraid she was sick or something. Elizabeth really missed having her with us."

"She said she was sick, but she's had company all morning. I don't guess she's too sick."

"Can I see Cassie?" asked Elizabeth. Her little voice was eager and it carried my heart through Cassandra's open bedroom window near the front porch.

"Are you trying to turn her away from The Church?" Mrs. Orgeron's question was so blunt and unexpected that I looked at Cassandra in surprise. Cassandra looked at her fingernails. They were bitten to the quick.

"Oh, no, we just invited her to go with us once in a while if she wants to."

"She has a church."

"Does she feel like we were trying to force her? We didn't mean…"

"I feel like you're influencing her in ways she shouldn't be influenced. She's had a hard life the last few years. She isn't strong enough to make decisions like that. She can be easily swayed in her state of mind."

"But she asked about our church, I just invited her to…"

"She went. She saw what you all do. That's enough. Now she needs to go back to her own church. You can come with us any time you want. Just don't be turning my daughter from her church."

"I can't bear this any more, Kate," Cassandra whispered.

I put my pencil down on her dresser. I closed my sketch pad. I gathered my pencils and pencil sharpener and my soft eraser into the blue zippered pouch I kept them in.

Helen and Elizabeth had started making their ways down the path away from the house. Elizabeth was crying because she didn't get to see Cassie. Mrs. Orgeron went to the kitchen. The house smelled rich with the pot roast that had been roasting all morning and my stomach growled as I thought of the savory meat dripping with onion gravy she had put in a warm oven before church to make sure it was ready by one o'clock.

"Don't go," said Cassandra.

"I have to," I said. I hadn't even started fixing my own family's lunch and suddenly my inspiration to draw had left me. I just wanted to go home. I would probably make tuna fish sandwiches and my father would complain that I hadn't started earlier and made a proper Sunday supper.

Cassandra wrapped a white sweater around her shoulders. "What am I going to do?"

"I don't know, Cassandra. What do you want to do?"

"I want to get out of here. I got out once and everything went wrong and now I have to start all over getting out and I don't know where I'll get the strength."

"I guess you're going to need a job."

"It would take forever to save money enough to get out of here. I don't have forever."

I put the sketch pad under my arm. I held the pouch of pencils in my hand.

"You can come with me," I said. Common courtesy. Without thought. Without preparation. "We still have that spare cot Helen slept on." Growing bravado. This was right, I knew. This was right.

"Come live with you?"

"You might as well," I said, not looking at her, not letting myself think about it. "You'll have to help me around the house. It won't be a free ride."

"I can help."

"Come help me fix lunch. We'll talk to Mom and Dad and come for your things later."

Mrs. Orgeron ordered Cassandra to stay home and eat the pot roast with her family. She was shouting at us by the time we managed to squeeze out the door. I don't know where Mr. Orgeron was. I think he had gone out into the back yard. I imagined he was already drunk, too drunk to care what happened to his daughter.

We went to sleep early that night. I had begun to realize what I'd done. My mother was tight lipped. My father sank down in front of the television.

The windows were open and the elephant ears slapped the screens. Cassandra seemed out of place in her robe, hesitating, wondering if it was okay to do the things she needed to do. We had taken her things from her room while her parents were at Sunday evening church. It seemed cowardly, but who cared? Cassandra chose not to leave them a note, saying she would talk to them in a couple of days when she felt better about it.

I didn't know for sure why I had made this offer. I didn't want anyone else depending on me, but I kept loading myself up with responsibilities. I didn't have time to think about what I wanted for myself. Less time still to do anything about it.

There are people who can spend their lives examining their motives and their ideals and their morals. I am one of those now. I have more leisure time than I would like. I'm often bored. But when I was young there was always work to be done. My job wasn't stressful, it wasn't stimulating and the tedium was exhausting. Evenings I came home and worked until I was exhausted. Mornings I was up before light even in the long swelter of summer. I cooked and cleaned and told people what they needed to do that day. I planned what would be expected in the house and told other people to do it. If they didn't perform the tasks I'd assigned, I yelled, I shrieked. I scolded, I nagged. I manipulated. I found out that guilt would motivate these people in my care better than anything else. I was promoted to assistant manager of Kressky's.

Finally I took back some time for myself. Sunday afternoons, I determined, were painting days. I passed out instructions from my easel to take the hamburger out to defrost or polish the shoes for work or sweep the kitchen, and I painted. When the daily tedium got heavy I planned in my head what I would be painting next Sunday, how it would be affected by light and shadow, what colors would enhance the mood. When Sunday came the painting was complete in my head and all I had to do was move the paint quickly from palette to canvas and I would be done.

I was lying in bed the Sunday night Cassandra came to us deciding how Cassandra would be placed on the canvas, getting ready for the next portrait of her in my house, before I even finished the one I had sketched her for earlier at her parents' house. "Cassandra The Guest". I wondered what all the Cassandra portraits would look like lined up on a vast white wall. What would they say to someone who didn't know Cassandra? Would they make anyone else weep they way they did me? Would it be a novella or a series of isolated snap shots? The child Cassandra captured by my immature lines of graphite on newsprint. The teenaged portrait of us both, the "Rebel Cassandra", the "Cassandra With Child", the unfinished "Madonna Cassandra", the "Mourning Cassandra".

Would the novella be about Cassandra or about me? Was I obsessed? Was I lazy? What would people think of a woman who spent her life perfecting the portrait of Cassandra, who never stayed the same, Cassandra who changed like water poured from vase to pitcher to pot, who froze then melted then escaped like steam? Would anyone notice that she wasn't really all I had ever painted? Would anyone see anything in these paintings about me?

I approached sleep that night in rare examination of myself. I should have been bored of painting the same subject, yet when I thought of something new to paint, it was Cassandra's face, Cassandra's hands, the way her weight rested tentatively on the chair, light as a bird ready to fly. Cassandra's being and nothing more.

Someone I met at work had asked me out on a date. It was a young law clerk who worked at the Court House and sometimes came in to eat at the lunch counter. He would buy a newspaper from me and flirt. I probably should accept, I thought, as I sank over the edge of sleep.

The pounding rumbled through the house. I shoved aside my pink curtains in my half sleep to close the windows so it wouldn't rain inside. But it wasn't thunder.

My father's footsteps fell heavily down the hall; I followed him into the living room. I could see a threatening shadow in a menacing dance against the white clapboard of the porch.

"Where is my daughter?"

"What's wrong, Gene?" Daddy still seemed disoriented after waking so abruptly. "She's sleeping. We were all sleeping. What's wrong?"

"I want my daughter back at home," said Eugene Orgeron.

"Well, it's my understanding she's staying here for a while," stammered my father. Poor Daddy, stuck in the middle of something as grisly as this. Half asleep.

"Like hell she is! She's coming home with me tonight!"

Cassandra had to have heard the shouts, but she didn't leave her little cot by the window with the burglar bars bolted tight across it.

"For heaven's sake, Gene, she's sleeping. Let her sleep and we'll talk about it in the morning."

"I want her back home now. Are you going to get her or am I going to come in and get her?"

"You're not coming in our house like this, Gene. You're drunk."

"I am going to get my daughter."

"Like hell you are!" Dad was wide awake now.

"Like hell I am!"

"Katie, call the police," said Dad, with concentrated calm. He didn't look over his shoulder. He didn't move. He spoke just as calmly to me as if he'd asked me to bring the salt shaker to the table. I hesitated, then went into the hallway. I fumbled in the dark for the phone book.

My mother came into the hall wrapping her robe around her.

"What is all the commotion?" she whispered to me.

"Mr. Orgeron is drunk and wants Cassandra to come home," I said.

"Is she out there?"

"No, she's still in my room. I don't know how she could be sleeping."

Mother opened the door to my room a crack. She squinted but said she couldn't see anything. I called the police and they said someone was on the way. Mother went into the dark room. Cassandra's cot was empty. We checked the bathroom and the sewing room. There was no sign of her.

"I'll tell her father she's gone so he will leave," I said.

"No," hissed mother. "We don't know where she went. Let him stay here 'til the police come."

Mr. Orgeron ranted and shouted on the porch until lights began to turn on up and down the street. The police arrived quickly and led Mr. Orgeron to their car. He gestured toward the house and shouted for a while. The officers stood on either side of him and spoke softly in soothing monotones. When he finally calmed down the policemen walked him to his own house.

They then came back to ours. They asked about the daughter Mr. Orgeron wanted. My father told them she was twenty-one, plenty old enough to stay where she wanted to stay. The police asked to speak to her and my mother told him she had gone. Things weren't good at their house, we said. She was afraid of her father.

The police officers scribbled a report and left, reminding us to call if there was any more trouble.

When Daddy closed the door, my parents and I stood looking silently at each other. Cassandra entered the room carrying my father's handgun. He got it when he had the burglar bars installed. To protect his family. Cass's finger was on the trigger, but she held the gun low and to her side.

"If he comes back, I'm going to kill him."

For thirty minutes Daddy negotiated with Cassandra to give him the gun. Finally she gave it up and watched him carry it into his room. Cassandra slept in my bed with me that night. She held to the edge of her bed, and every time I moved she froze. I could have dragged her from the bed to the bathroom and doused her with cold water, and she would still have pretended to sleep because that was how she got through the night when things got dangerous.

Cassandra wouldn't sit on the front porch after that. She would sit looking through a narrow crack in the front curtains but she wouldn't go outside at all alone. If my mother insisted on having the curtains opened, she would cower in my room. My father had to walk her over to Miss Lizzie's house and we had to drive her to the store or to church or she wouldn't go. Even when she was persuaded to go on errands with me she was terrified and would later be sick in the bathroom and go to bed without dinner. Before long we couldn't get her to leave the house at all. Her fear was a gradual implosion.

During this time Danny continued to call her. There were a few days when he was unable to reach her. She'd moved into my house so suddenly that she hadn't had time to tell him where she had gone. When she finally reached him he was angry.

Cassandra had urged Danny to move back to town and get an apartment with her. He refused to leave the old house. He said it was his and it was paid for and he didn't plan to leave. But Cassandra was sickened by the thought of it and wouldn't move back for anything or anyone.

It was better to stay in her father's house until she found her way to mine. But there was so much more to it than that. Cassandra and Danny were planning to be together again, but they didn't tell me for a good while longer.

A few days later Mr. Orgeron came back again. Again it was night as we tried to go to sleep.

"I want her to come home. She is *my* daughter, and you can't keep me from her." My mother and I watched again, huddled together in the hallway, as the huge puppet-like shadow swung over my father.

"She doesn't want to see you, Gene. Now go on home," pleaded Daddy.

"I'm not leaving without her, Bill! Get her out here or else."

I had dialed the police as soon as I heard his shouting. I heard Cassandra stirring behind her closed door. We had all just gone to bed.

"You stay put, Cassandra. We're taking care of it," I whispered through the door.

"I called the police, Dad," I said, loud enough for Mr. Orgeron to hear.

"The police are coming, Gene," said Dad. "You heard her. Go on home now so you won't get in trouble again."

"What you want to go and call them for, Bill? We been neighbors for ever."

"Just leave us alone and we won't call 'em, Gene. Get on now."

"I want my girl."

"No, Gene. You're drunk, now. Get out of here."

"I demand to see my girl, Bill! Now let me in before I tear your house down board by board!"

"You're not going to do that, Gene!"

"Like hell I'm not!"

"Calm down. This isn't getting you any closer to your daughter. I'm not going to let you within a mile of her while you're drunk!"

Mr. Orgeron went away, lumbering across the yard back to his own house. We checked all the windows and doors and huddled inside waiting for the police in silence.

Wham! The front door shuddered. Through the window we could see Eugene Orgeron's torso lunging and swaying. He had a wood ax and was trying to chop down the front door.

"NOOOOO!" Cassandra bellowed. She tore into the room bearing the same gun my father had taken from her the last time her father banged upon our door.

"Cassandra, don't make it worse!" Dad yelled at her. "Now, calm down, Cassie. We called the Police. They'll be here any minute."

"What good will they do me? They'll talk to him again and send him home and he'll come after me again. I have to stop this once and for all!"

"Cassandra!" Gene Orgeron yelled through the front door. "Is that you? Now you come on home now so we can stop bothering these nice people. Now come on out here. Come on." He panted and the pounding at the door stopped.

Cassandra inched toward the door, but Daddy moved in front of her.

"Stop," I cried. My mother was sobbing in terror.

"I can't stop until it is over. Get away from the door," Cassandra ordered. She pointed the gun at my Daddy. He looked at the gun and moved to the side.

"Please, Cassandra," I pleaded. "The police are coming…"

She opened the door and jumped back. A twenty foot shadow of her father was cast across the floor by the street light. Daddy shaded his eyes. He was standing there in blue striped pajama pants and bare feet. I wanted to jump in front of him and protect him. My mother was weeping. I stood up and she clung to my gown.

"Come on home, now, Cassandra," cooed her drunken father. "It's time for bed."

"I'm not going to bed with you any more," Cassandra shouted. My face drained. I sat back down, groping for the couch behind me so I wouldn't fall.

"Now, Cassie, whatever are you talking about? I just want you home under our roof where you belong."

"You rotten bastard," she screamed. "I'm going to kill you." Her face was red as blood even in the darkness.

"You are not, now, Girl," he said. She stood in the shadows in our dark house. "Just come on out here," he said. He was so drunk I could smell it on him.

Cassandra shouted, "You know that baby I had?"

"What? Now, let's just not worry about that," said Mr. Orgeron. "Let's just let the past be the past. No use crying over it now."

"That was your baby, you son-of-a-bitch."

"How could it be mine, now Girl? Don't go making these people think things about your Daddy, now." Mr. Orgeron looked to where my daddy was standing in shadow. "It's her nerves talking, you know. She's had a few hard years." It was amazing to watch him dart back and forth between cooing and violent demands.

"If I have bad nerves, you gave them to me. You gave me every bad thing I ever had happen to me. You're not going to do any more to me, Daddy. I'm going to kill you."

"Let's just go home and talk this thing though, Cassandra."

Cassandra stepped forward into the light. The gun was aimed at her father.

"Come on, now, that's it. Let's just go talk it out. I'm sure things will seem brighter in the morning."

"They will," Cassandra agreed. "They sure will."

Cassandra hitched the gun up in her hands and aimed. My father reached for her arm. "Cassie, no."

I'd seen this before.

The shot rang out loud and swift. Cassandra's father fell backward against the tall white porch post. He twisted and hit his head against the railing. He slumped with a soft whoosh and a leathery clatter and landed face down on the porch. The ax fell beside his hand. The street light glistened in the growing crimson pool. My head filled with the echoing memory of Danny's scream.

The police pulled up, wagging their flashlights, hurling questions, snapping orders, crackling messages through their car radio. They held their guns at ready until they saw that they were too late. They tucked my Cassandra into a squad car and her face flashed at me in the circling blue light.

The trial was brief. Cassandra spent three months waiting in county jail, wearing a faded gray wrap around dress, her face as dull as the fabric. She started smoking again while she was in there. She smoked like an assembly line now. She held her lighter poised in her right hand, her pack of Pall Malls in her left. She kept them moving. She was never not smoking. She stared through a smoky haze and cursed at her cell mates.

When they hand cuffed Cassandra that night I screamed a hole into my soul. "Take me," I yelled. "She hurts too bad already, can't you see?" But Cassandra wasn't crying. She seemed to have a small wicked smile.

Helen burst forth from her house, running to me with her robe flying behind her. Lizzie watched from her porch rocking herself back and forth in her own strong old arms. Helen wrapped me powerfully in her arms and stroked my hair and didn't try to stop me from screaming. She stopped me from running in the street. She pulled me home, up to my own porch and bear hugged me until I could stop the screaming. She wanted to scour Gene Orgeron's blood from my porch with Clorox and Pine Sol throughout the night after I finally fell asleep, but the police made her wait. They had to collect all the evidence. We stayed in a motel for a week.

I wept each night as I went to sleep. I took to sleeping away as many hours as I could and my mother began to come and place her hand across my forehead as if it would heal me. Our roles were completely ambiguous now. I was as much her mother as she was mine and it was her turn again.

I didn't go to work. Someone called and told them all that I had been through. But the store didn't have a policy for non-family member's deaths. They were unsympathetic.

The trial came and my parents and I all told the same story. He was drunk and trying to break in to get Cassandra. I called the police. She shot him in self defense.

The jury didn't come to a conclusion easily. They heard about the shooting she had done before. Shooting her own baby. Maybe she was crazy. But Eugene Orgeron didn't die after all. He was in a vegetative state, wouldn't ever wake from it, but he was alive. The bullet went into the side of his head, and he hit the back of his head against the railing, then slapped forward onto the porch and broke his nose. He was a waste, but he wasn't dead. I could have told them he was a waste before it ever happened.

Psychiatrists provided by the state which also provided counsel examined Cassandra. She told everyone flat out that he had been raping her since childhood, that she had a baby by him who was accidentally killed, and when he started coming after her again she had had enough and she shot him.

When she said those things in court I was there, sitting in the back. I wept into my hands throughout each long day of testimony. I missed so much work that I was fired from Kressky's. I hurt from a place deep inside me I never knew existed.

But Cassandra was stoic. She was straight backed and clear eyed. Her skin was sallow. I wanted to take her on long walks down the levee and make her strong as the current. I wanted to swim with her in the mighty Mississippi and let the troubles melt off in the sandy earth, churning out to the ocean to be food for whales. But it wasn't safe in the Mississippi River and they wouldn't let me near Cassandra.

Mrs. Orgeron came to court on the last day of the trial to hear the verdict and sentencing. She didn't look at Cassandra. She pretended she didn't see me. She was dressed in black, with a black hat with a veil that fell over her eyes. Funeral attire. But her husband wasn't dead. He was at a nursing home wearing a diaper and being spoon fed beef broth and Jell-O. Developing a bed sore on his right buttock. She visited him once a week and she reported to the church about his desperate state, but she stayed only moments, sometimes not even entering his room.

Cassandra blinked as the judge sentenced her to ten years in prison for attempted manslaughter. She moaned just once then raised her head with determination. She turned to her lawyer and said loud enough for all to hear, "It's worth it."

I was weak and shook on my way to hold her before she went away.

"You look terrible," she said.

"Thanks," I said.

"You can't let this tear you up like this."

"Cassandra," I said, "you're going to jail for what he did to you."

"But don't you see, Kate?" Cassandra crossed her hand cuffed wrists across her chest. "I almost *did* it. I'm closer to being free than I ever have been before."

The guards came and the taller one took her arm at the elbow and said, "Let's go."

"Cassandra," I said.

"Yeah?"

"I love you."

"I know. I bet you wish you didn't, don't you?" They led her away. She looked back over her shoulder and smiled big and strong at me. She lifted her chin. Her eyes were dry and clear. As I turned away from the door that closed on her, I saw Danny Boudreaux near the back of the room. His eyes met mine for an instant and he was gone.

Mrs. Orgeron was waiting for a cab outside on Poydras Street. I walked past on my way to the bus.

"Kate." I heard her say my name and stopped without turning back to face her.

"Mrs. Orgeron," I acknowledged her.

"I should have known you would side with her."

I turned. She was behind me and I knew I should walk on and ignoring her. But I was too young, too emotional, and too naive.

"It was the only side to choose," I said, looking at her veil where the eyes would have been.

"She has nearly killed her father. He's not much more than a vegetable. The doctors don't give him much hope for recovery. He could die any time."

"He deserved it."

"How dare you!" She screamed. People stood and stared or buried their heads in their newspapers. An old man took a drink from a bottle in a paper bag. Someone asked someone else if we were from the case that had been in the news.

"How dare I?" I screamed at her, "How dare I? How dare *you* sit by and do nothing while your husband was raping your daughter in her own bed?"

"How dare you!" She screamed back, "Support her taking away the bread winner in this family? How am I supposed to eat? How am I supposed to keep a roof over my head now? How am I to pay for his nursing care?"

"Is that what you care about? You did know, didn't you? You did know he was sleeping with her, sneaking into her bed at night?"

"It kept him at home!" I could see in her face that she hadn't meant to say that, to admit her complicity on a city street corner with an audience recording every word.

"It kept him at home? What did it do to her?" With each word I punched the air with my fist so hard that my feet left the ground. The man with the bottle stepped back. A man rustled his newspaper, looking over it at us.

"It kept her in clothing and food. It was a small price to pay!"

"It gave her a rotten marriage and a dead baby that had the same father she did! Did you know that, Mrs. Orgeron? Did you know she ran away from home and married Danny because your husband got her pregnant?"

"How dare you! I'll kill you, you little lying tramp!"

"Try it!" I threw my purse to the ground and braced myself.

She leapt toward me, fingernails scratching, fists pummeling the air and my face.

"You hurt her as much as he did!" I screamed at her. She slapped my face. I kneed her in the crotch and punched her belly. I whacked her chin with the top of my fist as if her head were a volley ball. She rolled onto her back and began kicking at me as I stood over her.

"You let him rape her all those years and didn't try to stop him. You are just as guilty as he is. She didn't have anybody taking care of her."

"I was trying to keep my family together! You wait until you have to try doing that! " She scrambled onto her hands and knees. "She had God looking after her!"

Someone said, "Amen!" Someone else said, "Jesus Christ!"

Her cheek was swelling and her knees were bloody. She got to her feet and waved her purse at me, panting. She had managed to keep it in her clutch throughout the brawl.

She snarled at me. "What do you know about it? She killed her baby and she's nearly killed her father! He may have committed incest but she's a murderer! At least he didn't hurt anybody!"

"Like hell he didn't," I howled.

"Who did he hurt?"

I took several breaths into the depths of my soul. I felt myself becoming
calmer, calmer.

"Mrs. Orgeron," I said as I smoothed out my skirt, "Look in the mirror. Look around you. He hurt everyone and everything."

I swung my arms expansively and as I did I noticed that my purse was gone, and so was the man with the newspaper.

"God works in mysterious ways," said Mrs. Orgeron, brushing off her dress with her hand.

I walked all the way home. I had no money for the bus now. No one offered to help me. A yellow cab splashed past me and I saw Mrs. Orgeron's black hat bobbing against the window. Her face was pressed into a handkerchief. I should have felt relieved that I had defended my loved one, but I felt like I wasn't good enough to drown in the swamps that sucked away at the edges of the earth.

Nineteen

Kate And Her Art

Now that I had no job I spent most mornings at Miss Lizzie's house. I went after breakfast and since there was little reason to hurry, I often stayed.

Elizabeth was four and growing tall now. You could see more of her mother in her each day. She was strong and fast. She hated wearing shoes and could climb anything that went up from the ground. She could scale trees that didn't have a foothold for ten feet straight up. Helen would shout at her to come down, circling the base of the tree. Helen had climbed trees as well as her daughter when she was a girl, even while Elizabeth was growing inside her, but nowadays she wanted her feet on the ground. Elizabeth did come down when Helen called her, but not ever right away. It was usually right after Helen made her realize it would be a very good idea.

Helen wanted to dress Elizabeth in ruffles and lace but Elizabeth wanted to wear shorts so that she could run faster and climb higher. Helen had never had a chance to enjoy being fixed up when she was a child and she ached to dress her daughter so that she would look like someone cared for her and doted on her.

Most of Helen's own clothes were still second hand. She only splurged on Elizabeth. She learned to sew on Miss Lizzie's old black Singer and Miss Lizzie reminded her to press out the seams with a hot iron so that they wouldn't pucker. Helen made matching Sunday dresses for herself and Elizabeth. During the week Elizabeth wore pink or lavender shorts that Helen made with the sturdiest lace she could find. Elizabeth didn't care what they looked like, she just didn't want them to slow her down.

I fretted each day about what to do about a job. I perused the want ads while Helen carefully wound Elizabeth's hair into neat braids. Sometimes Lizzie would come in from her garden with a handful of flowers she would arrange into a vase. Elizabeth would carry the ones with broken stems to my mother who lovingly put them into a jelly jar of water.

My parents were driving me crazy. Mama wanted me to do more and more for her now that I was out of a job. She said it was only fair since I lived with her and Dad rent free. She had a point, but I resented her. I planned to move out as soon as I was working again.

Sometimes I looked at my mother and thought she was starting to get old. She was only fifty four, but she had taken to doing needlework in the big chair in the light of the picture window for long hours each day. She didn't worry with make up. She cut her hair short so she wouldn't have to perm it. She was no longer depressed, but she was a lot less active. Menopause had been blamed for her sadness. Hormones running rampant inside her. But I was beginning to believe that some people were just of a nature to get sad sometimes.

I was frightened to realize that I would not always have her, yet it sometimes seemed as if it would be a relief. I was not ready to have her depending on me.

I painted a lot while I was unemployed. I spent money from my small savings to buy brushes and paint. I painted Lizzie and Helen and Elizabeth. Helen complained that she was too busy to sit there and be painted. I painted her snapping beans on the back porch. It took me all of harvest to finish that painting because she would finish far too quickly. I left my supplies in Lizzie's kitchen so that I would not waste any of Helen's brief stillness setting up to paint. I never felt that bean snapping painting was finished no matter how much I tried to touch it up later. Helen never commented on it. She didn't like looking at it.

I painted pictures of Lizzie's house and garden. I painted the storage barn and the lawn mower. I painted the sewing machine with a length of pink fabric hanging over it. Miss Lizzie scolded me for letting the fabric touch the floor where it could get dirty.

Helen grew annoyed with me when she found my easel in her path. I complained that I had to do something until I could find a job. "Well, please do something. Weed the garden! Something! Just don't sit here in the way!" Helen's new love was growing vegetables in the soil. She remembered what to do from her childhood, but rather than seeming like torture as it once did, to grow fresh vegetables to feed her daughter was the essence of mothering. Lizzie taught her to move the plants from one spot to another each year to keep from overworking the soil with one crop. She taught her that if you plant beans and squash and corn together the soil remains rich, but if you plant only corn in one place year after year the soil will no longer be able to support it.

I stayed unemployed for a year. I rarely looked for a job, and when I did it was for jobs I had no chance of getting. I guess I was still recovering from so much grief, and maybe I was showing that I had inherited my mother's tendency toward depression.

One day when Elizabeth was five or six I kept her for an afternoon at my house. She set to work rummaging through my dresser drawers and closets and other places she had no business being. I ignored her precocity, as always indulging her. When Helen arrived to get her, she had just pulled a painting out from the back of my closet. It was wrapped in yellowed newsprint. She peered under the wrapper.

"Can I take it off?" she asked.

"Oh, all right," I sighed. I hadn't looked at the paintings in some time.

"Don't be getting all Miss Kate's things out, Elizabeth!" scolded Helen.

Elizabeth asked, "Don't I know her?"

"Those are all Miss Cassandra," I said.

Helen leaned over her daughter's auburn hair and looked at the painting of Cassandra. It was "White On White" the one that didn't come out the way I planned. The one that showed how much Cassandra wanted out.

"Wow," said Helen. "When did you do this?"

"I was a kid. I painted it just before we graduated from high school."

"You paint good," said Elizabeth.

I tugged at a length of her hair. "Thanks, Boo."

"It's pretty. Beautiful," said Helen.

"I didn't know you really cared about art. You barely notice the paintings I've done of all of you."

"But this one. I don't know what it is."

I took the painting and propped it up on my dresser in front of the mirror. Cassandra's eyes seemed to dart toward the light of the window.

"It makes me sad," I said.

"Well." Helen silenced me. "Do you have more?"

"There's a lot of 'em in here," said Elizabeth.

Helen gave Elizabeth a look. "Sh, Elizabeth. Can we look at them, Kate?"

"Oh, sure. I guess."

Helen pulled out the painting of Cassandra when she was pregnant. Leaning way back in her chair, the mountain of her belly rising before her. I turned away and looked out the window.

"This makes me want to cry," said Helen. Elizabeth ran a little finger over Cassandra's round belly. I watched a squirrel outside. I fingered my curtains. The same ones I'd had as a child. I needed new ones. Soon as I got a job, I promised myself.

"You can tell just how she feels," Helen said softly. "Lonely and scared and lost."

"That's how it was," I said.

Helen and Elizabeth pulled out all the paintings and lined my room with them, balancing them against everything that would hold them up.

I felt Helen gazing at the side of my face. Examining me. She lifted a canvas and brought it to me and stood holding it so that I had to look at it.

"This is what you do. This is who you are."

I exhaled. "It doesn't put food on the table."

"Your daddy is still putting food on the table."

"No, he makes money for it. I buy it, prepare it and clean up after it."

"You're a painter, not a maid. Those people are your parents, not your kids."

"I am a family keeper who just happens to know how to paint." I turned to stare out the window. I put my back to Helen.

She edged around me, laying "White On White" on the bed. "It is high time you took care of yourself for a change. You need to take these paintings to someone to see how much they are worth."

"Who on earth would want a bunch of paintings of Cassandra?"

"I would. These are not just paintings, Kate. They're a whole story."

She spoke with such urgency that I had to look into her eyes.

"I don't know how to find someone to even look at them. I'm not sure I can sell them!"

"Maybe someone would see them and want you to paint a picture of their kids."

"I don't know how to find people like that. I can't just go door to door!"

"You can figure it out. Or you can keep house for the rest of your life."

"What would you do?" I added, "If you were me."

Helen held her chin in her fingers. "Let's look in the yellow pages." She grabbed the phone book from the hall. "What kind of people want paintings?"

"All kinds, I guess."

"Well, what kind of people buy paintings?"

"People without anything better to do. People with money."

"Where do they put them?"

"In their houses, I guess. Offices. Museums."

"Can you buy a painting from a museum?"

"Not usually. They are just exhibited there. Famous paintings."

"Well, if someone wants to buy a real painting where do they have to go?"

"Galleries, I guess."

Helen looked for 'galleries' in the yellow pages. She read a list of a few names of galleries. She got a pen from my dresser and circled them and folded the corner of the page back.

"Call them," she said.

"I'll think about it," I stalled.

"No, call them now, while I can be here with you."

"Are you going to *make* me do this?" I raised my eyebrows.

"No one can make you. I'm just going to stay here to help you be strong while you call some of these."

"For moral support?"

"That's it."

I sat on the bed. "Well, I guess they can only say no."

"Or yes."

"And I don't have a job anyway."

"So call."

Helen stayed with me while I made seven calls. Each was harder than the last, and that, she said, is why she stayed. She didn't want me to give up on myself.

"You didn't give up on me," she said.

Most of the calls lead to rejection. I soon learned to answer "Yes" to "Do you have a portfolio?" and that softened some of the later calls. Finally I managed to get one appointment. The following morning at ten. The Marseilles Gallery on St. Charles street. A small but well respected gallery.

I woke up at five and couldn't go back to sleep. This wasn't a job interview. It was judgment. Was I good enough to be who I am? Would they look at my work and find me worthless? Would they send me away to work for minimum wage for the rest of my life?

At six o'clock in the morning I lined the walls of the living room with the paintings I had selected the evening before. There were one hundred and forty seven canvasses. I had elected to take a series of the Cassandra paintings. I selected six that Helen, my parents and I considered worthy. "White On White", "The Wedding Portrait", "Cassandra With Child", "Cassandra Holding Child", "Cassandra Grieving", "Cassandra Alone".

I ate a small breakfast, showered and was ready to leave at nine. I planned to take the street car, but worried about my paintings. I had tied them together with twine, wrapped them in newsprint, but I didn't want the stretchers cracking against the benches, the canvas punctured by some umbrella.

I edged the paintings into the trunk of my father's car. He offered to take the street car that day. I wore a white suit and white heels and worried over a spot of darkness that smudged on my sleeve as I manipulated the bundle of paintings.

I hoisted the paintings up the steps to the building that had once been a genteel home. I opened the door and knew I was out of my league. The floors were lengths of shining marble, padded with magnificent beige carpets, bordered with prints of soft pinks and greens. The lights illuminated the masterful paintings along the walls. There was a Van Gogh hanging on a distant wall. A Picasso further along.

"Don't let those frighten you, my dear," a deep voice said. I turned to see a tall blonde man in a beige linen suit saunter into the room, hands in pockets. He wore a deep brown tie and a tailored white shirt. My face flushed.

He extended his hand as he approached me. My hands were rough from doing dishes. It hadn't occurred to me that I would shake anyone's hand. His fingernails were manicured. I folded mine into my fist.

"Place your work in here and let me show you the place," he said. I did as I was told, putting the bundle in an office.

"Hello," I said, as I returned, feeling foolish. I thought of my scuffed heels on my white pumps, the smudge on my sleeve shouted at me. My ears pounded with the clap of my heels on the floor. I followed the elegant man into another room.

"I am Morgan Foster," he said. "I am the curator here. You are Miss Breaux, I assume?"

"Yes," I said. "Yes, Kate Breaux."

"Here are some modern pieces we have selected from new clients. The first is— "A Portrait Of A Nude In Grey" by Stephen Prince. The painting was a series of shaded circles and black dots. I assumed them to indicate breasts, but five? There were three scribbled black triangles below the circles that I could see were meant to represent pubic hair. It was quite ugly. The brush had scraped the canvas as if it were removing graffiti, the colors, such as they were, were flat and dead.

"What do you think," Mr. Foster asked me.

I hesitated, then decided to bank on honesty. "Oh, boy," I said. He must have been mocking me with these paintings, is what I thought. They were ugly, I thought. They were lazy, I thought.

"What do you mean?" Morgan Foster could have been thirty or he could have been fifty. His hair receded but only slightly and his wrinkles were present but not deep.

"I mean if this is what you show here then I'm in the wrong place."

"Have you never visited the Marseilles?"

"No, I haven't." Suddenly it seemed as obvious as daylight that I should never enter a gallery that I have never visited, that I was making a grave tactical error just by being here.

"Rule number one," Mr. Foster said. "Know your market. Visit galleries multiple times before presenting your work. This way you will know they are right for you and visa versa and you won't waste the curator's time."

The air conditioner kicked on and my heart stopped for a split second.

"I'm terribly sorry. I'm new at this."

"I'm just passing along some good advice."

"Yes sir, thank you."

"It might be useful to you, as well, to know that most artists have photographs made of their paintings so that they can carry them in a notebook portfolio rather than carrying large canvasses."

"Thank you. I will do that," I said. I blushed again, feeling stupid, but he wasn't looking at me.

Mr. Foster continued along the wall of the room as if the conversation we'd just had didn't occur. I stood in place.

"Come here. This is something you might find interesting. We just got it." He ambled around the room in his silent Italian loafers stopping before a portrait of a pensive nude woman leaning against a pile of pillows. That she had been painstakingly posed seemed obvious to me. I couldn't tell what she was supposed to be thinking about, only that she was supposed to be thinking. Mostly I could see her breasts and pubic hair glaring at me.

"I haven't done many nudes," I said.

"What do you feel when you look at it. What was your first emotion?"

I hesitated. "Like someone was trying to tell me what to feel. I don't care about the model. This painting doesn't tell me anything about her. Except that all her parts are there. She looks too posed."

"Art isn't about feeling good all the time."

"No," I agreed. "But nudity doesn't guarantee good art."

"Touché. Are your paintings all going to make me feel as if I am sitting in a garden on a spring day sipping a mint julep with my lover?"

"God, no."

"What are your paintings going to do to me?"

"They are going to tell you a story."

Morgan Foster stood before the row of my paintings of Cassandra with his hands clasped behind his back. His office was constructed with a painting rack along one wall, a long wooden molding onto which paintings could be placed for viewing. It stretched across a white wall from end to end and was wide enough to hold all of my Cassandra paintings in order. The desk was spare, a thin Italian design with no drawers, just a table before a molded chair. The wall behind the desk was covered with book shelves on which a few books and many ornamental pottery pieces stood. A mahogany cabinet with wheels rested beside the chair. A narrow couch of gold tone on tone fabric was diagonally situated before a wonderful view of St. Charles Avenue. I was instructed to sit on this couch as Mr. Foster examined my offerings.

He side stepped from the first painting to the last, returning again and again to read the paintings from beginning to end.

"A very intriguing story," he said. "Someone you know, then."

"Yes."

"Is there more to the story?"

"Yes."

"How many finished paintings do you have?"

"One hundred and forty seven."

"How many of this subject?"

"Maybe sixty. Seventy."

"Where have you shown these?"

"No where. You're the first person I've talked to."

"You came to the Marseilles first?" Mr. Foster snorted. "That was gutsy. We have a bit of a reputation for being difficult, you know."

I didn't answer. I didn't know. He knew it was sheer ignorance.

"These aren't bad, Miss Breaux."

"They aren't?"

"You know they aren't."

"Yes." I did. I knew they were good.

He pushed a button on his desk and a middle aged woman in a pale blue, seer sucker suit appeared.

"Bring us some coffee, please, Mrs. Johnson?"

"Certainly," she said, smiling at me before she left.

I needed to go to the bathroom in the worst way. I didn't need coffee; I needed a bathroom break.

"If you would excuse me for just a moment I would like to get something. You may make yourself at home, wander about the gallery. Perhaps visit the facilities at the end of the hall."

"Thank you." As soon as he disappeared I did what I had to do. I stood in the bathroom and looked at my face in the mirror. My hair was wet and frizzy, my lipstick was smudged. My face was shiny. I scrubbed at the spot on my sleeve, but the moist spot was far more obvious than the smudge had been. I wanted to run away. I didn't know why he was keeping me here like this when he knew he wasn't going to show my pictures in this too good place.

I returned, relieved, to the office and found Mr. Morgan applying corner moldings to the paintings. Without turning he addressed me.

"Do you see how much different the framing will make?"

"Yes, yes, I do."

"Where did you study?"

"Delgado Junior College," I replied.

"Self taught, then?"

I looked at him. "I suppose," I conceded. "I just paint."

"I can see that you do."

"How have you been supporting yourself?"

"Until recently I worked at Kressky's. A friend got into some trouble and I was fired."

Mr. Foster turned and looked at me, then gestured toward the paintings. "Is this the troubled friend?"

I nodded.

"There are worse things than being fired from a menial job. It might be looked upon as a compliment."

"Thank you, Sir. I never thought of it that way." "Where is this friend now?"

I took a deep breath and looked at my hands. "She's in jail," I finally answered.

"An intriguing story, indeed. You never achieve joy with this model. What about the rest of the paintings. Is there a happy ending?"

Again I breathed deeply. "No," I said.

"You love her," he said.

I whispered, "Yes."

"Back to business, then." He strode to his desk and perched on the edge of it. "Your work is promising, but we only exhibit established artists."

"I see," I stammered. I knew it was too good to be true. I felt blood rushing to my face, my throat thickened and I was afraid to speak. I was so embarrassed. Ashamed.

"But, here." He reached into a drawer of the cabinet and withdrew a business card. Take your work to this man, Dennis Franks. He should see your work. He might be interested."

"Thank you, Mr. Foster. You've been very helpful."

"Before you go to him with your portfolio, visit his gallery as a patron. Look around. Visit many galleries, attend openings. Get used to the business."

"I will."

"And have some photographs made by a professional. There are several places around town that cater to fine artists. No more carrying that bundle!"

"Yes sir," I said.

"I will be watching for your work, Miss Breaux," he said. "Yours is no French Quarter drivel. This is good art." He tapped the paintings as we stacked them and wrapped them. I stumbled down the stairs to our old family car, and noticed him watching me through the office window. I blushed and crawled in the drivers' seat and scraped the curb with the tire rim as I drove away.

Twenty

Lizzie

I ended up taking a job at MacDonald's on Canal Street before the month was out. I was depressed that Mr. Foster hadn't taken any of my work, and to show it I took a job that I could thumb in Helen's face. See, the job told her, Kate is not capable of doing anything but handing out burgers.

But Helen was encouraged. She made sure I scheduled my day off on a week day so that I could spend the day taking my paintings to more people on the list of potential buyers we had made, and the people those people suggested. I used most of my savings to pay for professional photographs of my paintings. I purchased a sleek black leather portfolio. Later I had to buy two more. I bought two good suits on credit and a pair of good black patent leather pumps. I didn't want to feel as out of place as I had that day at the Marseilles.

Dennis Franks warmly welcomed me and my portfolio. I had waited until I had a selection of photographs to show him. It had taken a month and he scolded me for taking so long. Mr. Foster had told him to be looking for me. He took a long look at the Cassandra series. He said there was a great potential for a striking show just exhibiting the paintings he referred to as "The Cassandras". He also said it was important that people know who I was, so he recommended that I get gallery representation with a smaller gallery, host an opening and come back to him afterwards.

I was incredibly frustrated, but Helen wouldn't let me quit. Sometimes when I finished a new painting she took it herself to be photographed. She insisted that when I had five in a new series I take them back to Mr. Foster and Mr. Franks to show them what I was doing. They both seemed interested, but wanted me to be someone before they would let me be anyone with their galleries. I was irritated that Mr. Foster led me to believe Mr. Franks would take new artists. Mr. Franks told me that he had only taken three new artists in the past five years, and two of those had been disappointments, so he was reluctant to try again.

When I was twenty four years old a year had passed since I met Mr. Foster. Elizabeth was almost eight years old and Cassandra had been in jail for four years. It was in that year that the owner of a small gallery in the French Quarter called Esprit agreed to take my paintings on a trial basis for six months. Louis Lambert took a fifty percent cut on my sales. I had done a series of portraits of Elizabeth, and three of Lizzie, but they didn't sell. No one wanted to hang someone else's family over their couches. I traded them out for some small still lifes and landscapes and those sold within a month.

When I was down to six weeks remaining of my original agreement with Esprit, I took a week's vacation from my job at MacDonald's Fast Food Restaurant, set up my easel on Mr. Lambert's sidewalk and painted the buildings I could see from there. Most of those paintings were sold before they were finished. Tourists and business people walking down Iberville Street stood and watched me over my shoulder. It was unnerving at first. After that week I continued painting at Esprit on my days off, and after two weeks Mr. Lambert, or Mr. Louis, as he preferred to be called, said I was in for as long as I wanted to be. I quit the job at MacDonald's.

Mr. Foster said, "Well, it's a start, Miss Breaux. The tourist trade will get your paintings into homes, but not necessarily the right homes. Try entering some contests. See what happens there. All of this will look good on your biographical resume."

I didn't even know what a biographical resume was. I had never needed a resume of any kind. You don't need a resume to be a cashier at a junk food restaurant.

Helen and I were poring over some books I'd gotten from the library about preparing a resume one evening. Elizabeth was eight now, and was a handsome girl, feminine, strong and confident. She was lying in front of the TV pretending to practice spelling. Miss Lizzie was holding an afghan she had been knitting for months and couldn't quite seem to finish. By now I had decided she held it more to keep warm than to knit on it. Lately she had lost weight and was often cold.

"You need to turn off that show and do your studies, Elizabeth," nagged Miss Lizzie.

"I can study better with the TV on," said Elizabeth. They had only recently bought a new television set. Miss Lizzie's was an old black and white that was more snow than picture. Elizabeth was trying to catch up on what the kids at school were talking about.

"Not according to your last spelling grade, Young Lady. Turn off the television set. If you've finished your reading before bed time you can watch the rest of your show."

"It will be over by the time I finish reading all this."

"Then maybe tomorrow you will remember to do it as soon as you get home from school like I always try to get you to do," Helen said from the kitchen table. She rose and went into the living room. She turned the big black knob on the bottom of the set until it clicked. The black and white picture narrowed and shrunk until it was a tiny white dot in the center of a black screen.

Elizabeth stood up and stomped her foot. "You're trying to ruin my life!"

"Don't get me started, Elizabeth. I've told you what a ruined life is. You have to be educated, Elizabeth. That's pure survival. Nothing less. Now, get to the spelling."

Elizabeth snatched her notebook from the floor with an insolent look on her face.

Helen watched her daughter run into her room. The door slammed.

Helen clenched her fists at her sides. She looked at me. "I want to be a good mother to her, you know?"

Helen had finally started to look like a grown up herself. All the years of Elizabeth's babyhood, and during the time when she was a little girl, Helen had been mistaken for Elizabeth's baby-sitter or older sister. It would make her angry and she would firmly reply, "This is my own baby," no matter who it was, no matter if it would lead to questions about the baby's daddy. Helen didn't want there to be any doubt that Elizabeth was hers and she was taking full responsibility for her every step of the way.

Miss Lizzie was the one person to whom she would occasionally defer when it came to raising her daughter.

"I never had a mama," she explained. "I never had no one to teach me what to do to bring up a kid. Lizzie's my teacher. She's teaching me how to be a mama."

Miss Lizzie didn't move too swiftly any more. That evening when she heard Elizabeth's door slam she came slowly into the kitchen, bracing herself on the door sill as she came into the room.

"Oh, Honey, I'm no woo woo wah," she said.

"Excuse me," I said, "I didn't understand you."

"Wonna woo wah," said Miss Lizzie.

Helen took Miss Lizzie's arm. "You okay?"

A string of drool dripped from the left side of Miss Lizzie's mouth. She seemed agitated and kept trying to talk, but all she could say were woos and wahs.

The ambulance arrived shortly after our call. Lizzie was stabilized and placed on a gurney. The flashing of the lights took me back to the night Cassandra shot her father, a place I didn't want to go.

Lizzie had suffered a stroke and was taken to the hospital that night. She couldn't control her speech and her face was permanently twisted because half of it had no muscle response. She was terribly frustrated, and made sure we knew. She slapped the bed with her good hand when she didn't get what she wanted. Sometimes she kicked with her good foot, too. Often she cried in frustration.

Soon her children arrived and took over the house. Helen moved into Elizabeth's room with her and continued to cook and clean as always, but the visitors didn't help her. She had to pick up after them when they showered or ate. They called her 'Mother's Girl' when they spoke of her to each other. There were meals in progress nearly all day long. Helen rose before dawn and didn't go to bed until after midnight in order to take care of the guests. She was afraid to comment on their lack of consideration and things didn't improve.

Lizzie's older son, Bob, came for a week with his wife, Lynette. They spent most of their time at the hospital with Lizzie. They stayed in a hotel but took most of their meals at the house. They drove over to pick up the others for visits to the hospital, and left without saying much of anything to Helen.

The younger son, Dave, came only for two days. He visited his mother for a couple of hours each day, but went out each evening with his old high school buddies. He would stumble in late and sleep on the living room floor with a blanket and a cushion from the couch after waking everyone in the house with his slamming about.

Lizzie's daughter, Corrine, had three children. The two girls were Kathy, eight, and Donna who was ten. Mark was eleven and didn't want to be there. They moved into Miss Lizzie's room. Mark stayed holed up in Helen's room reading comic books most of the time. Even when Corinne and the children were visiting Miss Lizzie, Helen's room wasn't her own. Dave would move into it when the living room became too busy to sleep in. He came out several times a day to eat. Young Mark was very popular in his school back in California and hated missing school even for two weeks to visit his ailing grandmother. His mother reminded him that he might not get that many more chances to see her, and he shrugged. After all, he barely knew her.

Elizabeth was a sociable child and loved having the girls to play with. They were not interested in sports, but Donna could turn great cartwheels and both girls could roller skate well enough. Elizabeth tolerated having her hair put up in brush rollers in order to have skating partners. She managed to get them up into a tree some afternoons and they giggled at people passing beneath them.

Elizabeth resented it when she had to help with the cleaning and the other girls didn't. She really hated going to school in the mornings knowing that Donna and Kathy would be having fun without her.

It didn't last forever, though.

"Already?" asked Elizabeth as Corinne's family packed to go.

"Finally," sighed Helen.

Lizzie stayed in the hospital for a month, and saw some improvement, but she was still helpless. She needed help to walk, help to wash, help to eat. She couldn't talk and she was terribly frustrated and depressed. When Dr. Hale gave his okay Helen arranged with the children to have Lizzie sent home. It would save them money and Lizzie would be happier. She would see a physical therapist twice a week and Helen could work with her at home on relearning basic skills. She would not have to go to a nursing home as long as Helen could help it.

My father insisted that Helen ask Bob Giraud for more money for Miss Lizzie's care now that she required so much of it. Bob balked, but finally relented when his many telephone calls revealed that professional care would cost much more than Helen was asking. The checks came regularly. Corrine reminded Helen that the time may come when Lizzie would have to be placed in a Home. Helen told her that wouldn't have to happen if she would just be allowed to do her job.

"I'm cheaper, and I love her. She will be happier here with me."

I finished the last two in a series of six paintings of Miss Lizzie after she came home from the hospital. It was a poignant look at a mature and vital woman being beaten by time. In some of the paintings her hands were the focal point. In all of them her hands were featured. One of the most telling portraits was of Miss Lizzie smocking the white bodice of a dress for Elizabeth to wear on Easter. I painted the fingers as smears of paint representing of the speed of her work. The tendons were shown distinctly and strong. Another painting showed Miss Lizzie combing out Elizabeth's hair after her bath.

The last showed her hands lying helplessly on top of a quilt she had made out of the fabrics used in her life. A swatch of Corinne's blue nightgown from when she was a young girl; part of Bob's high school baseball shirt, white with a red stripe; a piece of Dave's white button down shirt worn on his first date. There was a piece of Lizzie's own mother's muslin apron; part of a linen handkerchief her husband had carried in his pocket on Sundays; some yellow gingham from an old set of kitchen curtains. Evidence and memory of all the work and labor of a long life well lived.

Miss Lizzie was more work than Helen anticipated. After three weeks of constant care Helen was haggard from fatigue. I went over and helped after painting in the sun all day, but again I was working and caring for my own family as well, and there was so little I could do. I managed to make extra casseroles and freeze them for Helen to use later.

Lizzie had to be spoon fed soft foods. She couldn't even use the bath room by herself.

She had to ring a small bell with her right hand. If the bell was not where she could reach it, there were sometimes accidents in the bed. These made Lizzie cry in shame. Helen went to a medical supply store on the advice of Dr. Dave and bought rubber sheets to place under the linens on top of the mattress to protect it. They were just like the one Lizzie placed under her when she gave birth to Elizabeth in my bed. She also bought a bed pan for use at night when she was too tired to take Lizzie to the bathroom and back.

Miss Lizzie's cousin brought over a wheel chair so at least there could be a morning walk. My dad built a ramp from the porch to the sidewalk. Sometimes Helen took Lizzie to the park and just sat there for an hour doing nothing. Miss Lizzie grunted in complaint, wanting to go home, but Helen ignored her until she was ready to go.

It was late in the year, Thanksgiving was approaching, when Lizzie's heart failed. Dr. Hale said that if it had been any more serious she wouldn't have made it. She went back to the hospital. Dad and I worried that she would never get back home. Lizzie was seventy-eight.

Helen prepared the house for Lizzie's children, making sure to stock up on snack foods, but this time only Corrine came. Her children were still in school, so she came alone. She spent many hours each day at the hospital. Helen and Elizabeth fussed and quarreled a lot. Helen was worried about what to do if the worst happened, but she couldn't look for a job and desert Miss Lizzie. Yet, she and Elizabeth had no where else to live.

Corrine called Bob every evening with news of Lizzie's condition. Dave called every other morning to see if there was any change. Corrine was silent when she was in the house, and I tried not to visit when she was home so as not to disturb her. Elizabeth came to our house to do her homework and watch television in the evenings with my mother and father.

Bob reduced Helen's salary while his mother was hospitalized since her duties were light then. She feared it wouldn't be long until there was no more job, but she was more afraid of losing Miss Lizzie, the woman who gave her this first job and taught her to be a mama and how to take care of herself and her daughter. Already she grieved for the old woman who had taken her in and made her part of a family.

Corrine stayed until Miss Lizzie's condition stabilized, then she had to return home to her own family. The whole of Miss Lizzie's family came out during Thanksgiving week, even Corinne's husband, Ron. Helen prepared a feast for them which took her four days to make ready, then she and Elizabeth ate at our house for the big meal. The Giraud family complained of turkey left-overs on Friday and Saturday. I told Helen they were concerned about their mother and didn't mean to be rude. Elizabeth was glad to see Donna and Kathy, but they spent a lot of time at the hospital at their mother's insistence, so there wasn't much time to play.

Miraculously, Miss Lizzie improved a little. After three months Dr. Hale agreed to let her go home. Corrine came out again to help her settle in. A few days later Bob came out. He set up a trust with an attorney to pay Helen's wages and Lizzie's medical expenses. Lizzie had left a confidential will with her attorney and after Bob settled the remaining business he went back home. Dr. Hale's nurse would see Lizzie twice a week, more if there were concerns. Lizzie seemed delighted to be at home. She spent lots of time on the front porch in her wheel chair listening to the radio. Helen was relieved to have her back, and didn't ever complain about how hard it was to care for her.

One evening Helen sent Elizabeth out onto the porch to wheel Miss Lizzie back inside to get ready for bed. Elizabeth went out and switched off the radio and gave Miss Lizzie a kiss on the cheek to wake her up. Lizzie often napped in the cool evening air. Lizzie woke up and seemed disoriented. Elizabeth helped Helen take her to the bathroom and put her back into bed.

Helen felt uneasy and slept on the couch all night, waking with every sound, just like she did when Elizabeth was an infant. She felt the air get lighter just before dawn and realized she'd been asleep for three hours. She rushed into Miss Lizzie's room, and just as she had when newborn Elizabeth slept longer than she expected, Helen slipped her hand in front of Miss Lizzie's face to see if she was still breathing.

The stillness stole Helen's breath as well. She tugged down on the window shade, making it snap open against the window. When the light spilled across Miss Lizzie's gentle face there was nothing there to save. She had died in her sleep.

Elizabeth heard her mother's heavy note of exhale, that sound people can only make in the realization of tremendous loss. Elizabeth would always remember that desperately lonely sound, recognizing it when she heard it coming unbidden from her own soul when the loss was her own.

Twenty One

Moving On

Helen wept silently in her place behind Lizzie's children. Corrine wept on Ron's shoulder. Donna and Kathy fidgeted. Bob's shoulders shook and Lynette patted his arm tenderly. Dave wrapped himself in his own arms, much the way his mother did when she was upset. Of all the children, he resembled her the most.

The Methodist Church was filled with congregation members, neighbors and friends, all of whom came to pay their respects to Mrs. Elizabeth Giraud. Some of them had known her since they were children; some had grown up with her. There were some tears, but everyone agreed it was Miss Lizzie's time to go.

The minister spoke of Miz Giraud's generosity, opening her heart and home to young women in need. He spoke of her strength, her motherly qualities. He assured us she would be waiting in heaven for us when we got there. He related stories Lizzie's friends had told about her humor and goodness and hard headed wisdom. How she never failed to bring a casserole to the sick, how she was always one of the last to leave the church whether it was a wedding or a cleaning day, how she loved to rock the babies in the nursery, how the young women she took under her wing turned into pillars of the community and would stand tall in her stead. He told how she hated being called a senior citizen. She was seventy when congregation members caught her showing the kids how to do a cartwheel. Helen and I looked at each other and laughed. We knew how sore she was after that little stunt.

The day was bright with sunshine when Lizzie was buried into her plot next to Mr. Giraud and the two babies they had lost so long ago. Those babies would have been older than Corrine, Bob and Dave were now.

Helen and I wore wide black hats to protect us from the sun. I wished the burial could have waited until evening. The sun didn't allow a secret space for privacy to mourn. We were all illuminated and bared. Each reddened nose, each tear streaked face shining in the sun.

Those who knew it sang an old standard hymn called "When We All Get Together". The women sang, "When we a-a-all…" and the men repeated in a low single note, "When we all…" "When we all get together, what a day of rejoicing that will be! When we all see Jesus, We'll sing and shout the victory!" It was somehow comforting.

Helen and I lingered for a time before climbing back into the car with my parents to go home. We were invited to Miss Lizzie's house for the feast of food brought by friends and neighbors. My mother had made a lemon mirangue pie from scratch. There was more food than the family could eat in the few days they had left in New Orleans. Some was frozen, much was sent home with the minister and with elderly neighbors. We took home the lion's share. I didn't have to cook for a week. Much of it had to be thrown away.

The next morning Helen heard Bob telling his brother and sister the details of the sale of the house. Most of the personal items were divided in the will, but there were some things yet to be decided. A realtor came and a sign appeared in the lawn in just a few days. Bob gave Helen a small severance check. She brought it to my house and sat in my living room and wept.

When the will was read and distributed there was $1000 left to Helen and $250 more for Elizabeth. Bob handed her a check for the total amount, his teeth grinding.

"You don't have to give me this," Helen told him. "She was your mother."

"Yes, I do," Bob said. "Legally, I do."

"But I loved your mother. I would have done everything I did without money. You shouldn't give me anything that is going to make you upset."

"Please don't take it personally if I am abrupt," he said.

"I don't," said Helen. "I will just save this in case you change your mind."

"I don't need the money, Helen."

"But you sure don't need to have hard feelings about me, either. You have enough on your mind."

I reprimanded Helen about this after Bob left. "You deserve that money!"

"Not at the cost of hard feelings from someone Miss Lizzie loved," she insisted. The money was put in an account. "I can only do what seems right. That's all I've got to go by."

There was nothing else to say once Helen made up her mind.

The house sold quickly. Strangers were ready to move in and before she knew it Helen had no where to go. She could have used the will money to get an apartment but she wouldn't touch it.

I invited her to move in with us just until she could find work. Dad was passive. Mama was angry, but she didn't say it. She kept quiet and the tension was thick as hot tar poured in the pot holes out in front of the house.

Helen and Elizabeth moved in despite the tension thick enough to hold them out. There was a surprising amount to move. Corrine had offered Helen an upholstered chair and a blanket chest. Helen crammed them both into the living room and there was barely room to open the coat closet door. We strung a wire in the garage to hang extra clothes on.

My mother dragged a chair into the back yard next to a stack of two cinder blocks. She sat out there all day, not saying hello or good-by. She had a stack of magazines and a radio. A few times I took her a tall glass of mint tea, and she drank it, but I couldn't coax her to come inside to eat. She fixed plates of food from the stove and carried them to her place in the yard. She didn't look at me at all.

Helen was ashamed of having to move back in with us. She started looking for a job right away, but it wasn't easy to find one that paid enough to support her and Elizabeth and pay rent and utilities on even a small apartment. With my father's permission she planted a garden on the north side of the house and in just a few weeks there were tomatoes for the table. Elizabeth did her best to stay out of Mother's way. Her grades dropped and Helen and I worried about her. I dreaded coming home from work, and I went to bed as early as I could manage just to escape.

I painted every single day. From Wednesday through Sunday I still painted in front of Esprit for what Morgan Foster called 'the tourist trade'. Monday and Tuesday afternoons I painted the things Mr. Foster recommended. I took his advice and painted what made me feel the most, not trying to make it anything I wanted it to be, letting it be what it was in my heart. What I painted was my mother and her cinder blocks in the back yard. I painted her from the back and from the side. I didn't want to paint her face because she was too angry at me. Sometimes when I took her tea out to her I would arrange a napkin and a vase next to her. When I did she softened her shoulders, said "Thank you". Nothing more.

I was angry at her for closing herself to me. I still felt the need to have a mother and my mother had quit the job. Thinking back I can see that she could have been right. I was an adult. She had to make me go on and live my life. But she would have been right only if she had intended to help me grow up. She was only acting to protect herself. And I suppose that was right, too. She wanted to grow gracefully old in a quiet house where grandchildren would visit. She wasn't Miss Lizzie. She didn't have it in her to support wayward girls.

Daddy carried Mama a TV tray each evening and sat with her in the softening light. Helen took over preparing the food and the quality of our meals improved a thousand fold. Helen was careful to set the table properly. She brought in roses and azaleas for the table. She put a small vase on Mama's tray. She was polite and subservient in my parents' presence.

I entered three national art contests from ads in the backs of some art magazines I subscribed to. My paintings were accepted in all three. A still life of Helen's muddy gardening shoes lying next to her hoe and a basket of tomatoes simply called "Helen's Shoes" was accepted in a prestigious show in New York City but didn't win an award. My "Cassandra In Gray", which was painted from sketches I did while visiting Cassandra in prison, won an honorable mention in Colorado. "Miss Lizzie's Quilt" won Best Of Show in a New York City exhibit where I was later told Georgia O'Keefe was a guest. I was told she said that my painting was "wistful and poetic." I couldn't afford to attend these exhibits myself, so the awards were mailed to me.

Mr. Foster never rejected my visits throughout my formative years. At first I hated going and only went because Helen nagged me into it. But years had passed and he had yet to offer to show my work, not even a piece of it. This time he smiled. A friend of his had seen the New York exhibit, and had indeed seen Miss O'Keefe there. He didn't know if she had commented on my work, but she had been in the same room with it. His friend had known the judge who selected "Miss Lizzie's Quilt" for it's 'depth of expression and the germane use of color.'

"I would like to see the whole group of Cassandra paintings this week."

"What for?"

"I would like to examine their continuity. I want to see how well they hold up under close scrutiny."

"Why?"

"It's possible we should discuss your future," he said. "Its time."

"The portfolio photographs, I assume."

"Bring the real things, Cassandra."

I brought in the paintings the next day, filling the trunk, the backseat and the passenger seat beside me. A young man was sent to help me unload them. He carried them carefully like treasures.

Mr. Foster directed me to a storage area behind the main galleries. He had a maintenance man help me carry the pictures in and lean them against the walls. Mr. Foster made a game of trying to guess in which order they were painted.

"Would you let me show these in tandem?"

"What?"

"Can you part with them for a long enough time for me to show them simultaneously? I think you're ready."

"You do?"

"You've been persistent. You've done as I've suggested, and it's paid off."

"But these are old paintings. The ones I had originally. Except for the prison picture these were all done before the day I first came in here."

Mr. Foster inhaled pensively. "There's more to it than having a pile of paintings. You've begun to be an artist. You've proven that you are consistent, determined. I don't want to hang the work of some spinster hobbyist and have her the next week down at the Baptist church telling how the Marseilles showed her "purty pitchers'. I only want artists who are artists to the marrow. Artists with the talent and the will.

"When you came in here I wasn't sure what you were."

"It took you all this time to figure it out?"

"Yes, it did. Quite frankly, at first I wasn't too impressed. I have to admit I was just toying with you. However, your work and your style of painting impressed me. I liked the way you were influenced very little by outside forces in your work. But you were so frightened of the process. And you looked a fright!"

"But painting, that's not hard. It's like breathing. It's like looking both ways when you cross the street. You just do it because you have to. Honestly, I can't understand what other people do who don't paint. But I've never been much of a people person."

"Some people have a passion, or just a survival technique. For some it is art or music- for you it is painting, for some it is having a lot of cats! Some people, like me, live vicariously. I display art as if I had something to do with it's creation."

"You do," I said.

"Excuse me?"

"You do have something to do with it."

"Only on the most superficial and removed level, my dear."

"What would art be with no place to show it? No one to appreciate it?"

"Perhaps. But then, does a tree falling in a forest make a sound? We shall never know, shall we?"

"I never dreamed my paintings would matter to anyone but me. Do you know what it has done for me to have you want them? Those contests! I would never have entered them without your advice. Without your help I would never have done more than breathe turpentine."

"Thank you, Miss Breaux. It's unusual for me to receive compliments of this nature. I suppose it has something to do with the presumed power I have over artists' careers." He chuckled.

"Themes no small potatoes," I said.

"Oh, Miss Breaux! Your way with colloquialisms!"

"You ought ta come over some time! Set a spell!" We sat back and laughed. After all the uncomfortable meetings we'd had we were finally laughing, with me confident in who I was, not ashamed of my origins, and him being interested. My shoulders relaxed, my face loosened, and for just a moment I felt wonderful.

For all those years I'd been coming every other month, sometimes monthly, with new paintings to force Mr. Foster to look at. I was never comfortable with the arrangement. I called each time I had finished a few, but it was only because Helen was at my elbow nagging me. If it weren't for her, I never would have had the guts to keep going back, feeling so inferior each time. So doubtful of my own chances.

I don't know why he continued to see me. I don't know why he took so long before deciding to exhibit my paintings. I think Mr. Foster, for all his poise and elegance, was bored with exhibit openings and wealthy people. I think I was a project for him, a hobby.

Fifteen months. It would be over a year before the show would hang. I left the paintings with Mr. Foster. Many of my paintings were old and in need of repair. Mr. Foster had staff artists to touch up scuffs and cracks on my paintings. This made me uneasy, but he said if he let the artists do it themselves they would repaint the whole painting. He was right, too. I wanted to fix so many things on those old pieces.

I wandered in several times a week to see how they were doing. The finished paintings looked as they had when they were new. I was embarrassed to show the oldest pieces, the old sketches done in childhood. They were naive and immature, but Mr. Foster insisted that they were part of the continuum. He said this exhibit was about me as much as it was about Cassandra. He said it showed my maturing process, as well as my disenchantment. He said it was a novel about my growth.

Mr. Foster warned me that offers would be made on these paintings, and that it was unlikely they would hang side by side again. I was terrified by this thought, but knew that if I did not allow them to be separated they would rot in my closet. It seemed that the Cassandras were taking on lives of their own. Why not let them live?

They were bordered in frames of elegant simplicity. No ornate golden frames like the old masters would have favored. No slick modern rectangles. These were sleek polished woods in natural hues, polished to a gloss. Linen liners gave depth to the paintings, and made them exquisite.

During this time of waiting I wouldn't let Helen and Elizabeth move out of my house. They could have done it if they had really wanted to, but Helen was afraid of the step out into the void. I told them I needed their support while I tried to deal with this moment in my life. Helen got a job at Winn Dixie, and came home at night to help with the details of the household. She cleaned and cooked to earn their room and board. I know her job was exciting for her, because it was new. She had never been employed in that way, and I think she was both exhilarated and afraid of the freedom it gave her. My daddy doted on Elizabeth, and she called him Daddy.

I knew there would have to be changes in our home life, but I wanted to wait until the exhibit was hanging before I trusted my success. It was too crowded in that little place. Everyone was irritable. Elizabeth's school work was suffering. My mother was sliding again. She didn't do well when the house was over full. Now even my father had episodes of silence and depression. I thought I would go insane, but I couldn't leave them. I prayed those paintings would save us all somehow.

It was seven years from the time Cassandra was incarcerated and two months after I learned that her portraits would be exhibited at Marseilles that she appeared at my door. She carried a paper bag of belongings. It reminded me of when Helen came to live with us all those years ago.

"What are you doing here, Cassandra? What on Earth? Come in here!"

I opened the door wide and stood, heart beating, until she wrapped her arms around me and we hugged each other hard and long. We were crying before we pulled ourselves apart. I looked her up and down. She was wearing a simple blue cotton dress and flat shoes. She had on a little make up. She was pale and smelled strongly of cigarette smoke.

"I'm out on parole. Good behavior," she said, laughing.

"I'm so glad to see you. Why didn't you call?" I drew Cassandra into the kitchen where the family was eating. "Look who's here!"

Helen got up from the table and hugged Cassandra. My Dad took Cassandra's little hand in both of his and said, "Good to see you, Young Lady." I noticed that Cassandra's fingernails were bitten into tiny half-moon stubs.

My mother was sitting at the table with us. My dad had brought her in from the yard and asked her to stay at the table until the family finished eating. My mother nodded at Cassandra, but didn't smile. Cassandra raised her eyebrows at me, but I could only shrug.

Helen said, "Elizabeth, do you remember Miss Cassandra?"

Elizabeth was nearly a teenager now. She said, "Sure. You used to come over a lot. You're the one in Kate's paintings."

"Do you still have those things?"

"Sort of," I said.

Everyone looked at me expectantly.

"Sort of? Is that all you're going to tell her?" Daddy patted my arm mischievously.

"Sit down with us and eat," I said. I pulled a plate from the cabinet.

Helen pulled up a work stool and offered her chair to Cassandra. Cassandra demurred, but Helen wouldn't have it. "You sit down, Cassandra. You're our guest."

"I don't know why we only have five chairs," I said. "Didn't we used to have more than this?"

"The other one's out in the yard," said Dad, looking at Mother with his eyebrows raised.

Mother rose from the table. "You can have this one. I'm not hungry."

"Mom," I started. She went to the bedroom and shut the door. Dad shook his head and stirred his mashed potatoes with his fork.

"I'm intruding," said Cassandra. "I should have called."

"No, you're not," said Dad. "You're fine. You're always welcome."

"Tell her about the paintings," said Helen.

"Yes, tell me!"

"Well, they're doing fine," I said, smiling.

"Tell me," Cassandra ordered with a mock growl.

"They are going to be exhibited all together as a series at an uptown gallery. The exhibition will be called "Kate Breaux's Cassandra Series.""

"Wow," said Cassandra. "What is the name of the place?"

"The Marseilles Gallery."

"Isn't that pretty hot stuff? My Dad used to get some of their staff in sometimes looking for antiques and things."

"Yes, actually, I guess it is." I ate some meat loaf. "Helen nagged me into hounding the curator for the last few years, and lo and behold, I finally wore him down."

"He wanted those paintings all along. He was just grooming you," said Dad.

Cassandra chewed a bit of meat. "Are they on exhibit now?"

"Not for another year. Can you believe that? Thirteen months left to go, actually." I ate some peas. "Hey! Mr. Foster would probably love to meet you. Why don't you come down there with me tomorrow and we'll look at the paintings? He's getting them framed so beautifully. Most of the work isn't going to be done until later but I can show you the frame samples. The frames are better than the paintings."

"Gee, Kate, that's incredible," said Cassandra. She was making a line of peas along the side of her plate.

"Don't you like the peas? I could make some corn, or…"

"I just don't think I can look at those paintings, Kate," Cassandra said. "I hope you understand."

"Oh, sure," I answered. "But they're going to make you famous!"

Cassandra pretended to laugh. "I'm already infamous. Isn't that enough?" The trial had been in the papers. The young mother who shot her baby and later her father. It was sensational stuff.

"You don't have to come. I just thought," I stammered, then stopped talking.

"Thank you, Kate. I know it's going to be just lovely. It's just that those paintings were of hard times. Kind of feels weird you didn't call me and tell me this was going on."

"I didn't know what you'd think," I confessed. "Will you let me paint you again? Good times?"

"I don't know, Kate. Maybe. In exchange for a favor."

"Anything. What do you need?"

"I need a place to stay for a little while."

We began to look for another house the next day, Cassandra, Helen and I. I made enough money to support us all, but just barely, now that I was a sought after tourist scene painter and had a prominent exhibit scheduled. Mr. Lambert had placed a calligraphy sign over my work station bragging about my credentials-to-be, and my sales increased by a third. Helen had her salary from Winn Dixie, and soon, we hoped, Cassandra would be working.

We needed a yard for the garden, and although Elizabeth was older now, she still needed a place to play. We needed four separate bedrooms. I needed a studio, and we needed a huge kitchen.

We looked at so many houses they began to run together. We hired a realtor named Darlene Neidermeyer. Darlene's hair was a big honey colored beehive listing slightly to the left. She talked incessantly in a loud, shrill voice. We stared out the windows of her Lincoln. Darlene asked where our men were and I simply said we didn't have any. Darlene's eye brows raised about half an inch and she didn't say anything for nearly two blocks.

This house was nice but the bedrooms were too small. This one was on too busy a street. This one had a cracked foundation. That one we simply didn't like.

We continued to search and to stay in my parent's shrinking house. My mother refused to come out of the bedroom now. We brought her chair in from the yard; it was ruined from the rain. We used it anyway, although we had to put a cushion on the seat to keep the splinters out of our behinds.

Daddy worried about us moving out alone without a man. I told him we were big girls and could take care of ourselves. I was afraid he wouldn't be able to handle my mother in the states they were in, but I had to get out. I couldn't stay there any longer. Maybe I kept bringing people in because I knew I would eventually be squeezed out that way. I would never have moved any other way. Dad was about to retire, and soon there would be yet another person in the house all day. I hoped Dad could handle mother on his own. Maybe with us gone, I reasoned, she would get better.

Dr. Hale wrote her a prescription for antidepressants. Daddy took off work, got the prescription filled and administered Elavil to my depressed mother morning, noon and night until she began to act normal again. Sometimes now the door of her room would be left open, and I would take it as an invitation. I would dust her dresser and take away her used cups.

Life was hot and cold, ecstatic and exasperating, hopeless and filled with boundless expectancy. Introspection was unavoidable as I sat blindly painting an image of the wrought iron balcony rails above me from a crazy upward perspective. I sat at the edge of the street some days, my stool occasionally falling off the curb, sometimes with me still on it. Mr. Louis thought I was losing my mind.

I sat in unlikely places to get strange angles, distortions in the shadows, in order to keep my mind meditatively interested in my paintings.

I painted in unfamiliar hues, adding unexpected still life items to the traditional scenes. At first it was just a dull red jump rope hanging from a plant hook on a balcony. Then a pair of high topped baby shoes soaking in a fountain. Later amid the wizened clay colored bricks and freshly watered ferns of a famous balcony on Bourbon Street and St. Peter I painted a brilliantly plumed turkey sitting on a red and white striped beach towel wearing glasses. Not clownish glasses, not great green goggles. Just tiny horn rimmed glasses like a science teacher would wear. In the painting, the people looking at the passersby on the street below didn't notice the turkey, which was reading the New Orleans Times-Picayune.

Mr. Louis didn't like it. He said I was getting too big for my britches. He said no tourist wanted to buy a painting of a fat lady paying for tomatoes in the French Market wearing purple Capri pants. Said there was no room in his gallery for paintings of carriage horses wearing great ropes of sausages about their necks. He said I'd better start painting what I saw out there and stay on Iberville rather than toting my easel all over down town.

I ignored him. I didn't really care. I had stopped painting the tourist scenes. They had long ago started to bore me. There were plenty of artists in New Orleans to paint tourist scenes.

To my surprise, as much as to Louis Lambert's, tourists loved what I was doing. My paintings were selling as fast as I could paint them, and requests for quirky things were placed.

One young woman asked if I gave lessons. Her name was Grace, and I told her I didn't. She asked if I would. She was just a girl, younger than me, but she seemed to know what she wanted. She was a hippi, living on her own. An orphaned native American girl with thick black hair that fell well below her waist. I told her I would give her lessons. Louis Lambert charged me to use his space. Grace was wise for her young years and she became a friend, one I would always cherish, even when she had moved away and we were unable to see each other often.

In my parents' house we cleared out the small bedroom Mother kept her sewing in and Elizabeth and Helen slept there on rollaway cots that had been stored in the garage for company. Cassandra slept with me. It didn't work for her to sleep on the couch because my mother wandered the house at night and they frightened each other at worst, at best were in one another's way.

Cassandra slept with me in my bed in my bedroom. I still had the same double bed, but had finally changed the curtains. Now they were lengths of yellow burlap tied back with macramé ropes over white shades drawn down for privacy at night. My bed spread was bought at an import store; it was a gauzy cotton throw in red, green, blue and yellow squares. I put a huge Japanese paper lantern over the light fixture and if we weren't careful we bumped it when we got up in the night to use the bathroom. I didn't like it, but I didn't take it down either. I enjoyed the absurdity.

Cassandra slept in a tight line she said she must have learned in prison. She barely interfered with my sleeping position at all. In summer she was afraid to sleep without covers even in the killing heat. In the winter she was always cold. She said she had nightmares of vampires, and of her father. The snores and moans of the other women in prison spooked her.

My sweet Cassandra was always in prison, every day of her life. I lay next to her in my private bed, the bed I'd slept in all my life, and couldn't sleep. I ached with her presence. If I hoped to hold her and caress her hair as I had done so long ago lying in the sweet grass behind her father's shed, I denied it. She was too damaged to take such chances, and I was too unsure.

Cassandra and I whispered until late in the night most nights. She was still afraid of sleep and I was often unable to do it. She told me Danny had called her regularly while she was in prison. I called sporadically, but he called every week without fail. It was all she could count on, she told me, besides the prison routine. It was all that kept her going.

I asked her if they would stay married. She said she had no intention of doing otherwise, but he would still not move from the house where Melinda died, and she would still not go to it. She said he was beginning to weaken, though, as the house grew older. It was difficult to manage. He gave up on the hens and the small garden was grown over. The oranges still grew and he would hire workers to pick them and pay them pittance wages. He worked at the refinery, had done so all the years Cassandra was gone, and he drove a pickup he'd raised up on giant tires that would keep his engine from dying when the water got high.

They thought maybe they would move into Belle Chasse, a town further up the river, closer to New Orleans. It was close enough to work for him, but far enough from Venice for her. I asked if she was afraid of him.

"Things are all so different now," she said.

We rented a big ranch house in Jefferson, just east of uptown New Orleans the next month. Mother cried when I left. I moved out along with Helen, Elizabeth and Cassandra. We unpacked our possessions in a day. It was obvious we couldn't get by for long without furniture. My father brought over a small rocking chair and an end table that evening. We nestled Helen's chair beside a window overlooking the yard. On Thursday afternoons I told Grace about our lives and even some of Cassandra's history. Grace was a good listener.

My father walked around the house and complimented us on our choice.

"It's just a rental, Dad," I reminded him.

He ran his hand along the walls peering closely to see if the angles were square. He shook the posts holding up the front porch.

"Looks like they're safe."

"Dad, it's a good house."

"We're going to miss you, Katie," mumbled my dad. His jowls had grown empty recently. His eyes had pouches beneath them.

How did I fail to notice his hair getting thin? When was it that his hands started to shake ever so slightly? Had he always hunched over that way when he walked? Had I ignored the way his voice shook when he spoke?

"Are you going to be okay?" Oh, why did I ask that, I thought. I was so afraid he would say, no, they would die without me, a slow and lingering death that would be my fault, my burden for the rest of my life.

"It's going to take a little while to adjust is all."

"Can you handle Mom by yourself?"

"What else have I got to do?" My father had retired earlier that year. He was sixty five and he said he felt it. He hadn't taken retirement well. He was bored and missed his colleagues. It wasn't the same when he took lunch with them occasionally. They still spoke of work and office politics. He had nothing new to add, no inspiration to offer. Things were changing more quickly than the lettuce grew in the little garden that my father would now be left to tend. He didn't even know that many of the people at his office any more and he had been gone less than a year. All Dad could offer his mate was old stories they had heard before. He felt useless.

"Don't let her wear you out, Dad."

"Katie, she is my wife. My love and my life," he added, melodramatically placing his hand over his kind heart.

"I've been taking care of you and Mom for a long time, now. In a way I was taking care of you before I grew up."

"You were just a good girl. I always expected you to be a good girl. It never surprised me when you were."

"But I never got to grow up, Dad. I never rebelled. I never rocked the boat."

"If you think it was so important, why didn't you?"

"I guess I didn't need to," I admitted. Our family beat the hell out of Cassandra's family. Or Helen's."

Dad took my hand. "Why are you moving in with all these women? Haven't you taken enough care of people? Isn't it time to be on your own?"

"Can't afford to, yet, Dad. Besides, they're my friends. They're adults. I won't be taking care of them."

"You can have friends without moving in with them. Maybe," he continued, "you need someone to take care of you."

"Who on earth would that be? Not you and Mom. Not Cassandra. She's a complete mess."

"Maybe you'll meet someone, settle down."

"I don't know, Dad. I may never meet anyone." I knew that I would never get married and settle down. I knew that about myself by now. I went on dates, even made some special friends, but I would never marry.

"Sure you will. You're a pretty girl. Any man would be lucky …"

"To have me, I know."

"There's always Helen. She's good at taking care of people, isn't she?"

"I couldn't even ask that of her."

"Why not? She did it for a living with Miss Giraud all those years."

I thought about that for a while. "That wasn't like work. That was getting family lessons. She was learning how to be a healthy grown-up person so she could be on her own one day. If I had her take care of me she would just be in the same boat I'm in after a few years. She needs to get a life of her own. Just like I do. This is just a middle place. We all need to get on with our own lives."

Dad and I looked out at the street for a while. "So, who's going to take care of you, Katie?"

"Dad, I think I'm going to have to be the one to do that."

Twenty Two

Cassandra's Way Out

We furnished the house sparsely with things we found at yard sales and thrift shops. Grace gave us an Indian Blanket we hung on the wall. When I suggested we pay full price for a couch, Helen was disturbed.

"It's not right paying that much. We don't need that. What we need is something to sit on."

She brought home a nearly new floral sofa in a homey early American style. One corner was tattered from a cat using it to scratch on. Cassandra and I teased her about it a lot. Cassandra's teasing wasn't always very nice.

"We could have spent more on a new one, but now we have a couch and we have some of the money," said Helen defensively. She patched up the torn corners on the couch as best she could and bought plastic sheets that she thumb tacked on to cover them.

Elizabeth came home from visiting a friend one day with a kitten. "Janie's cat had kittens and they're ready to have new homes. Couldn't I have him, please?" Elizabeth was a muscular teenager. She ran the boy's tracks and hurdles at school when they finished practice because there was no girl's team. Sometimes she got boys to compete with her. Often she won.

Helen called the landlord. He wasn't delighted with the idea, but said we could have him if we paid a security deposit.

"That takes care of the money and the couch," sneered Cassandra.

Cassandra still wasn't working. She was haggard and weary. Her attitude was always harsh and unyielding. Helen and I decided to give her a couple of months to adjust before insisting that she look for a job. She smoked so much that her fingers were yellow. I supported her cigarette habit, buying her Virginia Slims every time I bought my Benson & Hedges. In that house I smoked heavily, too. I didn't want to, but it seemed like I just couldn't help it.

Danny called Cassandra several times a week. He wouldn't talk to anyone but Cass. She would go into her room and talk to him on her extension that I paid for. She would never talk about it later.

As weeks went by, I threw myself into my painting at Esprit to take my mind off my upcoming solo exhibit at the Marseilles. My paintings were growing increasingly bizarre, but despite Mr. Louis' histrionics, they were selling better than ever. Several people told me that their friends had made them promise to come and buy something from me when they were in New Orleans. I even got a small write up in the arts section of the newspaper. It perturbed Mr. Louis abundantly, but I kept painting silly things, and people kept buying, and both of us were making a decent living as a result.

I was beginning to resent the idea of him making so much profit from my sales. I started pestering him to give me a larger percentage.

"After all, I'm doing all the work here!"

He refused. "I own the gallery. I gave you the chance when nobody else would."

"I'm getting out of here," I said.

With a week left to go before the opening of "Kate Breaux's Cassandra Series" I was without a job. Mr. Breaux threw me out but kept the prints that were still in stock in the store.

"I'll send you your cut," he said. I knew he wouldn't.

"Just hold on. After the show you'll have it made," said Helen. "Even right now you could go it on your own."

"We don't know that. It may flop. No one may even come," I replied.

"They'll come," said Helen. "Mr. Foster will see to that. But you have to be practical in the mean time. I can't pay the rent alone. I would if I could."

"I know you would. I have some money saved, but I don't want to use it if I don't have to. I'll think of something."

"Anybody want a beer?" said Cassandra. She listened to our discussion about my fate with grim amusement. "You should make up with Louis, Kate. No body's going to buy pictures of my fat ass." She snapped open the flip top and drank deeply.

Helen didn't drink. On occasion I had a beer or a glass of wine. Cassandra drank heavily and daily. She was hung over in the mornings and we had to protect Elizabeth from her. I knew that she was going to have to straighten up or leave. I kept hoping for a miracle.

Cassandra passed out on the sofa many nights. If Helen discovered her she would cover her with a blanket. I would just turn away and leave her uncovered. The gray striped kitten Elizabeth named Mister liked to curl up between Cassandra's knees. He kneaded her legs vigorously with his sharp little claws, and Cassandra didn't move. I sat looking out the window until the moon stopped shining through.

I set up my easel on Royal Street the next afternoon and just painted. I sold two quick paintings of absurd tourists before the sun set. The next day I set up on Barracks near the French Market because I wanted to paint the old mint building with a flying saucer sitting on it. I sold that painting and got two commissions to paint others. Some people recognized me from my old location and asked what had happened. I told them I needed to be on my own. Someone threw a ten dollar bill in my paint box.

Twenty Three

Kate Breaux's Cassandra

I wore a black mini dress with a scooped back and sheer butterfly sleeves. It would have cost me a month's salary if I were still working at Kressky's. A month earlier I had made an appointment at Albert Brown's Salon on Magazine Street to have my hair done by his best stylist, Henry. I wanted to make sure everything was perfect. I was a wreck.

Helen came to the reception with me. I couldn't get her to buy a new dress so I bought her one myself and surprised her with it the night of the opening reception so that she couldn't say no. I told her I would keep it myself if she didn't want it after the show.

"But it's not going to fit you," she complained.

"Then I guess you'll have to keep it."

Even Elizabeth came, wearing a blue gown Helen had made for her to wear to the sweetheart dance at school. Grace came and acted as receptionist wearing a long deep blue dress she had batiked herself, and a thick rope of beads.

Cassandra refused to go, or even consider the notion. I offered to get her a new dress and a haircut, too, but she refused. She refused even after I told her she could go incognito. She simply refused.

"The last thing I want is to have people recognize me as the jail bird in Kate Breaux's paintings."

"You should have told me sooner. I thought you would be happy for me."

"Who would be happy about having everyone know they're a convict? They must all know the story by now." She scanned the imaginary headline in the air with her hand. "Jail Bird Baby Killer." She looked at me fiercely. "What do they care about me, Kate?" She was already drunk. She started drinking screw drivers before I got back from the salon. There was orange juice all over the counter. Her drink was barely orange. It was mostly vodka.

"I care about you, Cassandra. Why didn't you tell me you felt like this before?"

"Goddamn you, Kate. Do I have to spell it out for you? You got some nerve selling my history. You got some nerve getting rich off of me."

I was horrified. How could I have been so blind? Of course no one would want to become known like this. What had I done to Cassandra? What had I done?

"Whatever I make, I will give you half, Kate."

"You keep your money," she snapped at me.

Helen led me from the house. "There's nothing you can do, now, Kate. You have to go. You can pay her for them."

"How can I compensate her for humiliating her? What have I done?"

"You've just been an artist. You just painted. She was willing to sit for all those paintings. You never did anything wrong."

"She didn't know they would end up like this. I can't do this to her. I have to call it off."

"It's too late for that. You have to do it. You've signed the agreement with Mr. Foster. People are coming from all over. We'll be there with you," Helen said. "You'll be fine. We'll work this out. It will be fine. We'll help Cassandra understand it later when she's sober."

"I'm really proud of you, Kate," said Elizabeth. "I've told everyone at school how great you are. We're even trying to get the principle to let our art class go on a field trip to your exhibit."

"Really?" I straightened my shoulders. I sniffed and dabbed at my eyes. "Well, then."

We took a cab to avoid being seen in my decrepit Buick. We walked between Jaguars and Rolls-Royces to get to the door. Mr. Foster met us with a flourish and then led me around by the elbow all evening introducing me to strange people who had more money than they knew what to do with. Helen tried to follow us for a while, but ended up leaning against a wall holding a glass of wine by the stem. She didn't like to drink at all, but she was afraid to say no. Elizabeth wandered around looking at the paintings and answering the inane questions of the guests.

"How old are you?" "What school do you go to?"

It was a terrifying evening. It was also fatuous. It lasted for four hours. I sent Helen and Elizabeth home after two. They were bored almost to tears. Elizabeth ended up stuffing herself on hors d'oeuvres and sneaked herself a glass of wine. Helen caught her before she drank very much.

I was afraid to go home. I was afraid of what Cassandra would be like when I got there. That thought stayed in my mind throughout the evening. Cassandra.

I arrived home to a darkened house. Helen and Elizabeth were asleep. I walked past their bedroom doors and listened for sounds of wakefulness. There were none. I went to my room and undressed. I pulled on my oldest cotton night gown. It was frayed at the bottom and torn under the arms. Once it was blue, now it was a dingy gray. It was soft and comforting.

I wandered out into the living room and went to Cassandra's bedroom door on the other side of the living room. It, too, was quiet. I assumed Cassandra had passed out by now. She drank herself to sleep every evening, then slept most of the next day, getting up in time to do it all over again.

I went to the kitchen and poured a glass of chocolate milk and rummaged around in the pantry until I found a box of Oreo cookies I'd hidden near the back. I went into the living room and turned on the radio.

Before I got good and comfortable on the sofa, the phone rang. I rushed to it, knowing it must be Mr. Foster. I didn't want the ring to wake Helen, who was a light sleeper.

"You were marvelous! We sold eleven paintings tonight, my dear, at remarkable prices!"

"You're kidding. How much?"

"We'll do a tally in the morning, but, you are on your way! You'll be out of that old wreck of a car within a week!"

"I made enough to buy a car?"

"Honey, you made enough to buy a very *nice* car!"

"No," I said. I flushed from head to foot.

"Yes," bubbled Mr. Foster.

"I can't believe it," I said.

"Yes, you can! I am making out a beautiful check to you tomorrow morning! Let's meet for lunch, and I'll give it to you!"

"How much do you get again?"

"Fifty percent, my dear, but don't let that trouble you. You're still going to be looking for an accountant to manage your wealth!"

"How did you manage this?"

"Didn't I tell you? I'm *goooood* at living vicariously."

I didn't wake Helen, but it was hard not to. I danced around the living room for a while, spilling chocolate milk on the carpet and laughing. Finally I sat down and stared out the window. I would hire someone to help my parents around the house. I'd get Cassandra into therapy. Right after I bought a new car! Nothing used, mind you. A red Corvette, maybe, or a Mercedes. Nothing practical. Not for me! My ship had come in! Glorious, glorious success! I sat in the moonlight and basked. Now everything would get better. Now I could fix everyone and we could all be happy.

I was so tired I decided to try to get some sleep, but I knew I wouldn't be able to. I took our newest Reader's Digest to my room and flipped on the light next to my bed.

"Hello, Kate," said Cassandra. She was lying on my bed, fully clothed. Her head was resting on the headboard, her legs were crossed at the ankles. I expected her to be sloppy drunk, but she seemed poised. She had definitely been drinking but she wasn't loose. She held up her right hand. In it was a small handgun.

"You dyed your hair," I said.

She ran her fingers through it. "Like it?"

"It's different. Yeah. What do you have that for?" I nodded toward the gun. "Did something happen?"

"Not yet," said Cassandra.

"What is going on? Where did you get that gun? What are you going to do with it?"

"I understand you have a little money now."

"Yes. Were you listening on the phone? I told you that you should have come with me. Everyone asked about you. I told them how much I treasure you. I want to make it up to you, Cassandra. I'm so sorry about the hard feelings."

"Oh, you're going to make it up to me, Kate."

"Cut it out, Cass, you're scaring me." I backed up and groped for the doorknob.

"Why don't you just stay in here so we can talk?" said Cassandra. "No point waking the girls up."

"Please put the gun down first. It's making me nervous."

"I like it." Cassandra ran her finger down the length of the barrel. "It's kind of sexy. Like a man, don't you think?"

"Cassandra, put it down. This isn't funny."

"Oh, what are you so scared of?" she demanded. "When did anything ever go wrong for you?" Cassandra swung her feet to the floor and stood up. She walked toward me casually. I backed into the corner. She reached to switch off the light. For a second the gun was pointed straight at my chest. In the same instant I could have grabbed it and put a stop to this insanity. I was too stunned to think of it. She was wearing jeans and a tank top. She had on her red suede boots.

"Is it just because you've never been with a man that you don't like my gun?" Cassandra laughed.

"Do you plan on using that on me?" I looked at the gun. I didn't take my eyes off that gun.

"If I do, you'll be the first to know. You'd probably love it."

"Jesus, Cassandra," I pleaded. "Give me a chance, here. You don't want to shoot me, do you?" I could literally hear my heart pounding in my ears. "I will do anything for you, Cass."

"You're going to get a chance, Kate. I just need a little help, and since you're such a big shot now, I want you to …. assist me, shall we say."

"What do you want, Cassandra? I'll share the money with you. You deserve it. After all, if I hadn't been painting you all these years I would never have had this luck. We're going to be sitting pretty from now on, Cass."

"That may come in handy. Right now, though, I have a job for you to do."

"What is it?"

"I went to see my dear, beloved father yesterday."

"What? Are you kidding?"

"Just walked right in. A nurse asked me who I was, but I said I was his niece. She told me I was the only visitor he'd had in six months. She said my mom calls every now and then, but never comes out there any more. I told her she just couldn't take it any more. Of course, they know they aren't supposed to let me in, but they didn't know what I look like.

"I don't know why he's still alive after all these years. He just lies there with drool running out of his mouth, looking like a pathetic skeleton. I looked at his chart and he's being treated for bed sores. Isn't that a joke? I guess God's finally paying him back. What goes around comes around. I didn't even fell sorry for him. He made me sick. I wish he looked more like he used to so I could really hate him the way he deserves to be hated."

"Sounds like you're doing a pretty good job hating him."

"Oh, sure, I hate his putrid guts, but he isn't dead, and that isn't right."

"Oh, come on, Cassandra! You're not thinking of killing him."

"I'm not? Funny, I thought I was," she said. She pulled a cigarette from a pack on my dresser and slid it in her mouth. She lit it with a silver lighter she snaked out of her pocket. She blew smoke out through her nose. Her eyes were slits to keep out the fumes.

"Don't do it, Cassandra. You already put him out of commission. He's suffering more like this than he would dead."

"Oh, but he's not."

"What do you mean?"

"You seem to have forgotten about hell."

I was pressed against the wall, each muscle taut with adrenaline.

"Hell's got to be worse than a nursing home. They still feed him, for Christ's sake. I want to think of him burning for ever down there in the hellfire and brimstone. They say brimstone stinks like everything dead. They say hell goes on and on forever. You can't escape. There's not even a drop of water. You just burn and burn and burn for eternally and always." Cassandra gurgled in her throat, a kind of self satisfied little chuckle.

"Cassandra, do you still believe in that?"

"I hope for that, Katie," she told me. "I hope it's worse than I ever thought so he'll have to suffer like he deserves to suffer."

"If there's a hell, Cass, don't you see that you'll be right down there with him if you kill him? Have you forgotten about 'Thou shalt not kill?'"

"It would be worth it just to watch his agony. Besides. God let the old bastard pop me all my life, I sure don't want to be hanging with God for eternity. I'll take my chances with old Lucifer."

"Cassandra, you can't mean that. You've already been through hell. Hell was right here on Earth. You lived through it."

"I don't know if I believe in heaven. I've never seen any proof of it. I know for sure there's a hell."

"This is just going to make things worse. Don't you see? If you kill him you'll go back to jail. You might even get the death penalty this time. Is that what you want?"

"If I have to, I'll do it. That old bastard haunts me every day. I can't get away from him. But he's not who I plan to kill right now. Him I could kill any time. It's my mother I have to take care of now. At least Dad's out of commission. She's still wandering around like nothing happened. Like she never did a thing in the world wrong."

"Cassandra, you can't mean this. You'll just get in more trouble. Please don't. You're going to go back to jail. Can't you see that?"

"What you seem to have missed is that I don't plan on doing it."

"Thank God, Cassandra. You had me scared."

"I plan," she said slowly. She took a puff of her cigarette before finishing her sentence, "to make you do it."

The thundering blood pounded behind my temples.

"I'm not going to kill anyone," I said. My voice was an octave lower than I remembered it. It was as if someone else had moved in to finish the conversation.

"Don't you think she's the scum of the earth?" asked Cassandra.

"Cassandra, I won't…"

"Don't you think I deserved to be protected?"

"Yes, of course. But I can't kill her."

"Not even for me?"

"No, Cassandra. Killing her wouldn't help you. She has her own hell."

"I think I might be able to talk you into it." She held up the gun and patted the barrel. "I think there might be a way to change your mind."

She ordered me to get dressed. My mind reeled trying to think of a way to escape, but she stayed a few feet away with the gun in her hand. I couldn't reach her to make a grab for it. I didn't dare run away. I loved her so much. I pulled on jeans, a tee shirt and tennis shoes. I had to think of something but I was too rattled.

"Don't try anything, Kate," she ordered. I was more terrified than I had ever been. Even more terrified than the night that gun shot sounded and the baby died.

"Open the door," said Cassandra. She was six feet away from me. I looked at her face, then at the gun.

"Don't even think about trying to get this gun, Kate. My finger is on the trigger and I don't want to shoot you," she said. Her voice was a slow terrifying monotone. My stomach wrenched in my gut.

I opened my bedroom door. I saw immediately that Helen was at the left side hiding in the shadows. She put her finger to her lips.

I thought Cassandra would see her, but I had no choice other than to walk on. I kept walking into the living room.

Helen tackled Cassandra and the gun went off. Ceiling plaster powdered us. Cassandra still had the gun in her hand as Helen wrestled her to the floor.

"Get back, Kate!" Helen screamed at me, "Get down!"

"Kate, if you move I'll shoot you," said Cassandra. I turned slowly and saw the barrel pointing straight at me. I was paralyzed.

"I've got the gun aimed straight between her eyes, Helen. You get off me or I'll shoot."

Helen slowly and carefully got to her knees. "Cassandra, don't do this. This is crazy. Kate's the best friend you've got right now." Helen's hands were in the air, not in surrender, but pleading.

"She thinks I'm her property," Cassandra snarled. "She thinks she can just take my life and make her fortune off it. If she wants my life she can have it, but she's going to have to participate in it. Now get up and get over there by her."

As Helen rose, Cassandra kicked her in the knee. Helen stumbled. Elizabeth's door closed softly and I knew she had been watching.

Helen backed over to where I was. "Cassandra, let's at least talk about what's going to happen."

"No need. Kate has told me all about how I'll end up on death row."

"No, not that. I mean, if you're going to kill someone you have to have a plan. We can't just walk in there and shoot him."

"Why the hell not?" Cassandra's cigarette had dropped during the struggle. She stood up.

"Cass, the carpet is burning," I warned her.

"Don't you try to distract me, Kate."

"Let me stomp it out," I said. Cassandra looked down and rubbed the smoldering cigarette out with the toe of her boot. She cast me the most evil glare I had ever seen.

"Let's get one thing straight here. You aren't going to get out of this." She looked at Helen.

"By the time the gun goes off, I will be long gone. Kate will be left holding the evidence. Damn!"

"What?" I said.

"I guess I have to take you, too," she said to Helen. "I can't leave you here to call the cops."

"Why not leave Kate here? I'll be more help than she would be."

"I'm not leaving anyone here to call the police. Where's that kid?" But she kept talking before we could answer. "The cops will find out soon enough the way we have it planned."

"We? Who else?" I stammered. "Us? This isn't our plan, Cass!"

Cassandra let out a loud breath. "Danny. Danny and I did a lot of writing while I was in prison. We came up with this plan."

"Hey, where's that kid?" she repeated. "Where's Elizabeth?"

"She's spending the night with Mom and Dad," I lied. "Went home with them after the show."

"Good. One less thing to worry about."

"Cassandra, we've been friends all our lives. I love you. Please don't do this. Please let's talk it over."

"We have it all planned. Danny will be waiting...," Cassandra stopped talking. "I'm not talking any more until we get there. I don't want you to have time to figure your way out of it."

"Where's Danny going to be, Cassandra?"

"No more questions! Now, shut up and go get in the car. Kate, you drive. Helen you sit up front. I'm going to sit behind you so I can make sure you don't pull anything. Don't forget that I'm the one with the gun."

Helen fidgeted with the torn seat cover in the front seat. I started the engine and turned on the radio.

"Turn that off. I have to think," said Cassandra.

I did. Helen turned around to face Cassandra.

"Cassandra, you've got to let me help you with this."

"What kind of help?" Cassandra covered her mouth with her hand. "hat the hell am I going to do? You guys are going to turn on me. We didn't plan this out with two of you."

"We're not going to turn on you, Cassandra. I can help you. I've done this before."

I gaped at Helen.

Helen leaned forward in the seat. "I had to kill my own dad. You're not the only one."

"What the hell are you talking about? I was there when your dad died, and he died of a heart attack," said Cassandra.

"You were there after he died. No one was there when he died but me."

"You better not be lying," said Cassandra.

"It's no lie," said Helen. "I've never told another living soul this before. It just never seemed like I needed to."

"So, if you killed him, how come everyone thought he had a heart attack?" Cassandra demanded.

"I told them he died in the bathtub drunk. They decided to say it was a heart attack. I didn't care. I was just glad he was dead. My daddy was the biggest drunk there ever was."

"Wrong," said Cassandra. "Mine was. 'Til I blew his lights out."

"My dad would pass out and you could just about run a truck over him and he'd never know."

Cassandra snickered. "Mine did that a couple times. I wish I would have shot him then. Why did you want to kill him your dad anyway? Did you mean to?"

"Oh, I meant to," Helen answered. "I'd been meaning to for a long time, but I had to wait 'til I had a chance. It was really scary. I was just a girl. I tried running away but people kept bringing me back. There wasn't any way to get away from him."

"What did he do to you?" Cassandra asked. "What did he do that was bad enough to kill him."

"He got me pregnant, then sold my baby."

I adjusted the air conditioner. Blow, cold air, blow.

"Then he let his friend get me pregnant. He'd hit me with anything handy just if he woke up feeling bad. Which he always did. The only days I didn't get hurt in one way or another were the times I managed to run away. Then I got beat up when I got brought back."

"Men are bastards," Cassandra said. Her voice sounded weak, exhausted.

"Not all," whispered Helen. I thought of my dad and what he would think if he knew what was happening to us now. "But some are for sure."

"A few months after he let his friend have me and I was pregnant with Elizabeth I stayed out in the orchard until after dark. He came looking for me. He had that sound in his voice. I knew what he wanted. He was drunk before supper. I knew if I could hold out long enough he would pass out.

"I climbed way up in the top of this one orange tree. It wasn't easy cause I was already so big pregnant. It wasn't the smartest thing I ever did. I managed to get up there, though, and I found a high branch. He wandered all through the rows yelling for me to come inside. He said he wanted me to cook. But that wouldn't have been the first thing he wanted me to do.

"I was starving and I just sat up there eating oranges. The mosquitoes were eating me like I was a picnic. He finally found me."

I remembered the scabs she picked in our kitchen the night she stowed away and came to live with us.

Helen went on. "I thought he was going to pass right under me, but he looked up and saw me. I just sat there. I was so far up I never thought he could get me. I shinnied up another branch, but that branch wasn't as strong. It bent when I sat on it.

"My daddy started teasing at me. He picked up this big stick and started poking at my feet with it. I pulled up where he couldn't reach me, and he climbed up in the bottom branches. I tried to climb up just one foot higher, and that was too far. The branch was too small. It cracked and I slid. I slid down until he got his hand around my ankle. I kept thinking about the baby, but there was nothing I could do. He had me. He whacked my butt with that stick and said I could go in the house or he could do it right there.

"I told him let me climb down. He jumped down first. I tried to run as soon as I hit the ground, but I twisted my foot and he took my arm and dragged me all the way into the house. He threw me on the bed and just did it while I tried to blank out. All I could think of was ending it, though. I had to get away. I had to stop him. Just like you, Cassandra. I had to get out of the way my life was. I made myself think about what he was doing to me, and I made myself get mad. I wanted to blank out, but I didn't let myself. I had to be mad enough to do something."

When Helen paused, Cassandra asked her, "What did you do?"

"Well, he got up from me and went to take a bath and told me to bring him a beer into the bathroom. We had this old tub with legs on it that was high enough to sit almost up in. Once in a while he used to fill it almost to the top and just sit in there and drink his beers. He never washed in it. Never used soap. He just sat in it like a disgusting prince of shit. I thought about running away when he passed out that night, but I couldn't see how it would be any different. I felt so bad. So filthy dirty. I was still having the sickness from being pregnant, and having him touch me was worse than eating a possum that had been rotting a week on the road.

"But something inside me kept saying I was too good for him. I don't know where it came from because no one ever thought I was worth the time of day, but I just knew there had to be a way to save this little baby." Helen caressed her stomach as if Elizabeth were still there. "Even if I wasn't worth anything, I'd have to pretend I was if I wanted to save this baby. I knew for sure she was worth something. It wasn't her fault she came about the way she did."

"So I took Daddy the beer. I handed it to him and when he didn't take it, I looked at him to see if he was asleep and he was. Passed out. I put the can on the lid of the commode and started to walk out. Then I turned back and looked at him again.

"The water was up to his chin and he was just floating in there. I thought I should pull him up or he'll drown. But I didn't. I didn't want to touch that filthy rotten body. I started hoping he would drown. I left him there and went and ate something, some crackers, I think. Drank a whole lot of water. I went back in and he hadn't moved. I knew that he would sleep all night if he was passed out on the bed, but if he was just sleeping in the tub he'd wake up later. I didn't think he'd had enough beers to pass out for good, but I didn't know for sure.

"I looked at how his legs were arranged. His hands were just floating in the water. He snored once and I ran out of the room. The water splashed and he mumbled. I thought I'd lost the chance.

"But he went back to sleep. After I was sure he was sleeping, I sneaked in and looked at him again. His head was falling to the side almost in the water. I went up behind him.

"As fast as I could I put one hand over his face and one on his shoulder and shoved a little to the side and down until his head was completely under the water. He woke up and started to struggle, but he breathed a big breath of water and started just trying to get up. He managed to twist around and get on his knees, but I still had his head. I took a fistful of his hair in each hand and just laid into him with all my strength. I was strong. All that work I did made sure of that. He looked up at me and I looked him right in the eye. He knew who killed him.

"He was sliding around, and finally he shuddered and let loose. I kept holding him face down in the water for a long time after. I couldn't take any chances. He had to be dead or I would be.

"After I let him go, he just floated, so I turned him over and his eyes were wide open, afraid. I should have got pleasure from that, you know, after all he put me through, but I was sick. I couldn't believe what I had done. I felt disgusted. I washed my hands in the sink again and again and I couldn't stop the feeling of his nasty hair and skin in my hands.

"I ran out into the trees again. I stayed there all night. I fell asleep somehow, and I was just covered with mosquito bites when I woke up. I went back into the house and it smelled like nothing you ever smelled. I covered my face with a rag and went into the bathroom. He had shit all in the water and the whole house just stunk. I shut the door. I called the police and told them my daddy died in the bath tub while I was sleeping and I woke up from the stink. They said he had a heart attack."

"Drive, Kate," Cassandra ordered me. "My dad needs killing," she said. "He got me pregnant, too. I never had a minute, a second of a day that was my own. I never knew when he was going to do stuff to me. I just had to shut down and take it.

"But, my mom," she said, shaking her head. "My mom was always over there telling me how God would send me to hell for my lustful thoughts. The only thing I ever lusted after was a safe place to go to. I was so jealous of Kate I could barely stand it."

I squeezed the wheel, driving, waiting.

"When other little girls were dreaming of being princesses," she went on, "I just dreamed of being Kate, living in a normal house with a dad who didn't get in her bed at night. I called her parents "Mom" and "Dad". Do you remember that, Kate?"

"Yes," I whispered.

"I know they hated it, but it was just a dream I had. It was the only little light in my life, pretending that they were really my parents. That someone like them would love me."

"They loved you, Cass," I said.

"Well, they didn't know me." Cassandra lit a cigarette, fumbling with the gun while she did. I watched her in the rear view mirror and instinctively turned around to help.

"Turn back around, Kate!" She adjusted the gun in her hand. "When Melinda died and I ended up back at my parents' house it was just a bigger and worse version of shut up and take it. My dad still came into my room. He'd even give me extra tranquilizers to make it easier. My mother just watched him go into my room. She'd even ask him to bring me my laundry or something like that. Give him excuses. He'd wake me up and be in there for an hour and she pretended she never suspected a thing. I'd walk out later and she would ask, 'Did you have a nice talk?' If I hadn't been so loaded all the time I would have killed her then."

She inhaled on her cigarette. I looked out the window.

"Once you told me, Kate, that when you were sick your mother always brought you hot tea and put her hand on your forehead. You said she would get out this old quilt her mother made and put it over you on the couch so you wouldn't be lonely back in your room. She'd make you Campbell's Chicken Noodle Soup and let you eat all the saltine crackers you wanted. What I wouldn't give for just one day like that when I was a little girl. Just one hour like that. Just to have a cold and have someone take care of me."

Inside the house Elizabeth went to the phone. I saw the curtains move. I held my breath.

Tears were running down my cheeks. "Can't you let us mother you, Cassandra?" I pleaded. "Won't you let me be what she wasn't? You can't change her. You can't change what she's already done, but you can start over."

"I can avenge myself. Let's go. Go to my mother's house and park around the corner. I'll tell you where."

"Vengeance is mine, sayeth the Lord," I said. I backed down the driveway.

"You spent too much time with me growing up, Kate. Look, the plan is set. I'm not changing my mind. Danny is waiting. I gave him her house key. He's going to unlock it before we get there, then wait in his car around the block."

She took a deep breath and exhaled slowly. "Then you are going to go in and shoot her. After I see that you did it, I will run out to where Danny will be waiting and we'll get away."

"Where are you going?" I asked.

"Wouldn't you like to know." I turned down the air conditioner. I drove as slowly as I dared.

"Why is Danny helping?"

Cassandra caught my eye in the rear view mirror. Helen was looking out the window.

"He always knew it wasn't his baby," Cassandra said. He could count the months. I admitted it to him right from the start. He knew about his own dad and Helen."

Helen spun around and looked at Cass.

"He knew, Helen," Cassandra continued, "But he didn't know what to do. He felt bad. He figures that helping me take care of my mom will help him repent for not helping you."

Helen turned and looked out the window again. I could not see her face.

"Danny still loves me. We'll be gone before the cops even catch you. Then, I figure with all your money you should be able to get yourself a pretty decent lawyer to get you out of this mess."

"I don't want to be involved in this, Cassandra."

"You have to, Kate," she said.

I started to cry. "Does Danny have a gun?"

"Of course," said Cassandra. "Here we are. I don't see Danny. Where the hell is he? Circle the block."

We came around the far end of the block and there was a dark colored Chevy. The headlights flashed once, then twice more.

"That's the signal. That means the back door of the house is unlocked. Let's go." I drove past the house, turned the corner and killed the engine and the lights.

"Helen, duck down so he won't see you," Cassandra ordered. Cassandra pushed me ahead of her and I knew the gun was pointed at me, tucked close to her inside her purse so that it would not be noticed if someone peered out a window.

"Her bedroom is back there," Cassandra hissed.

Helen suddenly appeared beside Cassandra. "We can do this a better way. There doesn't have to be such a mess. Let's think this over."

"Get back in the car!"

"We can do this a better way."

"No, it's too late! Get out of here!"

Cassandra touched the gun to the back of my head to let Helen know she was serious. She followed me to her mother's bedroom window. She rose up on her tip toes and peered in.

"She's asleep," Cassandra sighed. "Head around to the back door. I have another gun in my purse- your Dad's gun. You're going to shoot her with that."

I panicked. Daddy's gun! They had planned it well.

"I can't do this," I cried.

"Open the door, damn it, and shut up!" she hissed.

I turned the knob. It didn't move. I jiggled it.

"You try! It won't open!"

"No! I can't get my finger prints on it!"

I tried again to no avail.

Cassandra pulled her shirt up and wrapped it over the knob. It didn't budge.

Around the corner Helen darted from the car and darted along the hedges and leaned into Danny's car window.

"She wouldn't let me go. She said it had to be Kate. Did you make sure the house was locked?"

"Yeah, it's tight."

"Hurry," Helen said.

"When she finds out I tricked her, she's going to panic."

"Hurry, then," Helen told him.

I was terrified and began to tremble uncontrollably. I looked around, searching for an escape.

"What the hell is going on here?" Cassandra looked like a cornered animal. "He didn't open the goddamned door!"

"Maybe she locked it back," I said. "Maybe she had the locks changed and he couldn't!" I hoped.

"Then he wouldn't have given me the signal. The signal was only for if it was okay!"

Cassandra had selected the night of the opening of my exhibit almost as soon as she heard about it. She called Danny from my parent's house to tell him of the plan, and continued to call him from the house we shared, and I paid the long distance bills. She wanted to take my best day and ruin it.

Danny hated me. He hated me from the start. From the first night we rode in that fish smelling car he considered me a rival. When they communicated in the aftermath of their ugly time, their horror and their grief fed upon that of the other, and Danny convinced Cassandra that it was my fault. My fault that I never told anyone that teenaged Cassandra was in trouble, my fault that Helen moved away. It was even my fault she embarrassed him at their father's funeral with that big wad of spit on her dead father's face. Most of all, it was my fault that Cassandra shot Melinda and spilled her baby blood.

I was in it for the money, Danny told her. I painted the paintings, Danny convinced Cassandra, knowing they would someday make me famous, knowing they would make me rich. It was a plan to make it big with Cassandra as a sacrifice. So I owed her. That's what he told Cassandra.

"Maybe he opened the front door instead," I suggested. The cicadas were screaming from the trees.

"We went over this a thousand times. He was supposed to open the back door. Damn! Damn! Damn!" Cassandra darted back and forth in terror.

"Let's try the front door anyway, Cass. Maybe he panicked. Maybe he couldn't get the door open. Maybe he thought it was opened." Maybe, I thought, I could signal for help if we were out front near the street.

"The front door has a security chain on it," snarled Cassandra. We tried it during the trial run. Besides, he would only flash the lights if everything was okay."

"You came here before?"

"Shit, yes, we came here before. It was all planned. Do you think I'm just going to come over here and just do it?"

"Let God take care of her," I said. "Just forget this whole thing and let her get her own justice."

"God let them do this to me, do you really think God's going to punish her? He listens to her prayers, Kate, not mine."

Cassandra darted back and forth along the edge of the back porch. There were tall hibiscus trees on either side of the porch and occasionally she would stand up on tip toe to try to see over them, looking, I presume, for Danny.

"You told me one time that God never gives us more than we can handle," I said.

"Well, I was wrong." Cassandra got right in my face. I could feel her spittle. "God gives people more than they can handle all the time. That's all God ever does is give people more than they can handle. What do you think the jails are full of?" She leaned into my face and whispered viciously, "What do you think the loony bins are full of? People who could handle it?"

"I'll help you handle it, Cass. Helen and I will help you. You haven't done anything yet. Let's go before you get into a whole lot of trouble. I've got money now and …

She turned to me and hissed, "Life is trouble. Haven't you figured that out yet?"

"Look, let's just go see if Danny's car is still there. If it is, he can't be planning to screw you over. He wouldn't stick around if he was going to screw you around, would he?"

She didn't waste any time agreeing. "You go in front of me," she ordered, gesturing with the gun.

The skin along my back crawled. She was so agitated by now that I didn't know what she might do. I expected to feel the gun discharge into my back. I don't know how I walked around the house without falling apart.

When we reached the front corner of the house, Cassandra ordered me to go out and see if Danny's car was still there. I crept further out on the lawn, and sure enough, it was there. I couldn't see anyone in it, but the car was there.

I ran back to Cassandra and told her.

"Was he in it?"

"I don't know."

"Goddamn it, I can't just run out there if he's not in it. Go see."

"Okay." I walked out to the sidewalk. I realized I didn't need to hide. Nothing had happened yet. No one was in any trouble. I walked cautiously to the corner and peered into the car. Helen was in the driver's seat, crouching down.

"What are you doing?" she said in a loud whisper.

"What are *you* doing?" I asked.

"Get in the car, Cass. We've got to get out of here."

"I can't leave her here like this."

"Kate, she's gone crazy. You're not safe. Let Danny deal with her. He's going to try to talk her out of this. Let's get out of here. Let's take your car and go get the police."

"Where is Danny?"

"He went to talk her out of it. I think he's the only one that can right now."

"Why didn't you call the Police?"

"Elizabeth was doing it. I don't know why they aren't here yet."

"I have to go back and tell Cass. If she knows the police are coming she'll stop this before its too late."

"No, Kate, you can't. She's too wound up."

I ran down the street. I brushed against the bushes.

"Cassandra?" I called into the darkness. There was no answer but the rustling of the shrubs between the houses.

"They called the police, Cass!" I called, "Get out of here while you can!"

I heard muffled voices from the shrubbery. I carelessly went toward the sound. "Cassandra, I'm coming back there. It's just me."

Instinctively I held my hands up and moved toward the bushes.

"Get out of here, Kate," Danny said.

"I'm not leaving without Cass," I said.

"You have to, Kate," Cassandra told me. "I'm not coming out."

Danny's voice followed Cassandra's out of the darkness. "Get back, Kate. She's got a gun to her head. Get back or this will be on your shoulders, too!"

"Cassandra, you have to stop this. I love you. Please don't do this." Without awareness, I took another step toward the voices.

"Don't come any closer, Kate. I don't want you to see this," Cassandra screamed.

"Danny, stop her," I pleaded.

"Get out of here, Kate," Danny answered.

"Cassandra, I love you. Please…"

"Do you think it helps to be loved by a queer, Kate?" Cassandra sniped at me. "I'm not like you. You can't help me. Now, get lost!"

"You're my friend!"

"Don't lie to me. I know how it is."

Of course, she was right. I had loved her all my life. I loved her as a friend, as a mother and as a woman. I loved her in every way there was.

"I can help you! Look, I have money now. Things will get better!"

"Get out of here!" Danny stood up in the bushes and waved his gun in the air. The light came on in the house next door to the Orgeron's. Danny put the gun to his own temple as he sank back into the greenery and dark shadows.

I ran as fast as I could to Helen in Danny's car. "They're killing themselves, Helen! What are we going to do?"

"Both of them?"

"Yes, they have guns to their heads. We have to stop them. Run to my parent's house," I said. "Call the police again. I don't think Elizabeth got through. Tell them to hurry."

I ran with Helen to my parents' house. My father opened the door.

"What's goin' on? Kate, are you okay?"

"You tell 'em, Helen. Call the cops first," I ordered.

I ran to my car and aimed it to the place where Cassandra and Danny had been hiding. I shone the headlights on the shrubs and honked the horn. Lights began to come on up and down the street.

Mrs. Orgeron came out onto the porch in her robe and started shouting at me to be quiet. In a flash Cassandra was behind her on the porch with the gun pointed at her mother's back. I couldn't hear what they were saying, I just knew I'd reordered the sacrificial rites.

"Cassandra, stop!" I screamed at her. I jumped out of the car and ran to the porch. Cassandra followed her mother inside with the gun pointed at her back. She waved to Danny and he followed with the gun still pointed at his head. He walked backward looking from side to side, holding himself hostage. Mrs. Orgeron moaned fearfully.

The night grew bright with spiraling blue lights and screaming sirens just as the door closed behind the three.

I leapt from my car and ran to them. "They're going to kill themselves! They're going to kill her mother and themselves!" I was hysterical. I barely remember what questions the police officers threw at me. I don't know if my answers made any sense at all. My head was screaming and swimming in horror and fear. I think I told them how Helen and I had been taken. An officer shoved me behind a squad car protected by an officer who leaned over its hood with his handgun drawn. My parents' house was in my line of vision. The lights were on now, and I saw the curtains shift occasionally. In my mind I begged them to stay down.

I asked the officer if I could go home to them. After a brief conference with his superior, he said no, that they would need me for further information. Hostage situations were tricky, and when you throw in a potential double suicide, you need all your avenues open.

Remarkably, people began to emerge from their homes to stand on their porches and see what was happening. One elderly gentleman even came down to speak to one of the officers. With an amplifier horn they were ordered to go back inside; they were in a potentially dangerous situation. Go back inside.

But they wouldn't let me go in. The negotiating officer called me to huddle next to him near a squad car. He tried to extract a complete history in just a few seconds. He told me to be ready in case he had any more questions or wanted me to talk to Cassandra and Danny. He said I would be expected to stay handy because things could change quickly. They would need me to be nearby.

"I need to go to the bathroom," I said.

"You'll have to wait. When I can spare a man I'll send you to your parents' house."

I pressed my thighs together, clenched my teeth and pressed my head into my knees as I sat on the hard ground next to the blaring police car. I was trembling so much I bit my tongue, making it bleed. I still have a scar from that bite.

Seeing the blood, the officer beside me told another policeman nearby to get me to a bathroom. Because my parents' house was in the danger zone, we went around the corner and he knocked on a stranger's door and asked if he would let me use their rest room. The poor old man was too afraid to say no. He must have been about eighty years old. One eye was clouded with a cataract. He quizzed the officer on the commotion in a broken voice as I sat behind the bathroom door on his dirty toilet. I could hear the officer giving terse answers to his questions. I rinsed my mouth over and over with tap water that was orange with rust and tasted like metal. My tongue continued to bleed. I used a washcloth from his linen closet to press on it. It was red in no time.

"I'll get you another," I promised. Later I sent the man a whole set of new towels and wash cloths. It was the least I could do for scaring him half to death in the middle of the night.

The negotiating officer was named Phil Hammond. He was a tall, lean white man with a thick mustache. He shouted into the bull horn over and over until my ears were ringing.

"Come on out and no one will get hurt!"

"Send someone to the door. You will be safe."

"Please answer the telephone. We need to talk."

"They've answered," someone shouted. Then hush, everyone, hush.

"They're going to shoot themselves and the woman if we try to force entry," said the officer into my face. I stared at him.

"Do something," I pleaded.

They tried reaching the house again by phone several times but the phone just rang and rang. The bull horn was the only way to communicate to the three inside and they weren't talking back.

"Don't worry yet. No shots have been fired. We just need to get them to talk."

I don't know how much time passed before they decided it was time to get someone into the house. It seemed like hours. It must have been. It was starting to get light by the time anything happened.

Television reporters were on the scene now. New officers were brought in just to hold the media people at bay. They were pushed far down the street, blocked off with barricades. A helicopter circled overhead.

Eight officers with guns drawn surrounded the house. Four ran around to the back from opposite sides, leaping the short wrought iron fence and disappearing. Two officers positioned themselves at the corners of the house where they could look around to the front door and windows. Two officers approached the front door from opposite sides, weapons ready.

Sweat poured from my face. I had to wipe my eyes again and again just to see what was happening. Why didn't Cassandra answer the phone? Why didn't they open the door? Couldn't they just let us know what we could do?

My legs were cramped and my back hurt from my position on the ground. My left foot kept going to sleep and I couldn't stand up or even extend it fully to help it regain its circulation completely.

The officer on the left side of the house intercepted a message from the officers in the back. He relayed it to the officers flanking the front door. Each officer in turn placed himself so that he could look into the windows at the front of the house, then they returned to the front door. The first officer peered into the front door window. He tried the handle. It was locked.

With his Billy club he hammered the door knob powerfully. After several blows the knob came loose and he reached inside and unlocked the door. It was still attached by the security chain, so he gave it a swift kick and the door crashed open.

We couldn't see anything that went on within the house. Officer Hammond walked away from me to communicate with his squad on a walkie talkie. He gestured to another officer for me to be led away. The pins and needles in my foot caused me to stumble as I was taken to a squad car and urged to get inside. I laid down on the back seat, not knowing what to expect.

Suddenly there was a lot of movement. I peered through the window to see what was happening. Officers were rushing into the house. One began stringing yellow tape across the lawn indicating that it was the scene of a crime. I began to hyperventilate. An officer brought me water in a paper cup. I don't know where he got it.

"What happened?" I begged him. His dark face was wet with perspiration. His uniform was drenched.

"It's not clear yet, ma'am. Officer Hammond will be here to speak to you soon. The detectives are securing the scene so that no evidence will be tampered with."

"Are they okay? What's going to happen to them?"

"I'll tell Officer Hammond you are ready to see him."

I began to shiver. I was soaking wet with perspiration and suddenly my body was covered in goose flesh.

A woman came around the car to my door. It was my mother. My mother had come out in the danger. She was in a house dress in the middle of the night. She had on shoes.

"Mother, it's not safe out here! Go back!"

"Come with me!"

"I can't! They told me to stay!"

"It's okay. You can come in now."

"Mom, I'm so scared," I began to cry.

My mother's arms were around me and her chin above my head. She squeezed me with all the strength she ever had.

My heart broke, then. I couldn't stop the tears. My mother stroked my hair and held me for a life time leaning on that squad car. Eventually she pulled me out and led me to her house and sat me at her kitchen table. Helen and my father, my mother and I sat in silence, waiting. From the television news we learned that there had been a suspected murder and double suicide on our street. The story was still breaking.

Helen and I fell into each other's arms. My mother went to the stove, made tea and poured it into flowered cups for us. She made a coffee cake, and a pot of coffee. When Officer Hammond and Detective Smith came to tell us what happened she offered them breakfast. My mother cooked all day and into the evening. When the reporters called and came to our door, she helped my father tell them that we had no comment.

After Cassandra and Danny went into Mrs. Orgeron's house with her, Cassandra sat at the kitchen table and wrote a letter to me. I can't imagine that she just immediately sat down and started writing. I imagine her pacing and ranting for a while. The letter is frightening and lost.

Dear Kate,

This is it, you know. You should have helped me, but you didn't, so I have to do this final deed. There's no escaping it. Danny is here with me and we are going out together. He was the only one who ever stuck by me. All that time in prison, he was the only one I could count on. And he's the only one I can count on at the end.

Anything I have is yours. Just burn it, if you want to. Maybe you'll have the decency to burn this house down, too. All the years of being raped by my father with my mom doing nothing, they just come alive sitting in this stink hole.

You can keep on getting rich off my face, can't you? Imagine how much those paintings will be worth now that I've met such a tragic end? You'll be sitting pretty from here on in. Just don't forget where you got so rich, Kate. You were in love with an insane woman. Your main mistake.

This is the end. I'm going to die in a few minutes. If God has any mercy maybe he'll let me see my little Melinda before he throws me into hell.

I really loved you, Kate. You were my hero and my idol. I hope you understand that this is my only option now. I can't go on living this life. Hell has to be a better place.

> *Your friend to the end,*
> *Cassandra Dee Orgeron*

At some time during the evening Danny and Cassandra tied Mrs. Orgeron to a chair with belts and twine. They made a gag from some gauze and duct tape. They dragged her to the kitchen. The scratches from the legs of the wooden dining room chair were evident on the linoleum. They placed the chair next to the stove.

Cassandra and Danny made a palette for themselves from blankets and pillows. They drank some tea and someone ate a sandwich. They turned the gas on at the stove. They laid down together wrapped in each other's arms and went to sleep forever.

Twenty Four

The Final Portrait

There's so little I remember about the months immediately after Cassandra's suicide. If it weren't for Helen I would never have recovered. Helen took over and took care of me completely.

She enlisted my mother to come and help her each day, and my mother did. Helen cooked things to freeze for later. Mother made my lunch each day after Helen went to work. She cleaned the bathtub and the toilets when they were dirty. She braided Elizabeth's hair and nagged her about her homework. When Grace volunteered to come and help us out, Helen told her we needed to take care of ourselves now, but we would welcome her company.

Dad helped when mother could not do it all. He made sure either he or Mother was at our home when Elizabeth came home from school. Even though she was so mature for her age Daddy felt that children should have someone to come home to at the end of the day.

Helen became a manager at Winn Dixie. She took college courses in the evenings. She wanted to be a nurse.

I slept through the first month of my recovery. I wanted to die. I felt so empty and hopeless that I couldn't eat. What I did eat came up again. I took sleeping pills Dr. Hale gave me, and I didn't think about why. I started therapy with a warm woman who really cared, but I couldn't do anything but sit and weep.

After a while Helen decided I'd been idle long enough and told me it was time to get going. She brought me a non-threatening breakfast of toast, an orange and tea each morning and left it on a tray. She opened my window and my curtains wide so that the sunshine spilled over me in a wide ribbon. I hated it. I yelled at her. She told me that if I was irritated enough I could just get up and close them myself. Elizabeth's cat would knead my thighs and purr at me happily.

"Your Mama says it is good for you to get fresh air and sunshine, so if I have my way you're getting fresh air and sunshine!"

Helen took some long saved vacation time and stayed home for a week when she decided it was time for me to get up. She said that I'd never get better if I wasn't busy. She said people have to do before they can think. At first she only made me get up and brush my teeth and rinse out the sink.

"See?" she told me. "You did something useful. Now your mouth is clean and your sink is clean. And you did it. You can do something if you put your mind to it."

At first I balked. The truth is that at first I refused. Helen tricked me into getting up. She would steal the sheets off my bed while I was in the bathroom.

"While you're up," she would say, "would you wash those breakfast dishes? After you get dressed."

I would stand there and wash those damned dishes crying my eyes out. I hated her then. At least that's what I thought.

She told me that the most important thing to do while you are hurting is to take care of your body. She made me get up and bathe and dress every day, even when I wanted to be true to the stench I felt like.

She told me things that changed me. She said when it hurts the worst, so bad you can't bear it another second, that's when you have to get busy. If sweeping the floor doesn't stop the ache, then you mow the lawn. If mowing doesn't take away the torture, you dig a garden. If you start to think about Cassandra or anything else but the towel you are folding or the leaves you are raking, you stop your mind and bring it right back to your job.

If digging a garden doesn't even come close to filling in the cavern of agony, you run. You run for everything you're worth until you find a hill, and when you've run up the hill and you still can't see an end to your pain, you find a mountain, and you push your body up it until it can't climb any more.

When your body has taken you as far as it can and you are in pain and can't go another step and the hurt still owns you, you scream. You scream and scream and scream until the hurt and the fear and the grief don't have room to squeeze into your thoughts. You scream even though people think you are crazy, and you scream when there's no one to hear. You scream and you scream and you scream.

When you can't run any further, and you're too hoarse to scream, you feed your body with the best food you can get. Food from the earth. Food from the soil. Food from our garden. Then you go to sleep tired enough to rest and the next day you run again. You run and keep running every time the pain comes back, and one day your body will be strong and you will know you don't need to run away from the mourning any more. One day you'll be able to turn and look at your grief straight in the eye. One day you'll be able to take it all and make it your own. And finally, finally, finally, one day you'll be able to let it go.

My mother was a recipient of Helen's earthy wisdom, too. Each day as she gave us work, responsibility, life, she asked my mother what her family was like. She asked how her mother had made her red beans and rice. She asked how her father, a carpenter, would have repaired our broken door. She drew her through her life from her childhood, from how she planted sunflowers as a little girl and watched them tower over the fence a few weeks later, to what it had been like to hold a brand new baby of her own in her arms. When I would break down and cry, Helen would tell me stories about how when she was a young girl she could climb to the top of the orange trees and see clear into town. How she dreamed of going there and being free someday, and then we took her in. She said it took someone really important to take in a dirty little pregnant girl and give her a way to live.

One day when I was weak from mourning for such a long time and she was making me snap garden peas in the kitchen, I asked Helen how she figured out about recovering from grieving. I reminded her that she was only a little girl when she came to live with us. How was she the one that knew how to get better? She knew hell as well as anyone.

"I was never a regular little girl," she told me. "My mother died when I was a baby and I went to live with my Aunt Jeanne and Uncle TeeBo on the river. I was helping clean fish when I was three. Feeding the dogs before that. Uncle TeeBo used to hit Aunt Jeanne hard and finally she left him and took me back to live with my daddy. It was her that was at my daddy's funeral. You remember her sitting at the back that day?"

She looked at me and I nodded.

Helen was kneading dough on the counter with a big white flour cloth spread out across it. Her pounding became loud and rhythmic as she told the story of her wisdom. "Daddy didn't want me. He made sure I knew how much trouble I was. Then he figured out he could get some good out of me. He started…he was…sleeping with me when I was seven. Maybe before. I don't remember." She shook her head and looked at me, "But I told you already most of that."

"Yes," I said.

"I started trying to run away when I was little, just after he starting doing things to me. I used to go hide in the trees, but I'd get hungry and I'd have to come back and eat. If he was passed out drunk it was good. If he was just plain drunk I was in trouble. He'd beat me, and then do it to me."

It was hard to listen to her telling of her tragedy when I wasn't through with mine.

"Helen, you don't have to tell me."

"But you need to hear it. I have to explain something to you," she insisted.

"I told my teacher at school that I needed help and she got a social worker to go see my daddy. Daddy took me out of school after that. Said if they was just going to be poking around in our business I didn't need to be down at that school anyway. No one ever came out to see if I was okay. No one ever did.

"So I started running away. I decided if I had to eat raw fish and grass, that's what I'd do." Helen rubbed her face with her wrist and drew a flour line across her cheek. She went to the sink to wash her hands. "Problem was, people kept finding me and bringing me back. Usually it was Danny Daddy sent after me. Even when it was someone else they wouldn't listen when I told them my daddy was hurting me. Said I needed to mind my daddy.

"And every time they brought me back it was the same thing again. Daddy smiled and thanked them. Told them how worried he'd been. Then he'd take me in his room and beat me with his belt and do it to me. I don't know what was worse. Beating or raping. They both kill you inside."

I pushed the bowl of beans aside laid my head on my crossed arms on the table. I didn't cry, I just grew heavier.

"Then I figured out that I was pregnant. I didn't know what was happening at first. I started getting big in the belly though, then I started feeling her moving inside." For the first time, Helen's voice cracked. "I knew I had to get away. I started hitching rides in the backs of pick ups and cars and whatever was going far away fast.

"Once I even went to the police, and they took one look at my pregnant belly and drove me home to Daddy themselves. They told my daddy to keep a closer eye on me. I told them all what he did while they were driving me home, and they just shook their heads. I heard one of them say, 'At least they keep it in the family.'"

"The policeman said that?"

"One of them did. The other one said I was making it up to get attention. Said I'd surely been fooling around with some boy." Helen took a deep breath and swallowed. She hung her head over the sink and I thought she was going to be sick, but she went on.

"I don't know what he did with that baby. I just know he got money for her. It tears my heart out every day of my life not knowing. I know I'll never find her. Maybe she has a good life, but I have to just hope, because I'll never know. If I could have just gave her to a good family, that would have been the thing. But he took her. He stole her and I won't ever know where she is. That's what hurts. Not knowing if she's been okay. Not even knowing if she's alive or dead."

That's when she broke. She cried silently into her shoulder. She wiped her eyes and her sleeves.

"But here's what I did. I kept trying. When one thing didn't work I tried something else. When that didn't work, I tried something else. Finally there wasn't anything left but one thing. It was terrible, but it was the only thing left. And it was better him than me."

"You killed him," I said.

She turned around from the sink to face me. I lifted my head and looked into her eyes. The smear of flour was still across her face. Her hair was pulled back in a head band. She looked fifteen again.

It was bright noon outside our window as Helen told me this tale. It should have been stormy and dark, but the sun revealed her secrets like it showed the wrinkles on her youthful face.

"Did you ever try to kill yourself?" I asked.

"No, that was only if this didn't work," Helen said. "I wasn't the one doing wrong. I just always knew that. I was the one trying to get away." She wet a dishrag and held it to her face. When she removed it the flour smudge was gone.

Helen sat down at the table.

"The reason I never told you that story before is because I was afraid you would think less of me, or even that the police would come and get me. They might still if you tell. I killed my daddy as sure as day. But I had tried everything else I could think of first.

"Cassandra must have thought she had tried everything she could do, too. When your whole life is just hurting and people just keep knocking you down, you feel like you don't have many choices, but you have to see if you do."

Helen reached out and took my hand. "Cassandra lost track of who was hurting her. She didn't see that if she could have trusted someone she could have found a way. She never learned how to trust people, see? She got too sad to keep trying. You can't blame her for that. You did what you could. You took her in, and you loved her. You can't blame yourself for her dying. And you can't blame her either. She didn't kill herself. Not really. It was them that killed her."

And she meant Cassandra's parents and Danny and everything that was evil in the world.

"When you get hurt again and again you kind of lose track of what's real. The whole world starts seeming dangerous, and that doesn't stop just because your body grows up. What you have to do is keep looking for the answers you need, and some kids stop having the strength to do that after a while."

"What kept you going, Helen?"

"Elizabeth," she said. "Pure and simple. Elizabeth. Then you and Miss Lizzie. It was the fact that there were people who cared about me and that I had that little belief in me that I was worth something, no matter how little."

"Cassandra never knew that."

"I know. But that's not your fault."

"I loved her. I would have helped her anyway I could have."

"But she wasn't strong enough to help herself. That's not your fault. You can't help someone who can't want to be helped."

"I can't blame her for it. I blame those parents."

"Yes."

"Someone must have hurt them, too, though. How else would they get that way?"

"Look at me, Kate." I looked into Helen's face. "I could have ended up just like them, or just like my daddy. But I didn't. I looked at what my choices were. I dreamed of things getting better. And I tried things and tried things until I found a way out. Sometimes when Elizabeth is pulling one of her acts I just feel like slapping the stuffing out of her. Sometimes I just want to grab a stick and beat her blue. But I don't. That's the difference. I don't have to hurt her if I don't want to, and I don't want to, so I don't. I can decide to do better than what was done to me, and that's what I try to do.

"Cassandra lost the things that were important to her. Her baby. She carried so much guilt from that. Her faith in herself. That was preached right out of her. She never thought she could do anything right. That's dangerous."

"You mean because of her religion?"

"In her case, yes. Religion shouldn't be that way, but in her case it was. She was between a rock and a hard place a lot of the time. You do this, it's a sin and you go to hell. You do the opposite, you get some kind of punishment here on earth. She had no safe place. No where to hide. No orange trees, not even a pink bed where a mother could come and lay her hand on your head and say, "How you feeling?" Helen smiled at me.

"But my mother. Look at her. She gets her depressions."

"She's just loses her way. Everybody tells her she has to act a certain way, be a certain way. Some times she just gets lost. She's never far off track, though."

"Hard times made you strong."

"They did, sure. I could never be glad for what happened. I knew I had to live the life I had to live, though, you know?"

I nodded and she took my hand.

Helen continued, "I don't blame myself. I wish there were a way I could see to it that no other kid has to resort to that to get out of being hurt. I wish I could show kids what a terrible alternative that is. But I don't blame myself. I was in so much danger. I had to get out."

"I'm glad you got out."

"I'm glad, too. I'm not glad I had to kill someone to do it. But it was like a war. If there's someone going to shoot you, you have to shoot first. But daddy wasn't just shooting. He was torturing me all along the way. It was my own hell. He was the devil.

"But that's how I know how to grieve, see? I had to grieve for a family I never had, for a childhood I never had, for a little girl I'll never know, and for what I could have been. What I learned is that you just have to keep busy working away at your sadness until it makes sense and it makes you better."

My father found his own peace. He talked with Helen sometimes, too, but Helen was never comfortable with men. Daddy was gentle and always there when he was needed. I suppose I'll always regret that he died so soon after Cassandra's suicide. I wanted to spend so much more time with him. A year after we lost Cassandra, we lost Daddy. His heart warned him for years not to eat the rich New Orleans diet, but he said he'd rather die happy. I think he did.

After his death I knew what to do. I ran. I worked Helen's garden, and I ate what we grew. And then I looked at my father's memory and I let him go. We always keep those we love in memories, but I was never tortured by his passing in spite of all the sorrow I felt and tears I expressed. I'll miss him forever, but he's free to go.

Mother has managed to get on without my father. She is a blue haired old woman now, living in our old house, quite on her own and doing fine. We have lunch together at least once a week, and I am amazed at her energy. The depression lifted and left her alone after a time. She takes long walks with a little dog she got at the SPCA and she has more friends than I can count. She still tends the small garden Helen dug so many years ago. She grows the best tomatoes you ever tasted.

Helen finished nursing school and now works with nurses and doctors and all the people she used to be afraid of. She even became a midwife and now she goes to homes and delivers babies in the safety of their own family spaces.

Elizabeth went to college with Helen's savings and the money Lizzie had left to her so long ago. We also discovered the savings account Dad had started for her when we read his will. A lot of interest had accumulated over the years. Elizabeth majored in Physical Education and later became a Doctor of Divinity with a degree in Theology from Tulane University. She opened a counseling practice where she helped people through grief and abuse by integrating the healing of the spirit with the healing of the body. She says the spirit becomes enlightened when it's shelter, the human body, and it's voice, the human mind, are unified in health and freedom.

Helen did a good job of raising Elizabeth. She joined the First Unitarian Universalist Church on Jefferson Street and Elizabeth is a frequent speaker there. I make a point of attending when she will be speaking. Elizabeth is still very athletic. Her pet project is an annual 10K run she organizes to provide free therapy for abused children and adults who were abused as children. Elizabeth married a wonderful man named Kevin Combes and they have a daughter named Kyra Dionne.

All of the Cassandra paintings sold within a month of her death. The story was sensationalized in the papers and on TV. Her demise increased my celebrity. I suppose it would have been noble to turn all my earnings from her portraits over to a charitable organization, but I didn't. I contribute generously, don't get me wrong. I pay for the therapy of several of Elizabeth's patients who cannot afford it on their own. I've paid for midwife services provided by Helen for low income women. I even give to an organization that tries to help sexual offenders. But my contributions come from new earnings. The money from the Cassandra portraits I keep. It is very hard for me to take assistance from the living, so I allow Cassandra's memory to be my benefactor. Some people think that's selfish. I just think it's my turn.

I hired an assistant several years ago to help with my public relations and to screen social invitations. It sounds stuffy, I know, but I get so tired of it all. Sometimes I just want to take a nap. My assistant is named Lianne Crane. She is also my closest friend, next to Helen, and my companion. She shields me and guides me during our many trips to New York, which I detest. If it were up to me, I would not go, but she insists that I must. She makes it tolerable. She has moved into my big Garden District house with me, and I have felt at home here ever since she did.

We go to Europe once or twice a year. I especially like spending time in Nice although I am not yet fluent in French. Every so often we tour Europe with Mr. Foster. He is an elderly gentleman now, and he is wonderful company. He is a dear friend.

Helen lives with me in my uptown home. Her apartment is in the attached house once meant to house servants. In addition to midwifery, she now works as a home care nurse for women recovering from accidents, abuse and depression. Occasionally she will have a patient who has a terminal illness. She handles each case with caring and grace and energy. The first thing she does is to find something the patient can do, whether it's to clean up after herself or just to hold a pill while Helen goes to fill a cup with water. She says that people recover faster and even live longer when they feel useful. I treasure Helen more each day of each year. Helen never married, never fully came to trust men. She lives here in my house as my friend and in my heart, she lives as my sister.

During my mourning for Cassandra, after I had cleaned and repaired everything in the house we rented and after I had run until I could face my grief, I entered therapy. My therapist's name was Margaret Freeman, and she was the one who taught me how to see the grief through. She also gave me the tools to let Cassandra go. I will always be grateful to her.

I began a last portrait of Cassandra on Margaret's instruction. I painted her from memory. I put in every feeling I ever had about her, and worked on the portrait each day with the memory I awoke with. I worked twelve hours a day many days. I worked for three months with rarely a day off. The painting was the epitome of all I had ever worked for. It was my masterpiece. When I finished even I believed it was my best work ever.

Helen invited Mr. Foster over for dinner one night and showed it to him. She didn't know that the painting wasn't for sale. I never spoke to her about it. She thought it would improve my spirits to hear from him how wonderful the painting was. He pleaded with me to part with it, even opened his checkbook and wrote a large check with a promise of more after the certain sale. It was more than I had earned on the other Cassandras, but I declined. This portrait was part of my healing. It was mine.

"You'll change your mind with time," Mr. Foster assured me.

It was the middle of winter and we were experiencing a rare cold day. The world was gray and made me feel wistful like I did when I was a young girl and wished I could fall in love the way everyone else seemed to.

Helen, Elizabeth and I put on our winter coats and gloves and drove along beside the Mississippi River levee until we got to a place far from the city. A place where we could be alone and undisturbed.

We found a clear place and kicked away debris from a gravel track on the levee. We gathered the smoothest round river stones we could find and placed them in a large circle, about six feet in diameter. We spent a long time gathering logs and sticks and meticulously stacked them for a bonfire. When it was ready, I took Cassandra's silver cigarette lighter from my pocket and lit the fire. It took a long time to light, but when it finally did, the blaze shot ten feet into the air.

I went to the trunk of the old Buick we drove for the last time this day. I pulled out the portrait of my best friend, Cassandra. Evening was drawing near. I placed the canvas on the grass on the steep side of the levee away from the river. It just caught the west light. Elizabeth, Helen and I wrapped our arms around each other and gazed at our friend.

We wept openly and without shame. As our tears and mucous dripped from our faces we wiped them off on each other's coats. We used our hands to wipe the eyes of our sisters. We cried for such a long time we were hoarse for days. We wept until we couldn't stand up straight, and then we sat on the cold ground and cried some more. We went to the portrait and ran our fingers over Cassandra's face and hands and breasts, missing her from the center of our beings. We sat huddled together until we were no longer crying.

Helen nodded and Elizabeth withdrew from her pocket a letter. She read aloud.

Dear Aunt Cass,

Thank you for knowing me in spite of how much it must have hurt in so many ways. Thank you for letting me sit in your lap when I was a little girl. You were the only grown up who let me just sit there without ever moving unless I got up first.

I am sorry you never found a way to be happy. I'm so sorry you couldn't get away from your sadness and still have stayed with us. But I hope you are happy where you are, where ever that may be.

>   *I love you.*
>   *Elizabeth Kate Boudreaux*

Elizabeth, the young woman, lifted the single sheet of white paper and let it float gently into the fire. A single black remnant lifted in the wind and floated out onto the river.

Helen presented the dress Cassandra had worn to church the first time she went with her and Miss Lizzie. It was baby blue with a darker blue pattern of leaves on it, and had a narrow belt.

Helen was shy presenting this, even with us. "I brought this dress to represent the body it covered," she said. "This dress is for the Cassandra you could touch and feel. The one who breathed the same air with us. The one we could hear talking.

"I bring this dress in hopes that her soul is free of the load her body carried."

Helen brought the dress to me and wiped the tears from my face with its skirt. She did the same to Elizabeth. She carried the dress to the flames and pressed her own face into it. She held it to her face and her heaving chest for a while.

She held the dress straight out before her. The skirt billowed across her cheek in the soft wind.

"Cassandra," she said, in a clear strong voice, "Be free!"

The dress wilted and shrunk inside the fire. We waited until there was nothing left of the dress but the tiny metal buckle.

Helen walked back to where Elizabeth and I stood. She embraced us both, and we three looked at the portrait.

Finally I broke myself gently from their embraces. Helen and Elizabeth stood back and I looked at my painting for a lingering moment more.

When I tried to lift the canvas it seemed to weigh more than I could bear. I tried to drag it, but my hands shook and I kept dropping it. My fingers were stiff with cold.

Elizabeth tried to come and help me, but her mother held her back.

I got on the high side of the levee and picked up the corner of the painting and pulled it behind me to the top. I held it up on one end and looked at it one more time.

"Cassandra, I loved you," I said. I wanted more words, more time, but they were gone.

The wind picked up for an instant and the canvas lifted slightly from the ground. A flame reached out and licked it, wanting to be fed. I lifted the portrait high in the air with a searing moan of agony, offering the gods another chance. When they didn't bring her back, I hurled the final portrait of Cassandra into the angry flames.

The End

About the Author

Kellie Sisson Snider lived for fifteen years in and around New Orleans where this novel is set. She now lives near Dallas, Texas with her husband, their sons and several pets.

Ms. Snider is the humor columnist for Water Gardening Magazine. You can learn more about her work or contact her for speaking engagements by visiting her web page at: *http://kassarts.bizland.com*. Copies of this book are available through the web page or through the publisher.

Acknowledgements

My sincerest thanks go out to those who have supported me in this book's creation. Judy Sherrod, who encouraged me to dust off the manuscript and got me started again; my agent, Jerry Laycak, who saw the books merit from the start and directed the editing; Vickie Galante who commiserated with me throughout the highs and lows of this publishing process; the incomparable Wishcrafters and women's retreaters of Horizon Unitarian Universalist Church who give me enormous inspiration, and our old dog, China, who was beside me the whole way. And to my husband, Dick, and sons, Jesse and Micah, who make me laugh and make me very proud. You guys make it all worthwhile.